INCIDENT AT DAK TO

LOUIS EDWARD ROSAS

Louis Edward Rosas Copyright © 2021 American Mishima

All rights reserved.

ISBN:
ISBN-13:

DEDICATION

For all those who served in the Vietnam War.

In loving memory

Sven Johnson
1938-2021

CONTENTS

	Acknowledgments	i
I	1947	Pg 1
II	OPERATION PLEIADES	Pg 7
III	THE LBJ RANCH	Pg 30
IV	THE 4TH ID	Pg 53
V	PHANTOMS OF THE NIGHT	Pg 73
VI	ENTER THE MAN IN BLACK	Pg 92
VII	YANKEE STATION	Pg 107
VIII	MURDER IN III CORPS	Pg 124
IX	THE CENTRAL HIGHLANDS	Pg 153
X	THE LOST SENTAI	Pg 184
XI	POINT OF NO RETURN	Pg 212
XII	THE PERFECT CIRCLE	Pg 251

ACKNOWLEDGMENTS

We would like to graciously thank the following Vietnam Veterans for their service and their assistance in providing valuable information for the production of this book.

David Lucier U.S. Special Forces
Karen Offutt U.S. Army Ret.
Roy Martinez U.S. Army Ret.
Terry Hilliard U.S. Army Ret.
Dick Hanover U.S. Navy Ret.
Jim Barton U.S. Navy Ret.
Dan Kelly U.S. Navy Ret.
René Johnson ARC Ret.
Penni Evans ARC Ret.

Additional thanks for support goes to:

John C. Klice USMC Ret.
Joseph Galloway UPI Ret.
Tom Loehr U.S. Army Ret.
Marvin J. Wolf U.S. Army Ret.

CHAPTER I
1947

The American Southwest, a vast, picturesque, rugged landscape to behold. There, high up on a desert plateau leading down into a narrow canyon is where our story begins. From the outset, one could feel sporadic gusts of a south-westwardly breeze rustling through the dry sagebrush under the canopy of an overcast sky. It was an early October afternoon on that day in 1947 somewhere near the Four Corners Region of Arizona. From that vantage point, one could see the long-abandoned ancient ruins of the Anasazi that lined the canyon. The red-clay pathway was dotted with visible imprints leftover by coyotes on the hunt that followed the dusty trail. Moving forward, one could further see the discarded remains of a rattlesnake that had long since shed its outer skin. As one reached the outer edge of ancient round kivas, a faint hum resonated in the air. It was as if the centuries-old masonry were alive itself. This ghostly hum would occur with each passing gust like echoes of the past calling out from the spirits of those left behind. Mysterious and daunting, this was a place of many secrets. Its long silent sandstone walls bore witness to each passing equinox. And perhaps, there too, the stars above would somehow listen.

Moving deeper into the canyon, the cracks in the ground beckoned for the coming rains that loomed far off on the distant horizon. One could almost hear the thunderclaps echoing across the nearby canyons. It was then that a mirage-like figure came into view, appearing to rise above a desolate ridge.

It was the blurry figure of a man slowly who made his way on the trail. As he stepped closer, it was clear that he was a Navajo Elder in his late fifties. The gusts of wind quietly subsided as he slowly made his way up to the top of the barren ridge. He wore a black Stetson hat with a white beaded band around its brim. His faded blue denim jacket and jeans looked as weathered as his skin and his dusty cowboy boots. Once he had reached the top of the ridge, he looked out to the vastness of the lands he had traversed and sighed. With his hand extended, he gripped the palm of his six-year-old grandson who he helped up onto the rock so he could see the magnificent country before him.

The young boy in blue jeans had never ventured so far off the Navajo Reservation before this day. His deep brown eyes looked on with wonder as he wiped a wind-swept lock of his raven black hair from his eyes. He wore a red plaid shirt under a brown leather jacket that was lined with lambskin to keep warm. As he looked down, he noticed one of his brown leather shoe laces had come untied. Without saying a word, he tugged on his grandfather's blue denim sleeve. The Navajo elder looked down and see the boy's distress. Without hesitation, the grandfather knelt and tied the little boy's shoe.

"Are we almost there, grandpa?"

"More or less," replied his grandfather.

"How far do we have to go?" he asked.

"Not too far. It's just up ways along the trail," replied his grandfather.

Having tied his grandson's shoelace, they continued on their trek through the terrain. Like an omen, a large bird of prey flew up ahead. It screeched then soared in the direction of the path they walked.

"Is that the way?" the boy asked.

"You could say so," replied his grandfather.

"I wish my daddy was here."

"Me too, I miss him very much. You know, you are a lot like him when he was your age," replied his grandfather.

"Really?"

"It's true," he replied.

"Why did he have to go away?" the boy asked.

"The Empire of Japan made a great war across the sea," replied his grandfather.

"Was it at Saipan?" asked the boy.

"No, it started at Pearl Harbor. Saipan is an island further out in the Pacific Ocean where your father left this earth," replied his grandfather.

"But why did he have to go there?" he asked.

"It is not for me to say, but what came of it," replied his grandfather.

"Did you have to go to war grandpa?" he asked.

"Yes, a long time ago," answered his grandfather.

"Across the sea?" asked the boy.

"A different sea in 1917," replied his grandfather.

"Did you go to Saipan too?" he asked.

"Not Saipan. We went to the French countryside to stop the German Kaiser from waging war," replied his grandfather.

"What did you do in the war?" asked the boy.

"The same job your father did. Speak our words like the winds. Sacred words that you shall know. I will teach you as all Navajo Peoples should know," replied his grandfather.

"Was my father, brave?" asked the boy.

"He was the bravest of my sons and our tribe. One day, you must be brave."

Moments later, the grandfather and his grandson stopped and pointed to a large red rock face covered in ancient petroglyphs.

"Is that it, grandpa?" the boy asked.

"Yes, that's it. This is where we must go before the rains get here," said the grandfather. "

"Will we make it back home in time?" asked the boy.

"Of course, we will. But in this place, time has no meaning."

"Huh?" exclaimed the boy.

"One day, you will understand," said his grandfather.

With a deep sigh, the Navajo Elder surveyed the massive rock face and gazed upon its faint white etchings.

"You know, it looks just the same way as it did when my grandfather first took me here," he said.

"Like me?"

"Yes, I was once a little boy like you are now. For generations, we have come to this sacred place," revealed his grandfather.

It was then that the Navajo Elder reached into the inside pocket of his faded blue denim jacket. In his hand was a bundled sage stick. Holding a chrome-plated Zippo lighter, he lit one end of the bundled sage stick and quietly blew out the flame. As the smoke from the sage stick rose into the air, the young boy looked up to the sacred rock face before him. It was near the top where he could see carvings of primitive figures etched into the rock. Spirals and depiction of lights and strange looking people covered its face. The young boy's eyes focused on the high overhang of the rock face as his grandfather began to chant in the language of his Tribal Nation.

The boy stood in complete awe and wonder as the smoke reached the etchings. As the smoke filled every contour, the carvings seemed to come to life. It was as if the primitive figures animated as they moved and danced about. The animals grazed, the horses ran, and the hunters hunted. And then the more towering strange-looking figures resembling people wearing helmets with hoses and antenna protruding from them swayed with the smoke as the spirals and stars above them flickered. The young boy looked up and was not sure what he was seeing, nor could he contemplate its meaning. In a sense, they looked odd and inhuman to the young boy. He looked up as high as he could and took note of what appeared to be depictions of constellations of stars.

"Are those stars?" asked the boy.

"They were made by the Ancient Ones who lived here long before our tribe came to these lands. For generations, our peoples passed down the stories of the Star People who came here that I now pass down to you. Perhaps one day, you will pass on these stories to one of your own."

CHAPTER II
OPERATION PLEIADES

Blue, a crystal blue, that's how the skies looked over the South China Seas that day. That was the view from inside the white and blue Boeing 707 as it made its slow descent towards the scattered rain clouds that hugged the coast up ahead. From inside the airliner, a young blonde Pan Am Stewardess in her distinct blue uniform walked down the narrow aisle over to the two lone Caucasian men who were sound asleep in their seats. They had slept through the long night, and now it was time to wake up before landing in Saigon. Thus, the stewardess casually nudged one of them to awaken the two men.

"The story you are about to hear is one you may find incredible, if not, beyond belief. If I had not written this down, I am not sure if I would have believed it myself. Had I heard it from someone else, I would have told them they were full of shit. But I can assure you, that's not the case. They say dead men tell no tales. But if you are reading this that means one of three things has happened to me: I've been Sheep-dipped to another country, or I'm living anonymously in some boring suburbia, or I will have met my fate, and the cleanup crew has erased all records of my existence. Don't ask me when or where I found the time to write this down in my pocket journal. I am not sure how I did it myself. For reasons of

National Security, some elements of this story cannot be disclosed. But I will say this; if there is truth in such confessions, they must be told, for, in the end, they will say it never happened and I was never here."

"For the record, my name is John Anson Swift, or as my friends called me, Jay for short. That's me in the white short-sleeved shirt seen there asleep at the window seat of the Pan Am 707. That younger guy who could pass for an all-star quarterback sitting next to me with the blonde hair was Fred Mason. He was my go-to man of my team. He was a by-the-book former U.S. Army Weapons expert and MIT graduate. Notice how you see him adjusting his skinny black necktie into place before landing? Mason was a sharp kid who, after MIT, was snatched up by the Company and paired with me. I suppose it was because of our military backgrounds. He was none the less, a good man."

"Thirty-six hours earlier, we were in the middle of the Negev Desert pulling apart a piece of the latest Soviet hardware recovered from a downed Syrian MIG. That's when we got the call. We had to drop what we were doing and get our asses out on the next plane out of Tel Aviv to the Far East. Specifically, for an urgent assignment right in the middle of the war zone in the Republic of Vietnam. For reasons of National Security, I can't tell you all the particulars. But of what I can reveal, I will share with you here."

It was then that the overhead Fasten Seatbelts / No Smoking signs came lit up as the lead Pan Am Stewardess addressed the passengers over the PA system to ready for landing. Just as the two men fastened their seatbelts, the coastline and the brown muddy waters of the Mekong Delta came into view.

"The date was Sunday, October 29th, 1967, around 0700 hours, local time. Our plane was on final approach for landing at Tan Son Nhut. It served as both an International Airport complete with commercial terminals and as an Air Base for both the United States Air Force and the VNAF (Viet Nam Air Force). You see, Fred and I both worked as "field analysts" for the Company. Specifically, we were part of a small reaction team that would go out at a moment's notice to find, locate, and acquire exotic foreign technologies. Our mandate quite simple: We were to study and evaluate anything that would give the United States a leading edge over our geopolitical adversaries. And by acquire, I mean capture, recover, or steal anything of value that could be a potential threat to our national defense and to do so by any means necessary. Usually, we would take the Company jet, but as you can surmise, we had to make other plans in part due to an unforeseen mechanical issue. Thus, we took the first inconspicuous commercial flight out."

"It had been an interesting job up until that point, one that covered the last two years of my life since leaving the U.S. Military Advisory Command in Vietnam. It had taken me from one undisclosed airfield to another to virtually every part of the globe short of Antarctica. But now, I was headed back to the war zone. Fred and I had shared some tense moments working side by side over the last two years, but nothing like the dangers of Vietnam. We still didn't know it yet, but we were going somewhere that when it was all said and done, we would have bargained for more than anyone could have possibly asked for and never again."

It was then that the 707's landing gear touched down on the runway at Tan Son Nhut. The jetliner quickly shifted its four engines into reverse thrust to slow the plane down to taxi. Swift looked through the small window as the aircraft turned at the far end of the runway. On one side of the runway, you could see rows of old white DC-3's of the National Airline of the Republic of Vietnam alongside brand new Boeing 707's and DC-8 jetliners from the West. Moments later, the plane turned again, revealing a view of the opposite military side of the runway that constituted Tan Son Nhut Air Base.

"Hey, Fred, take a look," pointed Swift.

"Looks like brand spanking new F-4 Phantoms II's fresh off the assembly line," observed Mason.

"They didn't have them when I was here in 65," remarked Swift.

"Is that right?"

"Back then, these rows were lined with F-100 Super Sabers," recalled Swift.

"You know, I would sure love to get another close-up look on one of those Phantoms now that they have 20mm Vulcan cannons," said Mason.

"Well, Fred, you might want to be careful what you wish for. In Vietnam, you just might get it, and that's not always a good thing," warned Swift.

This was an ominous warning on Swift's part.

"For all my useful antidotes, it had never occurred to me that for once, I should take some of my own advice. If only I could have listened to myself at that exact moment. We were on a commercial flight wearing civilian clothes. Most guys said little or nothing. Fred and I liked to chat now and then, but in public, we kept things on the down-low. After all, we weren't spies, and we certainly weren't James Bond. To put it accurately, we were glorified technicians trolling around the globe for something to reverse engineer in hopes of giving our side an edge."

Minutes later, the bright outdoor light flooded the interior cabin as the door opened. The sudden tropical humidity impacted the cabin's threshold as the temperature hovered near eighty-six degrees while the passengers reached for the overhead bins. Fred Mason stood up and opened the overhead bin above his seat and retrieved a silver briefcase, and then prepared to disembark. Once at the threshold before stepping down the air stairs to the tarmac, one could smell that strange aroma of the tropical Southeast Asian Republic. It was a mixture of moisture from the damp ground of previous night's rains and something else. There, both men donned their Company issued Ray-ban sunglasses and stepped off the plane. Upon emerging into the open air, Fred Mason felt a sudden wave hitting his senses like some unexpected wind.

"Say! I know you said it was going to be hot here, but damn! And what the hell is that smell?" asked Mason.

Swift abruptly laughed, having remembered this same shock to the senses when he first arrived in Vietnam.

"After doing a tour here, I still couldn't tell you. Just smile at the pretty girls in Ao Dai's (Traditional VN Dress) and don't get too distracted. We have a job to do," advised Swift.

"Roger that!" replied Mason.

As the passengers stepped off the air stairs and onto the tarmac, they would walk another one hundred feet towards the terminal entrance. There, after clearing customs, they were greeted by smiling young Vietnamese women wearing colorful silk Ao Dai lining both sides of the doorway. The terminal at Tan Son Nhut was spacious with high ceilings, marble flooring, and wood-paneled walls, which were very modern for its time. It could almost pass for any contemporary European airport terminal. There was a mix of Western and Vietnamese travelers along with scores of posted ARVN (Army Republic of Viet Nam) soldiers that complimented the heavy Vietnamese National Police presence. This made for a tense atmosphere at the crowded baggage claim where the two men walked past carrying their unassuming black "Bugout Bags."

It was then that Mason and Swift noticed a middle-aged Vietnamese man. He wore a dark-gray Brooks-Brothers three-button business suit holding a small white placard with nothing written on it. He looked every bit like a plainclothes policeman or an RVN government official as he looked back at them through his black horned rimmed glasses. They suspected this might be their man, but to be sure, they would deliberately walk past him without a word. It was not until the two men exited the terminal and stood outside that the man walked up and stood next to Swift.

"Welcome to Saigon. My name is Ky. Please follow me to the car."

Swift and Mason followed Mr. Ky out of the airport terminal to an awaiting black 1965 four-door Peugeot 404. They could see another stern-looking Vietnamese man wearing a dark suit sitting in the front passenger seat as Mr. Ky popped open the trunk to load their black bags. Suddenly, a torrential downpour of rain came in out of nowhere that drenched the curbside of the terminal.

"What the hell!" exclaimed Mason.

"Monsoon season," said Swift.

"But, there were no rain clouds when we entered the terminal!"

"Welcome to Vietnam," laughed Swift.

Shaking his head, Mason quickly entered the car from the driver's side rear seat carrying his briefcase as fast as he could to get out of the rain. Swift got in the car and sat in the back seat opposite

Mason. Mr. Ky quickly turned on the ignition and activated the car's wipers before speeding away from the terminal. The vehicle drove towards the busy streets of Saigon. Even in the torrential rain, the busy roads were congested with many Vespa scooters, bicycles, old French cars, and many ARVN and American military vehicles. Suddenly, their car made an unexpected turn into a dimly lit narrow alleyway alarming Swift and Mason.

"Hey, this isn't the way to Thong Nhut Street!" observed Swift.

"You are correct; this is not the way," replied Ky.

Just then, the Vietnamese man in the front passenger seat turned around a pointed a small PPK Pistol at Swift.

"I presume this isn't the shortcut to the American Embassy either," said Mason.

Swift could see that Mason had already reached for his sidearm and had it pointed at the head of the Vietnamese man who sat in the passenger seat.

"I would not do that, Mister Mason. Mr. Cao will not hesitate to shoot should you fail to cooperate," warned Ky.

"That may be the case, but given this situation, my man here won't hesitate to shoot either," replied Swift.

Just then, Mr. Ky stopped the car in the dark alley.

"I must now ask you both for your credentials," said Ky.

Swift and Mason slowly reached for their identification while keeping their eyes on Mr. Cao. Mr. Ky quickly looked over their passports and then smiled before giving the nod to Mr. Cao for him to put his pistol away.

"My apologies, Captain Swift, we had to be sure," said Ky.

"What the hell was that all about?" demanded Swift.

"Sorry, I am not privy to such details. Our orders were to bring you from the airport and transport you to the safe house once your identities were confirmed," replied Ky.

"Well, now that's out of the way, can we dispense with the Dr. No treatment and get this show on the road?" asked Swift.

"Yes, Sir," complied Mr. Ky.

He quickly restarted the car and began to drive out of the alleyway and back onto the main thoroughfare.

"Say, Boss, do you think I look a little bit like Sean Connery?" asked Mason.

Swift placed his hand on his chin and pondered Mason's query.

"Hmm, we shall see, Moneypenny," laughed Swift.

Thirty minutes later, the black Peugeot drove into a small undisclosed French Colonial styled compound that was lined with tall trees. The gate was covered in heavy vines and manned by two young Vietnamese men in khaki civilian clothes. Behind the gate were two more men carrying M3 Grease Guns who watched every move as the black Peugeot drove into the narrow concrete driveway leading up to a covered carport. Mr. Ky parked the car next to an American Dodge Dart, and a pair of U.S. Army Jeeps with MACV painted in white on the side of its hood next to its serial number. As Swift and Mason opened the car doors, they could see another American car in the back pointed to a back gate leading to an alleyway.

"This way, gentleman," pointed Mr. Ky as Swift and Mason

followed him up the white wooden steps.

The interior of the house had a large sitting room with modern couches and chairs placed before the sheer white drapes that covered the sizeable French bay windows. Inside the freshly mopped dark wooden flooring, one could see a small desk near the door. Sitting there was a modern-looking Vietnamese woman wearing a white sleeveless shift dress complete with black beehive hairdo reminiscent of the former First Lady Madame Nhu. She presented a pleasant smile before returning to her work, typing away on a black IBM typewriter under the yellow flag with three distinctive red stripes of the Republic of Vietnam. Below it hung a black-framed portrait of Nguyễn Văn Thiệu, the President of South Vietnam.

Mr. Ky led Mason and Swift down the hallway to a pale sky blue painted conference room lined with white molding and baseboards. Cooling the humid room was an ornate white overhead ceiling fan spinning up above. On the wall was a large operations map of South Vietnam before a large mahogany conference table and wooden chairs. The furnishings' dark stains suggested it had been there as far back to the early French Colonial Period. And there at the center of the table was a silver serving tray containing a glass pitcher of water and crystal glasses. At either end were matching crystal ashtrays.

With the humidity being unbearable, sweat was taking hold of the newly arrived Americans. Thus, they both removed their jackets and loosened their skinny black neckties. Saigon CIA Station Chief William Colby entered the conference room shortly after that wearing a tan suit and thick black eyeglasses. Colby was joined by a U.S. Army General who arrived with his younger Adjutant, followed by two CIA agents in civilian clothes. As soon as the door closed, the Station Chief got straight down to business.

"Gentlemen, welcome to Saigon," greeted Colby.

The veteran CIA chief extended his arm and briefly shook both men's hands.

"Thank you, Sir," replied Swift and Mason.

"We're glad you're here," replied Colby.

"Sir, I only have Fred Mason with me. The rest of my team is still in Israel," replied Swift.

"That's alright; this comes from the Director himself. He felt your experience with Advisory Command would make up for that. So please take a seat," instructed Colby.

The general's adjutant pulled out a pair of thin packages Marlboro cigarettes made for the US Military and offered them to Mason and Swift.

"Could I offer you gentlemen cigarettes or some water?" asked the Lieutenant.

"Thank you, but I don't smoke," replied Mason.

"I'll take them. Trust me, these will come in handy later on," replied Swift.

Mason looked on as his boss grabbed both packs and inserted them into his shirt breast pocket as Chief Colby prepared to speak.

"Just to get introductions out of the way, this is my Assistant Director of Operations Richard Shaw, My Intel officer Bob Keene, General Lowe, and Lieutenant Tom Madsen, who's assigned to see to your needs. Of course, you have already met Captain Ky Nguyen of the ARVN Special Forces. I sincerely apologize for the cloak and dagger, but we're dealing with some rather extraordinary developments taking place in the Central Highlands near the

Cambodian border over the last thirty-six hours," said Colby.

"Sir, if I may ask, why we were pulled from the Negev Desert to come here?" asked Swift.

General Lowe looked over to Station Chief Colby for approval.

"You and Mr. Mason participated in Operation Diamond, did you not?" asked Gen. Lowe.

"Sir, we can neither confirm nor deny the existence of such an operation had we been aware of it," replied Swift.

"You further were involved in the interrogation of Munir Redfa piloting the Mig-21, which led to a physical altercation Major Ariel Sharon of the Israeli Army, were you not?" asked Keene.

"I know of no such involvement. That said, if such an altercation on Major Sharon had occurred by either myself or any member of my team, he probably deserved it," answered Swift.

Assistant Director Shaw chuckled at the notion.

"Are you familiar with Project Oxcart?" asked Keene.

"I never heard of it," replied Swift.

"You can cut the crap, Swift. We know both of you have seen an A-12 up close. Lieutenant Madsen is going to show you some photos and maybe you can help us," said Colby.

Following Chief Colby's instruction, Lieutenant Madsen opened a folder containing a series of 8x10 black and white photographs and placed them on the table.

"As you can see, this is an object recovered two nights ago from the crash site located three klicks east of Hill 875 near Dak To measuring four inches in diameter," explained Madsen.

The grainy photograph contained an unusual looking object that resembled a four-inch shard of white-blue crystal. It had what looked like a serrated tube running through it with burn marks at both ends.

"Have either of you ever seen anything like this before?" asked General Lowe.

"No, Sir," replied Swift and Mason.

"This could not have come from an A-12. It looks like a broken spar of some type comprised translucent material with fiber cable running through it. Possibly an advanced connector of some type," guessed Mason.

"That's classified," interrupted Shaw.

"What is it?" asked Swift.

"We have no idea. We just know is that it came from the crash site near Dak To," replied Gen. Lowe.

"That's where you come in," said Colby.

Lieutenant Madsen then placed two vanilla folders containing the official reports of the find on the conference table. Both Swift and Mason quickly looked over the papers inside and became focused on one line:

"Supplemental Conclusion notes that the object in question was recovered from a downed enemy helicopter?' remarked Mason.

"That is based on the eyewitness accounts by a squad from the 4th ID three kicks out from the crash site," said Gen. Lowe.

"Well, that's a new one!" exclaimed Mason.

"Somehow, I don't believe anyone is going to buy the notion of Uncle Ho having anything of this level of sophistication. While it's true that Charlie gets the latest hardware from the Soviets and Chinese, this looks way out of their league," assessed Swift.

"Well, Captain, that's what the Director wants us to say for the time being," replied Gen. Lowe.

"So, this is the cover story you're running with?" asked Mason.

"This comes directly from Langley. That's our story until you two can figure out what exactly what we are dealing with," replied Colby.

"Okay, so far, we have one recovered object of unknown origin or composition from a crash site. Take us to it," said Swift.

Station Chief Colby removed his glasses and rubbed his eyes as he sighed before speaking.

"Well, that's going to be a problem," said Colby.

"Why is that?" asked Mason.

The crash site is smack in the middle of an enemy tunnel complex that was nearly overrun last night by combined NVA and Viet Cong forces. Whatever crashed there is of deep interest to them. The 4th ID was pulled back to relieve the besieged Special Forces camp nearby. Until the site is secured, you will have to conduct your investigation elsewhere until we can chopper you in," revealed Gen. Lowe.

"Great! This gets better by the minute!" exclaimed Swift.

"Well then, if the LZ is too hot, then we should have a look at the recovered object," said Mason.

"That's the other problem," said Shaw.

"Please, by all means, indulge me," said Swift.

"The object has disappeared from the secure vault in the American Embassy basement," replied Shaw.

"Disappeared? How did that happen?' asked Mason.

"Oh, it gets even more complicated," said Keene.

"How so?" asked Swift.

Lieutenant Madsen placed another black & white 8x10 photograph on the table. The photo revealed to contain an image of a North Vietnamese Intelligence officer in dress uniform.

"Who is this guy?" asked Swift.

"This man in the photograph has been identified as an NVA Colonel Trung Ke Linh. He's from Hanoi. As far as we know, this man is an Intelligence Officer who answers directly to NVA General Võ Giap. This next photo was taken last Wednesday by our sources operating in Haiphong Harbor. As you can see in this photo Colonel Linh is seen talking with Soviet Military Advisors," revealed Keene.

Just then, Mason's eyes opened wide as he examined the photo. He then nudged Swift's elbow as the two men first pointed to a man in the picture then shook their heads in agreement.

"Is there a problem?" asked Colby.

"Yes, Sir," replied Mason.

"You care to explain?" asked Shaw.

"The Soviet Advisor seen on the left is General Sergei Kasakov.

He's a Soviet GRU Officer whose mission mirrors our own," revealed Swift.

"We've had two run-ins with this guy and his team in the Sinai and along the Turkish border. He's a ruthless bastard who plays by a different set of rules," remarked Mason.

"If Kasakov is here, then something big must be going on," assessed Swift

"We believe this may explain the recent increase in recent enemy troop movements massing along the Ho Chi Minh Trail," replied Shaw.

"That still does not explain how that object became missing," argued Mason.

"Well, that is why we are meeting here and not in my office at the American Embassy," replied Colby.

"Its clear security has been compromised by some unknown operative with one singular objective. Until we know more, this is what you will have to work with," explained Shaw.

"So tell us more about Colonel Linh," said Swift.

"He was captured in the tunnel complex at the crash site. He was later whisked away aboard a black UH-1 helicopter flown by what was believed to be CIA operatives," revealed Gen. Lowe.

"Believed to be? In other words, you don't know who grabbed him?" asked Mason.

"We honestly don't know. It could be Soviet KGB posing as CIA," suggested Shaw.

"That would be an unprecedented, bold move on the part of the

Soviets," remarked Mason.

"Sounds like the whole thing has been compromised. You've lost control," said Swift.

"They appeared to be American. We believe they are a rogue Black Ops team that Washington had somehow kept us in the dark about, but even that's doubtful. We're supposed to be running the show here," said Colby.

"Well, that may be the case, but it sounds to me like someone has other plans," remarked Swift.

"For now, that's all we can surmise. Just presume these operatives are dangerous. If you encounter them, use extreme caution. You'll be given all access clearance throughout the country. You are further authorized to use whatever deadly force or means necessary to complete your mission," instructed Gen. Lowe.

"There's another thing you should know," said Shaw.

"Oh? What's that?" asked Swift.

"As of this morning, Colonel Linh was found dead by local ARVN forces lying face down in a rice paddy near Long Binh. Approximately three klicks away from where the man who captured him is currently being held," revealed Shaw.

At this point, Swift and Mason looked confused.

"What do you mean by being held?" asked Mason.

"According to the report filed by the 720th MP Battalion at the LBJ (Long Bing Jail) Ranch, a veteran Staff Sergeant by the name of Wayne Thunderfoot of the 1/9 Scouts allegedly struck an officer in the field and beat him up pretty bad," explained Madsen.

"Say, Tom? Do you have that file on this Thunderfoot?" asked

Gen. Lowe.

"Ah, yes, Sir. I have it right here," replied Madsen.

Lieutenant Madsen reached for a file folder containing his file. Swift and Mason looked over the photo that was attached to the file.

"He looks like a big guy," observed Mason.

"He's six-foot-two. Believe it or not, this guy can fit in the tightest of tunnels. They say he is one of the best Tunnel Rats in the Central Highlands," said Gen. Lowe.

"His name is Staff Sergeant, Wayne Thunderfoot, born in Arizona on September 17th, 1941. He is the son of a 2nd Generation Navajo Code Talker who was killed by a Japanese mortar on Saipan July 4th, 1944. His mother died shortly afterward. Orphaned, he was raised by his paternal grandfather. He was a high school letter athlete and enlisted in the U.S. Army right after graduation. He is an excellent tracker and hunter. He is on his second tour, having first distinguished himself during a firefight with Viet Cong forces on his first night in-country at Camp Radcliff, September 3rd, 1966 earning himself the Bronze Star and the medal for Gallantry. He also has a Purple Heart for a wound sustained at Bong Song and numerous citations. He has served with distinction with the 1/9 and has earned a reputation of being one of the most feared Tunnel Rats in the Central Highlands to the point that both our troops and the Viet Cong call him The Chief. He is currently being held on charges awaiting military court-martial," revealed Madsen.

"Are you trying to tell me this decorated Tunnel Rat who just captured a high-value prisoner is being held on bullshit charges?" questioned Swift.

"CID (Criminal Investigation Division) couldn't get anything out of him other than he was dealing with a bout of nausea. What's odd about that is that Colonel Linh was also reported to be suffering from nausea and vomiting when he was last seen alive at Dak To," revealed Gen. Lowe.

Mr. Ky, who had been silent, smiled, and then placed a small medicine bottle on the table.

"This was found on Linh's body. The bottle says these are Potassium Iodide tablets. There were many found in his system," revealed Ky.

Swift slowly pulled out his small pocket journal and began to scribble down some quick notes.

"Potassium Iodide is a treatment for radiation sickness," explained Mason.

"You're correct, Mr. Mason. Given the flight path originating from over the Laotian and Cambodian borders, do you suspect the Soviets were testing a nuclear-powered aircraft?" asked Colby.

"Unlikely, nuclear powered flights were tested extensively by the United States and the Soviet Union throughout the 1950s. Neither Tupolev nor Convair-North American could get the concept to work without irradiating the plane or its crews. The smallest known submarine reactors are still too large and heavy for a fighter plane, making the whole concept impractical, particularly in the advent of mid-air refueling," explained Mason.

"Another possibility is that we're dealing with a top-secret supersonic Soviet prototype, something along the lines of a nuclear-capable fighter-bomber variant. It could very well be the rumored Tupolev Tu-150-1A," suggested Swift.

"My God! One of those things could swoop in and nuke our guys and be out of there before anyone knew what happened!" exclaimed Keene.

"Not likely, the Soviets love their proxy wars. They wouldn't risk a nuclear confrontation over a messy regional conflict in Vietnam," replied Mason.

"Assuming we are correct, this plane possibly broke up over the Central Highlands. If the 4th ID did see helicopters flying towards the scene, then that would explain Kasakov's presence in Vietnam. They would want to recover any wreckage found that wasn't destroyed by the plane on impact," suggested Swift.

"That might explain the radiation signature," remarked Shaw.

"So, in your expert opinion, what's the chance this could be something else? Suppose a meteor?" asked Colby.

"We would need to know more about what happened that night in question before we go out to the crash site," replied Swift.

"I'll again defer to AD Shaw," said Colby.

"On the night of the incident around 0230 hours, one of our PBR boats operating on the Sông Đà Rằng River reported being attacked by a bright light in the sky," said Shaw.

"A bright light?" asked Mason.

"Any survivors or recoverable wreckage?" asked Swift.

"By the time the Brown Water Navy showed up, the boat was obliterated, and no remains of the seven-man crew were found along the riverbank," replied Keene.

"Do you believe this incident is related to this rumored prototype?" asked Mason.

"Well, that's where the story for lack of a better word gets weird," said Colby.

Fred Mason raised an eyebrow as did Swift as they both became somewhat intrigued.

"Weird, Sir?" asked Swift.

"Just before the PBR boat was lost, an F-4 returning from a mission up North got the call. There was an E-2 Hawkeye on station from the aircraft carrier USS Oriskany tracking this thing when the Navy PBR boat called in for help. They said this bogey would appear then disappear off their radar. They said it moved at high speeds giving the F-4 chase almost to the Laotian border," revealed Shaw.

"Did they get a visual?" asked Mason.

"Well, yes and no," replied Keene.

"What the hell does that mean?" asked Swift.

"They could not positively identify the fast-moving aircraft in the night sky. It appeared as a glowing light in the night sky," replied Shaw.

"Assuming we are correct and the Soviets did indeed built this prototype and flew it over Vietnam, the glow may have come from the airfoil at high speeds above Mach 3 or better," postulated Swift.

"It would be the most logical explanation, particularly for the glowing light sighting. The A-12 was designed to deflect radar rendering almost invisible at high speeds, which tends to make its wings glow. So yes, based on what you have told us, we have to go with that assumption," said Mason.

"The F-4 pilot and his RIO (Radar Intercept Officer) both said this unknown aircraft banked at high-speed angles and then came at them. It damaged the F-4 before the object crashed up in the Central Highlands around Dak To," revealed Shaw.

"How long before you think the 4th ID will have this site secure for us to go in and investigate?" asked Mason.

"The site is still hot. The 1st PAVN (People's Army Viet Nam) Division is said to be massing forces along the Ho Chi Minh Trail on the other side of the Cambodian border. In response, 12th and 1/9 Cavalry will be mounting a larger operation in support of the 4th ID sometime in the next three days. As soon as the LZ is secured, we will get you there," said Gen. Lowe.

"In the meantime, AD Shaw will give you both a card with a number on it. Memorize it and leave it here in this room. That is the number you will call if you need a car, plane, or chopper to go anywhere you need until the crash site is secured," said Colby.

"To get to the crash site, you'll need to take a Company plane from Tan Son Nhut to Camp Radcliff at An Khe in the Central Highlands. From there, you will give your credentials to the CO (Commanding Officer). Should things go south, there is a secure line that will connect you directly to Langley (CIA headquarters) from the Signal Corps relay station atop the Hon Cong Mountain overlooking the base in a locked black box. You'll know it when you see it. Make sure to use the same combination you used in the Sinai," instructed Keene.

"Understood," acknowledged Swift.

"You both have rooms at the Caravelle Hotel in downtown Saigon for as long as you need to complete your mission. It has bulletproof glass, air conditioning, and modern amenities. I suggest you first interview Staff Sergeant Thunderfoot at the LBJ Ranch, then head on over to MACV and talk to that squad from the 4th ID who can give an eyewitness account of what they saw. There is also gun camera footage from the F-4 at Tan Son Nhut Air Base. Check with Colonel Randal Wallace at MACV. I believe you know him," said Shaw.

"I certainly do. We served together at Plei Me under Charlie Beckwith," revealed Swift.

"Good, he'll set you up with whatever you need there. Upon the conclusion of this assignment, all materials must be returned to the Saigon Station or be destroyed. This mission will be known as Operation Pleiades. Please bear in mind that this mission does not exist, nor will it ever exist," said Shaw.

"Understood," acknowledged Swift and Mason.

Having reached what seemed the natural conclusion of the briefing, Station Chief Colby stood up from his chair. He then recomposed himself before preparing to exit the conference room.

"Well then, gentlemen, I hate to cut this short, but I must get back to running our end of the war. I believe you have everything you need. Should any new developments occur, we shall apprise you of the situation," said Colby.

"Yes, Sir," replied Swift and Mason.

"Good luck and God Bless America,' said Colby.

Station Chief Colby quietly left the room with AD Shaw and Bob Keene leaving Swift and Mason alone with General Lowe and his Adjutant Lieutenant Madsen.

"Mr. Ky will drive you to the Caravelle Hotel. He's on loan to us and will handle any translations needed along the way. Keep your side arms handy. Remember, we are in an active war zone. When you get to the hotel, best change into the jungle issue fatigues we've provided for you, so you draw less attention. Given the sightings of these rogue operatives posing as CIA, we want you to blend in with our military presence here," instructed Gen. Lowe.

"Yes, provided they don't already know we are already here," agreed Swift.

"Agreed, any questions?" asked Gen. Lowe.

"No, Sir," replied Swift and Mason.

"Good, now get over to the hotel and get out of those civvies. With those white shirts and skinny black neckties, I swear you two look like a pair of Mormon missionaries. Now get out of here!" ordered Gen. Lowe.

"Yes, Sir!"

CHAPTER III
THE LBJ RANCH

Thirty minutes later, Mr. Ky's black Peugeot 404 pulled up along the busy curbside of the Caravelle Hotel. It was a beige ten-story building in the heart of downtown Saigon. It was also the home to both the Australian and New Zealand Embassies. As Swift exited the car, he looked up to the 5th floor and could see no trace of the damage left by a bomb that exploded there on August 25th, 1964. And while the marble flooring and sleek modern façade greeted one with a false sense of security, the danger posed by the attack on the 5th floor was not lost on Swift. Even in the confines of Saigon, the war was only a heartbeat away.

The Company had seen to it that Swift and Mason had adjoining rooms with balconies overlooking the busy Saigon streets. It was here that Swift had placed his black Bugout bag on the queen-sized bed before turning on the air conditioner. He could further see a pair of black combat boots and a suit bag hanging in the wardrobe. Unzipping the bag, he discovered a brand new olive drab green Jungle issue fatigues with the slanted pockets that were unavailable when he served as an Advisor. Swift could see his name patch opposite the U.S. Army patch along with his Captain's Bars on his shirt collar. Notably missing was his Special Forces patch, then again, he was working for the Company with a mandate to blend in with the American military presence there. Instead, the prominent MACV patch was on the shoulder. No sooner than he changed into his uniform and rolled up his sleeves, Swift then donned his fatigue cap and his gold-rimmed Ray-Ban sunglasses before looking back at himself in the tall standing mirror.

'Just like old times,' he thought.

Having worked for the Company, Swift either wore distinctive black fatigues or civilian clothes, depending on the assignment. But now he was back in the war zone, and this was the one way he could move about without suspicion. That's just the way the Company wanted it. As far as the general foregone conclusion of the involvement of other operatives was, blending in was a matter of anonymity. Awareness of such danger made this necessary ploy a matter of personal security that neither Swift nor Mason would take lightly. This time he was not there to fight the Viet Cong. His mission had nothing to do with the war. It just happened to drop into the war zone, and things were just getting hot.

Minutes later, Swift walked down the hotel lobby and was saluted by a Sergeant who was likely on an in-country R&R (Rest & Recuperation) leave. He could see Mason standing at the curbside in his new fatigues with his sleeves rolled up carrying his silver briefcase. He was also wearing the same issue gold-rimmed Ray-Ban sunglasses just like any other G.I. walking about in Saigon.

"There he was, back in uniform, Lieutenant Fred Mason, standing there looking so official. He could have easily got into Special Forces, but instead took an offer to go to MIT. You could say he made the better move. Well, at least, in the pay and perks."

"Looking sharp there, Lieutenant," said Swift.

"Thank you, Captain. Well, I have to admit this is better than trying to pass ourselves off as a pair of civilian aerospace engineers," remarked Mason.

"Although that too would have worked, people would assume we'd get in the way," replied Swift.

Just then, a canvas-covered U.S. Army Jeep pulled up. They could see MACV painted on the side of the hood. It was a young buck sergeant driving with the name Warner on his name patch.

"Captain Swift?" he asked.

"Who wants to know?"

"I have orders to drive Captain Swift and Lieutenant Mason directly to the MACV compound to see Colonel Wallace," said Warner.

"That sounds about right," said Swift as he climbed into the front seat.

Sergeant Warner waited until the two men were seated in the vehicle before putting the Jeep into gear and speeding off into the oncoming rush of Saigon traffic.

Just outside Tan Son Nhut Airbase was the big MACV compound or as some would call it the Pentagon East. It was a big white complex with multi-purpose buildings spaced behind a big wire fence and a small barren strip of land on the other side of the fence like the Green Line found at fire support bases out in the countryside. Tall narrow watch towers overlooked the perimeter of the compound that was manned at all hours. They quickly waved past the main gate and pulled up to the main building. Just past the hardened bunkers, there were two big flagpoles, one bearing the American flag and the other flying the flag of the RVN.

Moments later, Swift and Mason were shown to a back-office down a long corridor by a female soldier wearing olive-green fatigues. No sooner than the door opened, Swift could hear a familiar voice.

"Well, I'll be Goddamned! If it isn't Captain Jay Swift alive and well, in-country!" exclaimed Col. Wallace.

"Yes, it is, Colonel, good to see you again!"

Swift and Mason stepped inside the Colonel's office and saluted.

"Incidentally, this is my partner, Fred Mason," introduced Swift.

Mason quickly switched hands with his briefcase to shake hands the Colonel.

"Pleased to meet you, son, have a seat," said Col. Wallace.

"Thank you, Sir," replied Mason.

"So, how the hell are you, Jay?" asked Col. Wallace.

"I'm good, I just didn't expect to be back here so soon," said Swift.

"Boss, you had earlier mentioned that you and the Colonel served together?" asked Mason.

"We sure did. Colonel Wallace was my first C.O. in-country before the shit hit the fan in late 1965. Operation Shiny Bayonet," replied Swift.

"After what went down in Plei Me, I thought I would never see this guy again. It's too bad you're not here for the war because I could sure use your talents out in the field. Charlie is planning something big, and I need all my best men. We believe they are going to move three entire divisions and hit Dak To any day now," said Col.

Wallace.

Swift turned his head just slightly enough to look at his partner, who looked back at him with conviction. Colonel Wallace could see a grim certainty in their facial expressions heightening his suspicions of what was going on behind the scenes.

"I'm not a gambling man, but I'm willing to bet you know what's really behind all this," speculated Col. Wallace.

"Sir, you know we can neither confirm nor deny any such knowledge if we were aware of its existence," replied Swift.

"That's alright. You can spare me the standard CIA crap. I know something went down at Dak To and those little bastards and their Soviet benefactors want it. Otherwise, they wouldn't be so eager to fight us for it," said Col. Wallace.

"We don't know what happened at Dak To, but we're here to find out," declared Swift.

Colonel Wallace sat down at his desk and continued his conversation.

"So tell me, Lieutenant, how you wind up with this big lug?" he asked.

"Our skill sets were a good fit, Sir," replied Mason.

"This guy left the Army to get his Masters at MIT before he came to work with me," revealed Swift.

"Is that right?" asked the Col. Wallace.

"Yes, Sir, I did a year in West Germany then spent my last year working at the Pentagon before being sent to Langley," replied Mason.

"Outstanding!" said Col. Wallace.

"Thank you, Sir," replied Mason.

"Well then, are you two ready to get to work?" asked Col. Wallace.

"That's what they pay us the big bucks for," laughed Swift.

"Very well then, I've been apprised of certain logistical requirements of your mission. I have drawn up these orders, which you shall both carry with you. This will give you whatever you need," said Col. Wallace as he handed the orders in two folded envelopes.

"Thank you, Sir. Our first objective is to drive out to the LBJ Ranch and go talk to that Tunnel Rat they call The Chief who they say might know something," said Swift.

"Drive, why the hell you would want to do that for when you got a Company chopper?" asked Col. Wallace

"A chopper? Well, that's all you had to say!" exclaimed Mason.

Minutes later, Sergeant Warner drove Swift and Mason through the East Gate of the Air Base to a segregated unmarked hangar. There they could see an unmarked UH-1 Huey awaiting them on standby. No sooner than the Jeep came to a stop just clear of the rotor blades, the pilot started up the chopper. They could see the co-pilot pointing to them to slide open the side door as the rotors grew louder. Mason and Swift immediately slid open the side door and climbed aboard. Mason placed his silver briefcase on the seat. They next picked up a pair of headsets left on the back seat for them to communicate with, which they quickly put on to use.

"Where to, Captain?" asked the pilot.

"Bien Hoa Air Base," said Swift.

"Roger that!" replied the pilot.

A moment later, the unmarked UH-1 Huey lifted off the tarmac and into the air and started heading North East.

"It had been less than three hours since we touched down in Saigon. So far, I've had a gun pulled on me, I've been put back in uniform, thrown onto a chopper, and now we're headed to jail. And to think, this was only day one. The twenty-minute flight took us along the route from Tan Son Nhut Air Base to Long Binh following the path of the QL-1. As we looked out of the opened doors of our chopper, we could see a traffic snarl leading up to an ARVN checkpoint set up on the Newport Bridge. Having passed over the Song Saigon River, we could see the big ugly water treatment plant at Tu Duc. From there, we flew across the Dong Nai River to Bien Hoa. Just over on my side door, you could see the South Vietnamese version of Arlington National Cemetery just off in the distance. From the air, you could get an idea of the scope of the place. It was a sight to see with its grand main gate standing before hallowed grounds and manicured walkways. While being far from being our prodigal sons as far as nation-building goes, the South Vietnamese were well on their way. The Republic of South Vietnam was a beautiful country, but it was a troubled work in progress hanging on pins and needles. They had built much infrastructure in their short twenty-year existence, but the more they made, the more determined their foe to the north was out to tear it all down."

Just then, Mason addressed the pilot.

"Say! Any chance you guys can just skip Bien Hoa altogether and take us directly to the Long Binh Jail?" he asked.

"Sure, this chopper has priority to set down wherever we need to go," replied the pilot.

"Good to know. I would've hated to drive a Jeep from the airbase," said Swift.

"No worries, Captain. This might look like an Army chopper, but we don't work for MACV," assured the pilot.

Minutes later, the unmarked UH-1 Huey circled the Army stockade at Long Binh and landed just outside the main gate. Swift could see the MPs of the 720th Military Police Battalion went on full alert as Swift and Mason quickly exited the chopper. Each of the manned watchtowers had guns pointed at them. Right off the bat, two MPs rushed over with their heads low to avoid the Huey's blades while carrying their M-16's as they tried to shout at them over the loud *whup-whup-whup* of the UH-1.

"Sir, you can't land here! This is an Army Stockade!" shouted one MP as Swift quickly pulled out his orders.

"I have priority clearance! We need to talk to somebody you're holding," informed Swift.

The MPs briefly looked over his orders in the prop wash of the rotor blades before handing them back to Swift.

'Yes, Sir, sorry about that, right this way!"

Ten minutes later, Swift and Mason sat at a table in a gray florescent-lit interrogation room. Mason had placed his silver briefcase on the table and opened it, removing a file folder, a small writing pad and pen, and a tape recorder. Just then, two large MPs brought the handcuffed prisoner to the door and knocked.

"Bring him in," ordered Swift.

The door opened, and in came Staff Sergeant Wayne Thunderfoot. At six-foot-two, he cut an imposing figure. They could see he had a light brown complexion and a small scar on his right cheek as he was sat down across from them.

"You can take those cuffs off," directed Swift.

"Are you sure, Captain?" asked the MP.

"Positive," replied Swift.

"Yes, Sir!" acknowledged the MP.

The MPs unlocked the handcuffs and stepped out of the room and closed the door. Thunderfoot sat down on the chair opposite Swift and placed his hands on the table.

"Are you my lawyers?" he asked.

"Nope," replied Swift.

"Are you here to get me back to my unit?" he asked.

"Nope," replied Swift.

"Then, what do you want from me?"

"I am Captain Swift from the Special Operations Group. Lieutenant Mason and I are here to ask you a few questions."

"For the record, I would like you to say your name," instructed Mason.

The bemused Navajo Scout became tight-lipped as he sat back and folded his arms in silence.

"If you aren't lawyers, then I ain't saying shit," he replied.

Seeking to garner his cooperation, Mason pulled out a thin red pack of Marlboro Cigarettes and placed them on the table.

"Would you like a smoke?" asked Swift.

"Sure, but I'm still not telling you shit," said Thunderfoot.

"We're just here to ask you about what you saw that night at the tunnel complex at Dak To," explained Swift.

Thunderfoot reached over and grabbed the entire pack of Marlboros. He methodically unwrapped the clear plastic wrap covering the package and opened the gold inner wrap. He then pulled out one neatly packed cigarette and placed it in his mouth. Mason reached over and pulled out his chrome US Army issue Zippo lighter and lit his cigarette for him.

"Alright then, my name is Staff Sergeant Thunderfoot of 1/9 Scouts. Wayne is my last name, but the Army always gets it wrong. There's not much to tell. 4th ID found the tunnel complex near a large impact site. The 8th Engineers were bogged down at Bong Song. We were closer and already in the air, so we arrived on the scene before the MPs."

Mason then looked to Swift as Thunderfoot took a drag off his cigarette. It was then that Mason opened the file folder and placed a black and white 8x10 photograph and slid it across the table. Thunderfoot looked for a moment and then turned his head to look away.

"Have you ever seen this object or anything like it before?" asked Swift.

Thunderfoot continued to look away in silence. He appeared apprehensive and took another drag off his cigarette before putting it out on the black ashtray that sat atop the table. The photo had disturbed him, yet, he said nothing. At that point, Mason produced another black and white 8x10 photo and slid it across the table.

"Have you ever seen this man before?" asked Swift.

Thunderfoot glanced at the photo and again turned his head away, saying nothing.

"Shall we show him?" asked Mason.

"Do it," said Swift.

Mason then slid a third black and white 8x10 photo across the table.

"The man you are looking at is NVA Colonel Trung Ke Linh. He was found dead this morning in a rice paddy not too far from here," explained Swift.

It was then that Mason slid a fourth photo showing Colonel Linh and General Kasakov together in Haiphong Harbor. Thunderfoot became increasingly agitated as he lit another cigarette.

"We're just looking for some information. Your cooperation could go a long way to helping you clear up this mess you're in," said Mason.

"Look, buddy! I don't know who you are. But until you get me a lawyer or get me the fuck out of here, I don't have anything more to say. You dig?"

It was then that Swift switched off the tape recorder. Mason then reached out over the table and collected the photographs to place them back in his file folder and back into his silver briefcase before closing it shut.

"What, that's it?" asked Thunderfoot.

"Yup, the clock is ticking. If you have nothing to say, then we're wasting our time here," replied Swift.

"Guards!" summoned Mason.

Right on cue, the door burst open and in-stepped the two large MPs to escort Thunderfoot back to his cell.

"Stick around, we'll be in touch," said Swift as the MPs led Thunderfoot away.

"So what do you think?" asked Mason.

"He's holding back," replied Swift.

"Yeah, it's obvious by the way he tensed up the minute we showed him the photos," remarked Mason.

"Are you hungry yet?" asked Swift.

"I'm starved!"

"Alright then, let's get out of here. There's bound to be a decent steak at that fancy hotel they put us up in," said Swift.

"Sounds good to me," agreed Mason.

The two men got up and walked out the door.

"We immediately left the LBJ Ranch and boarded our chopper for the flight back to Tan Son Nhut. We couldn't tell if the MPs were more pissed about us setting down so close to the Stockade or because they knew they couldn't do anything about it. When it came to the Company, the MPs were ordered to look the other way. Nothing to see here! That's what they were taught to say at the sight of a black helicopter or a Spook. But that wasn't us. We were just field analysts on an assignment and not the guys in the black choppers. I suppose our unmarked choppers are what distinguished us from the real spooks working behind the scenes. But to the MPs, it was all the same. They didn't ask questions, and we didn't volunteer information. After the Pleiku Campaign, I was convinced that nothing was what it had seemed. But unbeknownst to us, the real truth was out there, and it would kill to keep its secrets. One hour later, we were back at the Caravelle Hotel. We changed out of our uniforms and back into civilian clothes before meeting downstairs at the Hotel's cocktail lounge. They had nice round leather-covered booths with little table lights. A Vietnamese waiter in a white jacket and black tie sat us down in a booth. Right away, we ordered some stiff drinks. Fred and I indulged ourselves with some steaks with all the trimmings. We were served by a beautiful Vietnamese girl with a beehive hairdo who wore a gold-silk Ao Dai. We had gone almost the whole day since we had last eaten. Well, I can't say the steak compared to the last one I had in the States, but after the day we had, it would just do. I just wasn't ready to dig right back into the local cuisine just yet. Fred, on the other hand, couldn't resist his curiosity to try a small bowl of whatever they called it and a *Saigon Sling*. After a few rounds, we were both ready to call it a night."

Later inside Swift's hotel room, he prepared to retire for the evening. The long day and the time difference had taken its toll leaving him tired. Swift sat at his bedside in his boxer shorts and a white undershirt. On the nightstand sat a small brass base lamp with a canvas cover. There was also a beige-colored rotary telephone and a small analog clock. He had earlier taken a small glass from the bathroom and set in on the tiny nightstand. He next dropped three ice cubes that came from an ice machine that sat outside at the end of the 10th-floor hallway. Swift then poured himself a drink from a small whiskey bottle he had taken from the plane. He then reached for a cigarette and put it in his mouth. Like many former soldiers who had served in Vietnam, Swift sported a chrome-plated Zippo lighter of which was used to light his cigarette. He took in one drag and blew out the smoke from his lungs. At that moment, Swift stared at the inscription of his lighter. DE OPPRESSO LIBER it read, this was the Special Forces motto meaning To Free the Oppressed. A second later, a flash of light caught Swift's attention. Curious of what it might have been, he opened the long sheer French drapes and stepped out onto the small balcony. It was an illumination flare one mile away with the sounds of distant helicopters buzzing about. No matter how tired he was, he could not ignore where he was. And yet, he was far from the battlefield; the war was still all around him.

Flashback to October 1965. The monsoon rains had just subsided after a torrential downpour drenched the helipad at Camp Holloway. Captain J.A. Swift appeared in green tiger stripe fatigues with the distinctive Green Beret bearing the insignia of the 5th Special Forces. He carried an M-16 as he walked through the wet clay to the awaiting UH-1 Huey bound for the Plei Me Special Forces Camp. No sooner than he took his seat, a helmeted U.S. Army Avionics Specialist who looked about his mid-twenties appeared wearing olive-drab green stateside fatigues and a heavy flack vest. He carried an M-16 in one hand and a green canvas toolkit in the other as he tried to speak to the pilot over the loud turboshaft engine and the *whup-whup-whup* sound of the main rotor blades.

"Hey Niles, you going to Plei Me?" asked the Specialist.

"Yeah!" replied the pilot.

"Got room for one more?"

"Hop aboard!" replied the pilot.

Captain Swift remembered that moment.

"The Specialist wore the gold and black horse patch of the 1st Air Cavalry. He had come from the division base camp at An Khe, which at that point was still under construction. By now, the chopper's rotors had become so loud that one had to either use a headset or shout to talk. At first, I couldn't make out the guy's name was when he introduced himself or remembered what read on his name patch, Rosas-Luca? All I remembered was his name was Luis and mentioned he was with the 15th Transportation Battalion. He was on his way to fix a radio on a troubled chopper. You wouldn't know it from looking at his light complexion, but he was an immigrant from Mexico City. I wouldn't have known it had he not told me. I suppose Uncle Sam wasted no time drafting his ass before sending him to The Nam as soon as he got his Green Card. And from what few words were exchanged, he seemed like a nice guy with a big smiling grin. Hopefully, he got out of there before nightfall."

"The hours seemed to tick away accelerating with each passing moment as the glowing red sun sunk deep into the tree line. From every direction, one could feel eyes watching you from the bush watching, waiting, and ready to pounce. Preliminary intelligence precluded that an attack by the 33rd and 320th NVA Regiments was imminent. The resulting tension in the camp was reaching a boiling point where you'd be lucky to hold down your C-rations, knowing what was coming. It was not the night for doling out the ever unpopular ham and lima beans! I suppose Charlie had it worse living off days old stale rice and rat meat if he could find any. In any case, we knew he was hungry for a fight, and we were prepared to give it to him."

"As the sun dipped below the horizon, the last three Slicks lifted off towards Camp Holloway. They were taking out a small number of Vietnamese and American personnel. Those of us left behind comprised a dozen Green Berets, fourteen ARVN Special Forces, and some two-hundred seventy-five Montagnard fighters that made up Detachment A-225. *The Yards,* as we called them, were armed with old M-1 rifles, M-3's and crudely assembled crossbows that along with us and our M-16's were left to defend a small patch of high ground against an estimated force of over two thousand attackers. Whatever was going to happen, it was going to be a major maelstrom, and we'd be lucky to survive it."

Captain Swift checked his wristwatch as Lieutenant Scott Corbett led out the patrol beyond the perimeter with his Montagnard Mike Force.

"The small camp sat on a low rise bluff that was cut clear of the dense jungle. From the air, Plei Me looked like a triangle etched with earthen trenches, sandbags, and a barren death zone forming the defensive perimeter surrounding the camp. But in the dark, you could see nothing but the stars, and there were many shadows all around. We remained vigilant in our bunkers and trenches as we peered out through our Starlight night scopes. There, we waited for Charlie to make his move."

The time had reached 1900 hours as an eerie silence loomed over the camp. It was as if the wildlife in the jungle had packed up and moved out to avoid the oncoming storm of lead and phosphorus. It got so quiet that even crickets where nowhere to be heard. Suddenly, a crackle came over the radio. Radio operator Staff Sergeant Lockard picked up the receiver.

"Come in, over," whispered Lockard.

((Static))

"Come in, over," repeated Lockard.

((Static))

Just then, a small dimed red light flashed twice northwest of the tree line.

"The Mike Force is early," whispered one Green Beret.

"Something's not right," replied Capt. Harold Moore.

"I agree," concurred Swift.

"Jay, take a squad over to reinforce the Southwest," ordered Capt. Moore.

"Will do," complied Swift.

Swift quickly grabbed his M-16 and quietly climbed out of the trench when out of nowhere, a tripwire on the Southwest perimeter set off an illumination flare. Dozens of Vietcong could be seen crawling through the death strip cutting through the wire. A second later, an NVA whistle screeched into the night, bringing with it green tracer fire from all directions. Just as Swift made back to the safety of the trench below him, a tremendous blast from a recoilless rifle knocked him off his feet. The concussion briefly muffled his hearing leaving him in a momentary haze as green tracers shot overhead. Swift immediately got back on his feet and grabbed his M-16. At that instant, a Viet Cong Guerrilla jumped into the trench to bayonet him. Instinctively, Swift used the stock of his M-16 to deflect the bayonet charge and knock his attacker to the ground. With savage fury, he pummeled him with the butt of his M-16 cracking the man's skull before moving on.

By now, enemy whistles sounded from all directions. Shouts of enemy soldiers echoed as they charged across the death strip in a full-frontal assault amidst the red tracer fire from the defenders. Running to another position, Captain Swift looked over and spotted three NVA regulars carrying AK-47's with fixed bayonets scaling over the command bunker. Swift switched to full auto and pulled the trigger unleashing a fury of 5.56 millimeter rounds before they could penetrate the bunker. Meanwhile, mortar fire erupted as illumination flares exploded, turning the night into day, revealing the sheer number of enemy forces attacking the camp in a pincer move that threatened to overrun the base. Swift had to move again and joined the dozen ARVN Special Forces, who pulled back to a fallback position with a group of wounded Montagnards. In the cacophony of the siege, Swift could remember hearing radio operator Lockard before being wounded shouting out:

"Spooky inbound!"

In the thick of the battle, Swift hadn't noticed that a bullet had pierced his left side and exited out the back. His adrenaline had somehow dulled his senses. But before too long, the shock would start to set in as he raced back to an adjacent bunker, holding his side while firing his weapon. By then, everything began to blur as a mortar round exploded near him. There were Viet Cong within the wire and a sea of NVA swarming all around them. Swift continued firing his M-16 until he emptied his magazine, killing two Viet Cong that came within inches of bayonetting him before collapsed from his wounds.

"The last thing I remembered before waking up at the field hospital at An Khe was the sound of Puff the Magic Dragon, also known as Spooky, coming in for the kill. You couldn't see the AC-47 gunship in the dark, but you could sure hear that unmistakable high-pitched buzz saw sound of its 7.62 mini-guns. High above the camp, the unseen gunship fired a red laser-like torrent of death. The rapid rate of fire allowed no time for screams of agony for Charlie caught in its red tracer beams of destruction. Like a high-speed meat grinder for humans, the enemy was reduced to unrecognizable pieces of shredded flesh. One could almost taste the clouds of pink mist. It was such indescribable horror to witness up close. The lasting imprint was one you could not un-see or ever forget. Wherever Spooky pointed its red death ray of lead, it wiped out everything in sight."

Moments later, Swift woke up in his Saigon hotel room in a cold sweat. The sounds of gunfire that haunted his dreams echoed in his memories. Then it occurred to him, he really did heard something and it was taking place outside. Instinctively, he reached for his 45 caliber pistol and stepped out onto the balcony. As soon as he looked down below, he could see it was no big deal. It was just a small group of poor Vietnamese kids lighting firecrackers before being chased away by a pair of angry National Policemen.

"Kids," he remarked.

Though relived, Swift could still feel his heart pumping. It was clear that he could not go back to sleep. With nothing more to see, Swift stepped back inside his room and reached for a cigarette. Just as he was about to light it, he noticed large vanilla enveloped was shoved through the bottom of his hotel door. Out of precaution, Swift gripped his pistol and carefully approached the door. Quietly chambering a round, he placed his other hand on the doorknob. With a sudden tug, he flung open the door, but there was nobody there. Swift stepped out into the hallway looking both ways, but found no one.

"What the hell is this?"

Still barefoot in his boxers and undershirt, he walked next door to Mason's room and knocked on the door.

"Hey, Fred."

"Yeah?"

"Are you awake?" asked Swift.

"Yeah, somewhat," replied Mason.

"Can you come over?" asked Swift.

"Sure, just give me a few to get some clothes on, and I'll be right over," replied Mason.

Minutes later, Swift had changed into his fatigues before opening the door. Mason appeared in uniform and quickly stepped inside and followed Swift and sat down by the small round table lit by an overhead lamp.

"Can I get you something to drink?" asked Swift.

"Nah, I'm good, thank you. I was still trying to sleep off those Saigon Slings when those firecrackers woke my ass up. I take it you couldn't sleep either," said Mason.

"I tried, but this place has a way of making you remember things you'd like to forget,' replied Swift.

"I can imagine. So what's going on?" asked Mason.

Swift grabbed the large vanilla envelope and placed it on the table.

"Someone slipped this under my door," said Swift.

"Did you see who it was?" asked Mason.

"No, they disappeared before I could open the door," replied Swift.

"That's no good. Shall we call the front desk and move to another floor?" asked Mason.

"I think we should hold that thought, but keep the Bugout Bag ready. Until then, take a look at this."

Fred Mason reached over and opened the envelope emptying its contents. There were several black and white photos with arrows, circles, and scribbled notations.

"These look like satellite photos. Notice the curvature of the earth," observed Mason.

"You're right."

"But what's this blurry object?" Mason asked.

"I don't know. The notes say Tu-150-A1 flying from Eastern Siberia on a southward track. But this doesn't look like anything. Even if the photos say it is a plane, why on earth would the Soviets deliberately fly it this far south to a warzone? It sounds too damn convenient," remarked Swift.

"Well, based on what I can ascertain from these images, whatever this was broke apart at high altitude near the edge of space. Theoretically speaking, this thing should have disintegrated or self-destructed to avoid capture. If their secret planes are like ours, they would have packed self-detonating explosives so nothing could be found," postulated Mason.

"Ah, but something was found!" exclaimed Swift.

"Found and later stolen from the U.S. Embassy basement vault," added Mason.

"Tell me, from our own observations, have you ever seen anything that remotely looked that object they recovered?" asked Swift.

"Not even close to any Soviet hardware we've ever come across. Do you think it is an elaborate forgery to implicate the Soviets to entangle them into a larger war? Perhaps, dare I say, as suggested by Keene, a nuclear war?" asked Mason.

"Unlikely."

"Do you think Colby's people sent this?" asked Mason.

"Your guess is as good as mine. Had it come from the Station Chief, they would have called us in or met us at a safe house or the MACV compound," reasoned Swift.

"What's the chance that Kasakov sent this? I mean, think about it. If he knows we are here, then he knows we're hunting for his plane, and should we find it first, he's going to want it back," speculated Mason.

"That wouldn't make any sense. Me in his position wouldn't want us to see these photos," reasoned Swift.

"Could it also be that he can't find it, or can't get to it since it's on contested ground?" suggested Mason.

"If we still can't publicly acknowledge the existence of the A-12, they sure as hell won't be sharing intel on their bird, provided it exists. I suspect we're on a fool's errand to lend credibility to a bullshit cover story to hide something we're not privy to," speculated Swift.

"But Boss, come on, enemy helicopters? Everyone knows a helicopter can't fly that high or that fast. Who would believe such nonsense?" reasoned Mason.

"I honestly don't know. We have a crash site we can't get to, a dead NVA Colonel last seen whisked away in a black chopper, a jailed Navajo Tunnel Rat who won't talk, stolen evidence, and now convenient satellite photos delivered to us by some anonymous source. All this, while Men in Black roam around passing themselves off as us leaving a string of dead bodies and we're just getting started!" complained Swift.

"I agree; this whole thing sounds crazy. What do you think we are really looking for? A meteor or sensitive Soviet hardware?" asked Mason.

"I could make a better cover story than the one they want to go with. Everyone knows a meteor can't change course, nor can a satellite engage a supersonic fighter plane. In any case, we still got more work to do before we can get out to the crash site. Let's say we get some morning chow and then talk to those 4th ID guys in Vung Tau. Perhaps, they'll have something useful to tell us," said Swift.

"I couldn't agree more!"

CHAPTER IV
THE 4TH ID

It was now Monday morning, October 30^{th,} 1967. Swift and Mason drove a Jeep to the seaside resort city of Vung Tau. There, they meandered through scooters and military vehicles down tree-lined streets to the large open plaza known as Flags Square. All around them were bars and dancehalls named after American cities. They were packed with Vietnamese girls and the latest Acid Rock not played on Armed Forces Radio. In the center of the square, stood a free-standing wall monument that displayed a small map of Vietnam with the South shown in Yellow and Communist North Vietnam displayed in red. The map was flanked on both sides by the flags of all the countries helping the fledgling South. On the back of the wall had a large inscription in the center flanked by two yellow flags of the Republic of Vietnam. Moving past the Flags Square was the busy central outdoor marketplace. From there, they took a turn past the old Roman Catholic cathedral down past the old French Colonial houses. No matter where they went, American GI's were everywhere on R&R from the Recreation Center to the white sandy beach.

"Cap Saint Jacques Beach they called it. I remembered it from my first tour with Advisory Command. It was a popular place going back to the French Colonial Period. It was lined with concession stands selling drinks and anything else they could get you to fork your Piasters (currency) for. So popular in fact, you could see scores of Americans, Australians, New Zealanders, and bikini-clad Vietnamese girls carrying about as if they were at Redondo Beach. I suppose for many, that was the point. It seemed the only thing that reminded you that there was a war going on was the sight of the distant American Navy ships anchored offshore and the occasional UH-1 patrolling overhead. As far as one could see, everyone was either frolicking about in the water or taking in the crystal blue skies in the eighty-two-degree fall temperatures. For all anyone knew, Charlie could've been there on R&R, probably dipping his feet in the same water next to the same Americans he might have fought only days earlier in the field, and nobody would've known it."

"I wasn't supposed to care about these details, for I was no longer part of the regular army nor part of their war. But there was something about putting on that uniform that just did it to you especially while traversing the countryside. And while it wasn't the same, I couldn't help but feel like I was supposed to be back out in the field. It was a nagging feeling that I could not share with Mason. It just didn't sit right with me, but I suppose I should have been more thankful to Fred. Without him, I would have lost focus. Sure, I knew there was bullshit going on. But just how much behind the scenes was something we couldn't talk about, particularly to those who were still doing the fighting."

"The day's agenda had us driving down this narrow beach road towards the Grand Hotel at the base of the hill near the end of the bay. It was a beautiful place adorned with lush greenery, colorful cabanas, and delightful local girls in Ao Dais, but unfortunately for us, we were there on business. We had a squad from the 4th ID who were to give us firsthand accounts of what they witnessed. They were waiting for us in a conference room where we would conduct our investigation. After making our way into the marble-lined lobby, Fred and I stepped into the big room with sheer white drapes that obscured the view of the beach outside from prying eyes. It was there that the twelve-man squad of 3rd Platoon, 2nd Battalion, 12th Infantry Regiment, of the 4th Infantry Division anxiously awaited us."

"The men sat patiently at the long mahogany conference table in their neatly pressed khaki uniforms and newly pinned combat medals. For a bunch of young guys, they had more medals than the men who came back from WWII. Such terrible things they must have seen! But just ask anyone who stepped out into the field long enough and they could tell you how they got their share. Lord knows, I had seen mine. As soon as we stepped into the room, they all stood up at attention. After putting them at ease and asking them to take their seats, Fred opened his silver briefcase and began recording and took notes. Leading this squad was their twenty-four-year-old Sergeant, Sean Eldridge of Bridgeport, Connecticut. He had a distinctive scar that ran under his left eye. I'll assume that's how he got his Purple Heart. He seemed to carry some apprehension and couldn't wait to get this over with. Then there was his second in command, Corporal Ray Fuentes, who was said to have come from Cuba in 1959. Next was their RTO (radio telephone operator) Specialist 4th Class (SP4) Billy Langford of Butte Montana. He was a medium-sized blonde kid who looked like he grew up on a big ranch and T-bone steaks. There were four Black troopers who sat together on one end of the table whose names were Pfc. Alan Coolidge of Houston Texas, Sp4 Jermaine Johnson, Pfc. Clayton Baker, and Pfc. Emmet Eckerd of Athens, Georgia. Rounding up the squad was a Los Angeles Chicano named Pfc. Johnny Sanchez. Then there was the M-60 operator Sp4 Robert Lawson, Pfc. Trey Pearson of Portland, Oregon, Pfc.

Peter Rozano of South Philly, and Pfc. Stan Kozlowski of St. Paul, Minnesota. And while we were on our fact-finding mission, they looked at us with suspicion and the uncertainty of what would become of their testimony. For this reason, I spoke to them in a calm, relaxed manner."

"I am Captain Swift, and this is Lieutenant Mason from Special Operations. We've asked you all here to learn what happened that night of October 27th near Dak To. So, if you will, Sergeant Eldridge, please tell us what you witnessed there."

"Well, Sir, we had earlier humped five klicks on our patrol before dusk and hunkered down in the bush for the night. Our position was three klicks south of the impact zone near Hill 1338. Coolidge and Sanchez were on watch," said Eldridge.

Lieutenant Mason looked at the nervous nineteen-year-old private and looked at him directly.

"Your name is Alan, right?" asked Mason.

"Yes, Sir," replied Coolidge.

"Where are you from, son?" asked Swift.

"Houston, Texas, Sir," he replied.

"Boy, I'll tell you what!" chuckled Swift.

"Yes, Sir, that's something you'd hear down there," replied Coolidge.

"Can you and Sanchez tell us what you witnessed?" asked Mason.

"Well, you see, Sir, there's not too much to tell. I'm not even sure what I saw that night," replied Coolidge.

It was then that Johnny Sanchez looked up and started to talk.

"It was around 0230 hours when Coolidge and I were rounding up our watch. We were tired after a long day of humping the rough terrain. It was then that a bright white-blue light erupted high up in the sky. Then it looked like a blue-white fireball shot from it and hit something three klicks away," said Sanchez.

"Whatever it was, it hit so hard we could all feel it from where we were. It woke everybody up," added Coolidge.

It was then that Corporal Fuentes spoke up.

"As soon I got up, I could see a few of us spotted what looked like distant red rotating beacons flying towards the crash site from the east. They looked like choppers, but they didn't sound like Army Huey's or Marine choppers," described Fuentes.

"According to the mission report, you had spotted enemy helicopters. Is that what you witnessed?" asked Swift.

"I don't know what else they could have been," replied Fuentes.

"I'm inclined to agree. Only Coolidge and Sanchez saw the first bright light in the sky. The rest of us saw the rotating beacons flying in from over the Cambodian border. At that point, I had our RTO radio in. The Special Forces camp on the other side of the hill claimed they didn't see anything. They already had a patrol out five klicks in the opposite direction, so we were instructed by our LT who was with 1st Platoon to saddle up and proceed to the impact site," revealed Eldridge.

"Around what time did you arrive there?" asked Swift.

"We got there by 0530 hours just before dawn," replied Eldridge.

"That's when that weird fog came out of nowhere," added Sanchez.

"*Conio*(dude)!" whispered Fuentes.

"*Cállate*(shut up)!" shrugged Sanchez.

"Was there something you two wanted to add?" asked Swift.

"No, Sir. There's nothing remarkable about it. It dissipated by the time we were ordered out," explained Fuentes.

Swift and Mason could see there was some tension between the two Latinos. They could also see Coolidge was sweating nervously.

"Does anyone else want to add anything?" asked Swift.

"Sure!" said Rozano.

"Go ahead," instructed Swift.

"I was on point when we arrived on scene. Whatever happened there, it looked like we got there too late. There were dead Gooks everywhere," said Rozano.

"What else did you guys see?" asked Swift.

"We saw bits of smoldering brush around a large impact crater, but there wasn't much to see beyond that," replied Eckerd.

"We looked around and didn't find anything. Then Kozlowski nearly tripped on a hidden ventilation shaft that led to a tunnel entrance. We all took up positions and radioed in. Thirty minutes later, the 1/9 arrived and sent in a Tunnel Rat. As soon as he went down into the tunnel, the MPs arrived. They made us move back to set up a perimeter. Minutes later, the Tunnel Rat came up with a sick NVA prisoner, and that's when a black chopper arrived which we were told not to look at. By 0730 hours, we were ordered out," explained Eldridge.

"You said the prisoner was sick? Like, how so?" asked Mason.

"Oh, man, that dude looked sick and vomited this yellow-white muck when he came to the surface as they took him away," said Fuentes.

"Vomited?" asked Swift.

"Yeah, that dude threw up some major chunks like you've never seen before! I about lost mine just watching him," described Baker.

"Lord, have mercy! That Dink was sick! It was like he puked up all the stolen lima bean C-rations nobody wanted to eat," exclaimed Eckerd.

"It could have also been that diseased rat meat Charlie eats," suggested Kozlowski.

"I still think it was a meteor. I used to see them back home at night," remarked Pearson.

"Maybe," guessed Langford.

An uncomfortable silence filled the conference room. Swift and Mason could see Sanchez eying Coolidge, who appeared nervous as the rest of the squad either stared at the ceiling fan or looked out the sheer white drapes as they waited for what would come next.

"Well, gentlemen, I think that's all we need for now. We know how hard you've worked, so for your cooperation, Lieutenant Mason will be passing out hotel room keys. You guys get to spend the next twenty-four hours here on our dime before we need you back at the MACV Compound barracks. They expect you there by 1400 hours tomorrow. In the meantime, have some fun and relax. You're dismissed," said Swift.

The entire squad stood up and saluted before filing out of the conference room one by one with each man casually taking a key. As soon as the room emptied, Swift closed the door to speak privately.

"Well, what do you think?" asked Mason.

"I'd say these guys were told they didn't see anything. Standard operating procedure when the black choppers arrive," replied Swift.

"Probably, so, the sooner we can get to the crash site, the better we can wrap this up. I don't see why we can't just skip all this and drop into the site? It can't be worse than the Golan Heights," reasoned Mason.

"Fred, I hate to tell you this, but take it from someone who's been here. The difference between what we've seen in the Middle East and here is you can see people coming at you at a thousand yards. In Vietnam, the enemy can be a few feet away, and you wouldn't know it until Charlie was right up in your grill ready to get the drop on you. It's better to wait until we get the go code. Trust me, things can go south here real quick," said Swift.

"All right then. You're the Boss," replied Mason.

"You damn right!" replied Swift.

Minutes later, the two men walked through the spacious white marble-lined lobby of the Grand Hotel when an older Vietnamese maid dressed in a white maids dress uniform flagged them down.

"Sir! Brown GI told me to give you this," she said in broken English.

The maid presented a folded matchbook that bore the hotel brand name on the white cover. Swift tipped the maid a few piasters then quickly flipped open the match cover. On the inside, he could see written in pencil "Rm 215/10m."

"What's that?" asked Mason.

"I think someone wants to talk," replied Swift.

Minutes later, Swift and Mason walked down a long corridor. With a nod from Swift, Mason knocked on the door of Room 215. They could see someone had quickly looked through the small peephole before opening the door.

"It was Johnny Sanchez who had something to say. It was clear from the interview that there was tension with Corporal Fuentes. But now that we could sit down with him in private, we'd finally have a chance to have a real talk."

With the sheer white drapes drawn and the balcony door closed, the three men walked inside the hotel room. They sat at a small round table by the balcony door. They could see Sanchez appeared nervous. Sweat protruded from his forehead and was noticeable on his white undershirt that peaked from the blouse of his khaki uniform. After a deep sigh, Sanchez looked at Swift and Mason intently as he took his chrome Zippo lighter and lit a cigarette.

"Thanks for coming. Coolidge was supposed to be here, but I guess he didn't want to risk losing his ticket home," said Sanchez.

"Is he a short-timer?" asked Swift.

"Yes, Sir, they promised him a ticket home early in time for his wife's delivery if he kept his mouth shut," revealed Sanchez.

"Who promised you?" asked Swift.

"The fuck if I know," he replied.

"And what did they promise you?" asked Mason.

"Extended R&R and a cushy spot in the rear and maybe an extra stripe," answered Sanchez.

"Who made this offer?" asked Swift.

"Some creepy older white dude in his fifties dressed in black who talked to us when we were pulled back to base camp," said Sanchez.

"Creepy, how?" asked Mason.

"Look, I don't know. The man was just creepy. We assumed he was CIA, but now, I don't know. I had seen him at Dak To when the MPs told us to look the other way. He took off with that NVA prisoner on one of those black choppers they told us not to look at," explained Sanchez.

"Did he give a name or who he was with?" asked Swift.

"Frankly, I don't remember. He didn't say shit, but for some reason, we listened to this guy. There was something wrong about him and I can't put my finger on it. All I know is he gave us the creeps," replied Sanchez.

"Did he threaten you?" asked Mason.

"Maybe, well, not really. I'm not even sure. The man implied there might be consequences if we went off script," revealed Sanchez.

"Off script? Do you mean you were told what to say to us?" asked Swift.

"Yeah, they told us we would be interviewed by a CIA team working with Special Operations. That's you, right?"

"Yes, that's us," acknowledged Mason.

"So, you guys are not real Army?" asked Sanchez.

"We're real Army. I was as an Advisor from 64 to 65. My partner here is a weapons expert from Quantico. We work for the Company as field analysts. We were told you had seen some enemy helicopters. We're here to find out if Charlie is introducing choppers to the field. You understand that if there's any truth to that, it could change the war," revealed Swift.

"My apologies, Sirs, but like I said before, nothing makes any sense. They told us what to say if anyone asked what happened there, and it didn't sit too well with me. I grew up in Whittier, so I don't take kindly to veiled threats. Normally, I would have told this guy where he could stick it, but for some reason, I couldn't. I don't know who he was working for. All I know is that guy gave me the creeps!"

"So tell us what happened on the night of October 27th," asked Swift.

"It all started as we said. We were hunkered down for the night 27th in the bush after a long day of humping. Coolidge and I were on watch around 0230 hours when we both noticed a big bright white-blue light high up in the sky. It looked like an explosion but without a red-orange fireball. Part of that light streaked across the sky and crashed three klicks south of hill 875. The sound of the impact was loud enough to wake up the entire squad. We told Sergeant Eldridge what we had seen. No sooner than our RTO radioed in, we spotted what looked like a pair of distant red rotating beacons from helicopters, but they weren't ours."

"You're certain they were helicopters?" asked Mason.

"Look, man; this is a helicopter war. I've seen enough of them and flown in them enough times to know a helicopter when I see one.

Those red beacons could have only come from helicopters. We couldn't hear them from where we were. All I know is that they weren't Hueys, and they sure weren't Marine Choctaws. I never heard of Charlie having choppers, so we didn't know what to think. There wasn't any radio chatter that would have indicated they were ours, so they had to be one of theirs. But no sooner than the choppers disappeared, a second light appeared out of the sky."

"A second light?" asked Mason.

"No, it was like that light in the sky," replied Sanchez.

"Like the one you and Coolidge witnessed?" asked Swift.

"Sort of, but different."

"Different, how?" asked Swift.

"This one moved much slower. It moved just above the treetop level, and it didn't make a sound. The guys called it the Star of Bethlehem because it reminded them of those 1950's biblical movies. We followed it to the crash site, only this didn't lead us to no baby Jesus. It reminded me of something I had seen as a kid," replied Sanchez.

"You followed it?" asked Mason.

"Yes, just like the three wise men," replied Sanchez.

"You said you've seen this kind of thing before," said Swift.

"I have. Back when I was around eight years old, my grandmother and I would take the Greyhound Bus to Mexicali every summer. We'd go there to see my grandfather, who lived on the other side of the Mexican border. The bus always took the same two-lane desert highway through Imperial Valley. I'll tell you, it was a scary place at night, especially for a kid. On some nights, you could see some distant, weird lights in the sky that I knew weren't stars or planets."

"How did you know they weren't an atmospheric phenomenon or your imagination?" asked Mason.

"I don't know. I just did. My grandfather, who was part Yaqui told me to ignore them, and they would leave us alone. I used to have nightmares about it. He never explained what they were, and my grandmother told me not to talk about them. That's what that second light reminded me of. It was the same color, too," revealed Sanchez.

"That's interesting, so what happened next?" asked Swift.

"Silver Actual ordered us to proceed to the impact site and await further orders. We knew there was a Special Forces camp on the other side of the hill. They already had a Mike Force out five klicks out in the opposite direction, but we were closer to the impact site."

"What time did you arrive?" asked Mason.

"0530 hours," answered Sanchez.

"What did you see once you got there?" asked Swift.

"We told you what they wanted us to tell you. Now I'll tell you what they didn't want you to know."

It was the morning of October 27th, 1967, around 0530 hours. The moon was slowly sinking below the horizon as Sergeant Eldridge led his squad on orders to the impact site. What their commanders in the 4th ID did not know is that they were following a slow-moving object at treetop level leading them to the impact site. It moved without sound and emitted an eerie blue-white glow that illuminated the path through the thick elephant grass in the early morning dew. The squad, whose call sign was Sapphire Six, tailed the glowing object at a distance equaling that of a football field. One could say the pace of the object was almost deliberate as if it were leading the squad there. The indescribable light source moved just above treetop level, lighting up the difficult terrain exposing tripwires and booby-traps along the way. Not knowing what lay ahead kept the soldiers on edge and yet at the same time beckoned them to keep pace with it.

By now, they neared a small ridgeline that silhouetted in the eerie glow that melded into a fog bank that appeared out of nowhere. Illuminated tree branches cast shadows in all directions exacerbating the tension within the weary squad. It was then that Rozano stopped dead in his tracks and held his breath. A moment later, he took another step forward when he thought he heard something move nearby. Immediately, he put his left hand up in a clenched fist, signaling the squad to halt their dangerous trek through the bush.

"Rozano, what is it?" whispered Fuentes.

It was then that Rozano hand-signaled to alert the squad of enemy movement just over the ridge. Sergeant Eldridge quietly directed his men to spread out to create a kill zone.

"Ready on that sixty," whispered Eldridge.

Lawson got down on the ground in a small earthen depression and readied the M-60 machine gun as the squad anticipated a firefight. Coolidge quietly switched his M-16 to full auto when suddenly; sounds of men running could be heard. And then it happened. A dozen North Vietnamese soldiers wearing chin strapped pith helmets carrying AK-47 rifles raced over the ridgeline. They unknowingly ran straight into the Americans waiting in ambush.

The squad savagely opened fire on the fleeing soldiers, killing them as they ran from the glowing light.

"Cease-Fire!" shouted Eldridge.

"What the fuck were they running from?" asked Eckerd.

"Probably that freaking light,' replied Baker.

"There could be something over that ridgeline," said Johnson.

It was then that the fog crossed over the ridgeline enveloping the squad. They could see a silhouette of an old man slowly walking on the ridge. Stan Kozlowski aimed his M-16 at the figure but strangely couldn't fire his weapon. Sanchez and Pearson both tried to open fire, but they too could not fire discharge their weapons. It was as if their M-16's had become disabled.

"What the fuck? I'm jammed!" exclaimed Sanchez.

"Me too!" echoed Pearson.

Each man checked their weapons when they noticed the figure of the man had disappeared.

"Hey! Where did he go?" asked Langford.

"I don't know!" replied Rozano.

"All right, pass the word, fix bayonets," ordered Eldridge.

Then men quickly attached their bayonets and re-chambered their M-16's before moving over the ridgeline. The men were spread out as they cautiously walked up to the ridgeline and crossed into the wall of glowing mist. Once they had wandered over the top of the crest, they could see a large impact crater one hundred yards from them. All around, they could see dead bodies and smoldering embers of burnt brush as they walked into the blackened earth.

"Hey, there's more, over here!" said Rozano.

"My God, what hit this place?" asked Johnson.

"Dead Gooks everywhere," muttered Baker.

"Man, this place is giving me the heebie-jeebies," said Coolidge.

"Keep it down! There may be some still here," warned Eldridge.

Corporal Fuentes did a sweep of the impact crater and reported back to Sergeant Eldridge.

"There's dead VC and NVA on the other side of the crater, but no blood trails. There are no bullet casings either. I don't know what to make of it," reported Fuentes.

"What do you think, Sanchez?" asked Eldridge.

"He's right. It looks like something zapped these guys without firing a shot," replied Sanchez.

Sergeant Eldridge knelt on the ground and removed his helmet. He scratched his head before signaling to Billy Langford to make the call on the PRC-10 radio strapped to his back.

"Sapphire-Six to Silver-Actual, do you copy?" radioed Langford.

"Silver-Actual, go ahead, Sapphire-Six," crackled the radio return.

"I got Actual on the horn," said Langford.

Sergeant Eldridge reached over and grabbed the handset from Langford to speak.

"This is Sapphire-Six, we've reached objective, over."

INCIDENT AT DAK TO

"Roger, Sapphire-Six."

Just then, Rozano, who was walking thirty yards away, noticed a faint blue-white light coming from a ventilation shaft.

"Sergeant!" alerted Fuentes.

"Silver, standby," radioed Eldridge.

"Rozano found a tunnel, and it's got that creepy blue-white glow inside it," relayed Fuentes.

"Silver, we got a live tunnel complex at the impact site. Requesting Engineers, over," radioed Eldridge.

"Sapphire-Six, standby, (static) Sapphire-Six, hold your position. I repeat, hold your position. 1/9 is inbound, and they're bringing in The Chief."

"Roger that, Silver. Sapphire-Six out."

"Oh shit, man! You hear that? They're bringing in The Chief! Charlie is in for it now!" exclaimed Johnson.

"Chief! Chief! Chief!" they chanted.

Fred Mason raised an eyebrow upon listening to this point of Sanchez's account.

"Did they mean Staff Sergeant Wayne Thunderfoot of the 1/9 Scouts?" asked Mason.

"Yeah, we had all heard of him. So had Charlie and they were scared of him. He's a famous Tunnel Rat from the 1/9. Big Navajo guy who I heard took trophies from any Dink-Slope that crossed him down below. I don't know how he could fit in that tiny hole, but he got down there quick. He went right to work as the MPs from the 173rd Airborne showed up at 0700 hours. They quickly took up positions around the impact site and ordered us to set up an outer perimeter. Fifteen minutes later, two black choppers landed just as The Chief surfaced, dragging up that sick NVA prisoner."

"Colonel Linh," remarked Swift.

"A team of men quickly jumped out of those black choppers. They wore black fatigues and dark sunglasses. We assumed they were CIA. They wasted no time taking the prisoner from The Chief. Then out of nowhere, that weird old Vietnamese man reappeared out of the fog."

"The same one that appeared when your weapons jammed?" asked Swift.

"Yes, the same one, I think. I'm not entirely sure. We didn't get a good look at him when he first appeared on the ridgeline," answered Sanchez.

"Can you describe this man?" asked Mason.

"He was a little taller than your average Vietnamese National. Really thin and looked a little bit like Uncle Ho himself complete with a long white beard. That's when it happened," said Sanchez.

"What happened?" asked Swift.

"The Men in Black were going to grab the old man when The Chief held up this weird blue crystal looking object that glowed," said Sanchez.

It was then that Swift nodded to Mason, who then opened his silver briefcase and placed a black and white photo on the table for Sanchez to see.

"Did it look anything like this?" asked Swift.

"Yeah, that's exactly what he had in his hand! It glowed in the same color as those weird blue-white lights. What the hell is that thing?" asked Sanchez.

"That's what we are here to find out," replied Swift.

"So go on, tell us what happened when The Chief held up the object," urged Mason.

"I had never seen anything like that before. Whatever that thing was, it sure got the attention of the Men in Black. They tried to take it from him and they got into a scuffle. One of them hit The Chief on the back of the head with the butt of an M-16. By the time that ruckus ended, the old man had disappeared. The next thing you know, they had loaded up the NVA prisoner onto one of the black choppers and turned The Chief over to the MPs. That was it. An hour later, we were ordered to regroup with the rest of Baker Company to a new LZ two klicks west. From there, the Slicks came in, and we were flown back to base camp. After our CO debriefed us, we were interrogated by that creepy older white dude. An hour later, they loaded up our squad onto a Chinook helicopter and flew us out to Pleiku, and from there, we were on a Caribou to Tan Son Nhut where we have been ever since until we arrived here at Vung Tau and that's it," said Sanchez.

It was then that Mason nudged at Swift.

"What do you say, Boss? I think we should put him in protective custody," suggested Mason.

"Sir, if it is all right with you, I would like to stay with my unit. It would look suspicious if I disappeared. Besides, there are a lot of pretty girls out on that beach, and it's been a while if you know what I mean," said Sanchez.

"All right then, you stay here and stay out of trouble. We'll check on you tomorrow evening at MACV. Until then, don't talk to anyone about this," advised Swift.

"Thank you, Sir," replied Sanchez.

After shaking hands and saluting, Swift and Mason left Sanchez in his room. Nothing was said until the two men exited the hotel and drove away in their Jeep.

"So what do you think, Boss?" asked Mason.

"I'm starting to get a bad feeling about this," replied Swift.

"How about those rotating beacons?" asked Mason.

"The official report says they spotted enemy helicopters. I think these guys might have seen Kasakov's team chopper in from the other side of the Cambodian border. That would make the most logical sense. But what attacked the PBR boat and the F-4 could not have been a helicopter or a meteor, so I don't know," said Swift.

"Do you still think we're still chasing Soviet hardware?" asked Mason.

"Based on what we got so far, your guess is as good as mine. I say let's marinate on it for a bit and get a bite to eat. Afterwards, we can see what those Phantom pilots have to tell us. Perhaps, they can shed some light into this mystery," suggested Swift.

"That sounds good to me!"

CHAPTER V
PHANTOMS OF THE NIGHT

Three hours later, Swift and Mason drove their jeep over a red clay road to a back gate of Tan Son Nhut Air Base. Over the course of the day, the weather had changed considerably with intermittent rains. For this, as well as for anonymity, they drove with the green canvas up. Being aware of the possible surveillance by the mysterious Men in Black as they had come to know them, they needed to further blend in with the military population. All cloak and dagger aside, they never knew when a sudden torrential downpour might catch them in the open. To the casual observer, things appeared routine. Two U.S. Army Special Operations officers displaying proper credentials pulled up to the security checkpoint. Without further scrutiny, they were waved in by the U.S. Air Force Security Air Police guarding the base.

"When Fred and I made it back to Tan Son Nhut, we drove up to this small one-story building used by the 12th Tactical Reconnaissance Squadron for their mission briefings. We could see they had air conditioning units sticking out the few windows that lined the sides of the building that leaked trickles of water. For this meeting, the Air Force had half-dozen of their Air Police deployed around the building. They were the Air Force equivalent to Army MPs. While the U.S Army guarded the outside of the base and the VNAF guarded the perimeter against the Viet Cong, the Air Force made sure that once you were inside, you knew it was their base."

"Everything had been prearranged by General Lowe at the behest of CIA Saigon Station Chief William Colby. There, we would meet with the F-4 Phantom pilots and their Commanding Officer, Colonel Davis. We had been given the heads up that Air Force Brigadier General John Harris would be sitting in on this. While he was not part of the 497th Tactical Fighter Squadron based at Ubon Air Base in Thailand, this was still his squadron's mission briefing room. Whatever was to take place there, he was going to be in on it."

Having parked, Swift and Mason walked past the Air Police sentries who, like their Army counterparts, wore helmet liners and carried M-16's. They stood guard covering the front and back exits of the air-conditioned building as Swift and Mason entered. They walked past a few small offices down to a large briefing room. By appearance, it resembled a small dark theater lined with comfortable high back cushioned chairs. At the front of the room was a large wall-sized map of Vietnam with icons from recent operations. There was a big pull-down movie screen of which they were to watch the gun camera footage that a young red-haired Air Operations Lieutenant in a khaki uniform prepared. Upon entry, they would first salute the higher ranking officers before making introductions.

"As we walked in, the two most senior officers stood at the forefront of the room. General Harris was seen his khaki uniform with a single silver star on his collar that gleamed in the overhead fluorescent lights. He stood at the edge of a desk with his arms folded as he chomped on a cigar. General Harris was a robust square-jawed man in his fifties. He looked every bit the tough

WWII veteran who took out five Nazi ME-109's over Germany that made him an Ace. One look at this officer, and you knew he was all business."

"Colonel Davis, on the other hand, was just nearing his 40's. He wore an olive drab green flight suit. By all indications, he must have just flown in from Thailand. Colonel Davis had blonde hair and looked like one of those All-American leading man types who was getting up there in years. He would look very comfortable on the side of a gridiron coaching a big PAC-10 university football team. Rather, Colonel Davis was leading a squadron of brave pilots who took on every surface to air missile and occasional MIG, the Soviets, and their Communist allies could challenge them. With mounting losses of men and machine, I imagine he must have written many letters to grieving parents explaining how their sons died on missions with little or no military value. I didn't envy his job one bit. Then there were the pilots who we had come to interview. Piloting the F-4 Phantom II was Captain Chuck (Buster) Wheeler. He could not have been more than thirty years of age, with over forty-five missions over the North. He had come with his twenty-five-year-old RIO (Radio Intercept Officer) Lieutenant Rob (Swiggler) Cook. They both sat down in the flight chairs in their olive-drab green flight suits. One look at these guys and you could tell they had seen more than their share of death over the skies of Vietnam, and their tour wasn't over yet."

As Swift and Mason stepped inside to the main squadron mission briefing room, they could see a small table to the side. Mason walked over to it and placed his silver briefcase on top of it and opened his case. He took out his tape recorder, a pad of paper and pen as Captain Swift prepared to speak.

"Gentlemen, I am Captain Swift from Special Operations. Before we get started, my partner Lieutenant Mason and I would like to thank General Harris for letting us use his mission briefing room. We would also like to thank Colonel Davis for joining us here. We know you have a lot of work to do, so let's get to it," said Swift.

"For our investigation, we will be recording this session on audiotape," said Mason.

"Furthermore, this meeting is classified. This comes from both the NSA Directive and from Langley. Anything discussed here stays here," said Swift.

"Very well, Captain, you may proceed," said Gen. Harris.

"First off, can we both have you state your names, squadron, base, and crew position?" asked Mason.

"My name is Captain Chuck Wheeler, call sign, Buster. I fly with the 497th Tactical Fighter Squadron Ubon, Thailand. I pilot the F-4 Phantom II."

"I am Lieutenant Robert L. Cook, call sign, Swiggler. I, too, am from the 497th Tactical Fighter Squadron Ubon, Thailand. I sit in the backseat as the Radar Information Officer."

"Thank you. We would like to review the recorded gun camera footage taken on October 27th, 1967, at 0230 hours. Then we would like to get your statements as to the event that occurred on the night in question," said Swift.

"Just so you are aware, the gun camera footage is less than thirty seconds in length. And from the look of it, there's not much to see," said Col. Davis.

"Thank you, Colonel," said Swift.

"You're welcome. Now, if you please, I'd like to know what happened to our Phantom," said Col. Davis.

"That's what we are for, Sir," replied Mason.

"Who would like to start?" asked Swift.

"I guess I will," said Wheeler.

"By all means," replied Swift.

"We were on a night run to keep an eye on some Thuds (F-105's) while they made their milk run up North. A MIG-17 decided to crash the party, so my wingman 'Jester' and I gave chase. We burned up a lot of fuel in the process," said Wheeler.

"Did you get him?" asked Mason.

"Captain Martin, call sign 'Jester' fired an AIM-7 Sparrow missile at him, but it turned out to be a dud and the MIG dove back into the clouds and got away. I guess it was that MIG pilot's lucky night. Afterwards, we met up with a fuel tanker after we crossed back over the DMZ. Our wingman was in the process of gassing up when we got the call from the Navy EC that one of their PBR boats was being attacked from an aircraft at high altitude. That didn't make any sense, but were close by, so we left Jester with the tanker. We used our afterburners to haul ass over the help, but it was too late. By the time we arrived on scene, all we could see were bits of flames on the banks of the river below as we circled. Whatever hit the PBR boat did so in the blink of an eye. That's when we saw it," said Wheeler.

"Saw what?" asked Swift.

"It was this weird bright blue-white light that appeared out of nowhere twenty miles away at 10,000 feet," replied Wheeler.

"Did you get a radar return?" asked Mason.

"We sure did, but I couldn't tell what it was other than it was coming at us fast," said Cook.

"Lieutenant Sparks, let's go ahead and pull down the screen, dim the lights, and run the gun camera footage," ordered General Harris.

"Yes, Sir," replied Sparks.

"Captain Wheeler, walk us through this footage step by step as it happened," said Swift.

"All right, I'll tell you again in about as much detail."

The night was October 27th, at 0215 hours. Somewhere over I Corps (northern South Vietnam) flying south of the DMZ flew two U.S. Air Force McDonald Douglas F-4 Phantom II's flying at an altitude of twenty-thousand feet in the night sky. They had just returned from escorting a flight of a dozen Thuds (F-105 Thunderchiefs) from a bombing run on the Ho Chi Minh Trail in Communist North Vietnam. Under the moon's light, they could spot the KC-135 tanker off in the distance.

"This is Jester 909 to tanker."

"Go ahead, Jester," replied the gray painted military converted 707 tanker.

"We need some go-go juice for the RTB," radioed Jester.

"Roger that. I'm sure we can accommodate you. Pull up, and we'll lower the boom for you," radioed the tanker.

"Much obliged," radioed Jester.

"You go on first," radioed Buster.

"Thank you, Buster," replied Jester.

INCIDENT AT DAK TO

The F-4 Phantom II slowly approached the aerial tanker, where they could see the long boom lower from underneath the tail. Captain Wheeler's Phantom flew alongside as Jester extended his refueling nozzle and made contact with the refueling boom.

"Contact, fill her up with premium unleaded, and if you can, please check my wipers and bumpers for me," radioed Jester.

"We got you covered, Jester. Initiating fuel transfer," radioed the tanker.

One minute into the air to air fueling process, a crackle came over the radio.

"This is Navy EC to Flight 909, do you copy?"

"909, acknowledged, go ahead, EC," replied Buster.

"We have a PBR boat under attack urgently requesting air support by unknown aircraft attacking them from high altitude one hundred twenty nautical miles southwest of your position," radioed the EC.

"Stand by, EC."

"Say, did he just say their boat was being attacked from high altitude?" asked Swiggler.

"That has to be a mistake. They'd never fly a MIG this far down south!" exclaimed Buster.

"Even if they could, they couldn't attack a small plastic boat at night from high up at night. They got to be joking," argued Swiggler.

"Hey, they call, we haul," replied Buster.

"Roger that! What's our fuel situation?" asked Swiggler.

"I'd say we can squeeze ten extra minutes with what we got, but we'll have to make it quick," said Buster.

"909, do you copy? 909," radioed the Navy EC.

"Roger, EC. 909 Buster 310 is on our way!"

"Go get em, Buster!" radioed Jester.

"See you back at the barn!" radioed Swiggler.

In an instant, Captain Wheeler's F-4 Phantom II dropped altitude to break formation and then turned southwest. The supersonic fighter immediately released its two drop tanks and fired the afterburners to race over to the scene.

"See anything?" asked Buster.

"I got nothing. Wait a minute, something keeps fading in and out ninety miles southeast at thirty-thousand feet," replied Swiggler.

Captain Wheeler's Phantom raced through the moonlit skies towards the hills around Dak To when his RIO noticed a blue-white light moving across the horizon.

"Hey, do you see that?" asked Buster.

"Yeah, it's also there on my scope, then gone the next. Hold it! I got a fix on it. It's turning toward us at fifty-five nautical miles!" replied Swiggler.

"We're going weapons hot. I'm going to try to get a lock before we close the merge," said Buster.

Suddenly, the gunsight piper lit up and made the distinct growling sounds that indicated Buster had a missile lock.

"Fox One!" cried Buster.

An AIM-7 Sparrow missile fired off, heading straight for the target as Swiggler tracked the missile's progress.

"Miss! Aircraft coming into close visual range!" alerted Swiggler.

The bright blue-white light raced towards them then suddenly shot up twenty-thousand feet at a steep angle.

"What the hell!" exclaimed Buster.

"He's coming around! He's going to try to scissor us!" alerted Swiggler.

"Not if I can help it!" replied Buster.

The F-4 Phantom II quickly banked high into a dirty roll then tried a classic wagon wheel evasion maneuver at high speeds. The bright light just kept pace.

"What the hell is that?" exclaimed Buster.

"I don't know! Hold it; he's gone!" cried Swiggler.

"Gone?"

"He disappeared. He's not even on my scope anymore," explained Swiggler.

Bewildered, Buster looked at his fuel gauge and saw that he was running out of fuel when suddenly the light appeared again heading straight for them.

"Shit, there he is again!" alerted Swiggler.

"I'm going for guns this time!" said Buster.

As the light closed the distance, Buster opened up his 20mm Vulcan cannon. In the span of a second, the furious burst from the

Phantom's gun came to an abrupt stop just as the blinding white-blue light collided with the plane and passed right through port wing brushing the left intake.

"What the ….?" asked Buster.

"Oh shit, look! Something happened to the port wing," revealed Swiggler.

Buster turned his head looked over at his port wing. He could see in the moonlight that the green and brown South East Asian camouflage paint was wiped clean off over half the wing and the mouth of the port intake. To his horror, his port engine began to flame out.

"Oh, no-no-no! Come on, baby! Restart!" cried Buster.

The port engine failed to restart after several tries. As the crippled fighter began to lose altitude, the sputtering sound started to affect the starboard engine.

"We're on fumes!" revealed Buster.

"What do you want to do?" asked Swiggler.

"Be ready to punch out when I call out Eject-Eject-Eject. If I had the fuel, I would like to try to make for Biên Hòa Air Base, but we don't. I'm going to try to gain some altitude and see if we can't limp her in," said Buster.

As Captain Wheeler went on to recount the strange events of the night of October 27th, 1967, he went on to detail the aftermath of his aerial encounter.

"We declared an air emergency and were set to land at Biên Hòa. We didn't have the fuel, but somehow we came within sight of it, but then the loss of flight controls made us overshoot the approach.

I have no idea how, but somehow, we managed to stay in the air long enough to make a hard stick landing at Tan Son Nhut Air Base. I know it sounds crazy, but that's what happened," revealed Wheeler.

"You mean to tell me you glided a crippled plane without fuel for an additional ten minutes without the benefit of sufficient altitude? You do know that's theoretically impossible, right?" decried Col. Davis.

"I don't know how else to explain it, Sir. We were ready to eject, but somehow, the plane just managed to stay in the air. I know that sounds crazy, but that's the God's honest truth. Trust me, I know we should be dead, and we're lucky to have walked away from that one. I'll tell you I am no religious man, but as cliché as it may sound, I believe somebody was looking out for us," remarked Cook.

Silence filled the room as the officers were left shocked in disbelief. It was then that General Harris stood up and made his remarks.

"General, your thoughts, Sir?" asked Col. Davis.

"Sounds like they ran into Foo Fighters," replied Gen. Harris.

"Begging your pardon, Sir? Uh, did you just say, what did you just say?" asked Swift.

"Foo Fighters, that's what we called them in the big WW Two. We had heard about them from the English Lancaster crews flying over Dresden. We thought they were nuts until we started running into them ourselves. I remember one of them buzzed my Mustang over Hamburg, late November 1944. At the time, we believed they were the new Nazi wonder weapons Hitler bragged about. But in the end, they turned out to be some weird atmospheric phenomenon nobody could explain to us, or at least that's what they told us. After a while, we got used to seeing them in heavy clouds and just blew them off like a flight of random geese. I hadn't given much thought about them since then until today," remarked Gen. Harris.

"With all due respect, General, are you suggesting my men encountered this same phenomena here in Vietnam?" asked Col. Davis.

"Colonel, I believe your men are telling you the truth. I also believe these two gentlemen from Special Operations might have an opinion on the matter," replied Gen. Harris.

"Officially, Sir, we have no opinion on the matter as of yet. Our initial intelligence leads us to believe that this may be a yet-to-be identified Soviet prototype that had illegally entered the war zone at high altitude. We initially suspected it to be a supersonic reconnaissance plane that flies near the edge of space. Based on Captain Wheeler and Lieutenant Cook's accounts, that early assumption lacks evidence to support such foregone conclusions. Thus, we will need to examine the plane to make further determinations," said Swift.

"Fair enough, Captain. Let's say we all go out to Captain Wheeler's plane and take a look," suggested Col. Davis.

"I thought you'd never ask," replied Swift.

Minutes later, Swift and Mason, along with General Harris, Colonel Davis, Captain Wheeler, and Lieutenant Cook walked over to the fortified redoubt that was lined with sandbags to protect the F-4 Phantom II from a mortar attack. They could see the plane was still being worked on. More noticeably, the South Asian green camouflage paint was wiped clean off a large section of the port wing and part of the port intake. A faint white substance coated that portion of the wing to which no one could identify.

"Well, I'll be damned! Look at that!" exclaimed Mason.

"That's still throwing me for a loop," remarked Cook.

Swift rubbed his fingertips along the edge of the wing and intake manifold. He then smelled his finger then put it in his mouth to taste it.

"What do you think, Boss?" asked Mason.

"It's not paint, and it doesn't smell or tastes like anything. Most remarkable! Can we get photos of this?"

Mason agreed and brought out a small Leica camera and started taking photos of the wing and intake. Both Colonel Davis and Captain Wheeler looked on with disbelief as a tall black Master Sergeant with the name patch reading Miller stepped forward.

"Master Sergeant, did you run the inspection on this plane?" asked Col. Davis.

'Yes, Sir, I inspected her myself. We pulled out the port engine and found nothing. We checked it a second time and still came up with nothing to indicate a bird strike or a collision with another aircraft. As far as our quality assurance can tell, she is airworthy," said Miller.

"Thank you," thanked Wheeler.

"Sir, would you like to have her re-painted before you take her back to Ubon?" asked Miller.

Captain Wheeler was just about to reply when Swift noticed the unmistakable sound of incoming mortar fire.

"We've got incoming!" shouted Swift.

"Oh, shit!" exclaimed Mason.

A second later, the first two explosions could be heard near the flight line as the alarm siren could be heard throughout the airbase.

"We have bunkers close by, follow me!" shouted Miller.

The men quickly raced over from the redoubt and followed Master Sergeant Miller to the fortified sandbag lined bunker. One by one, the men rapidly escaped the rain of incoming mortars as they took shelter in the bunker. The ground shook as explosions, and gunfire could be heard.

"We had run to the safety of the nearby bunkers. A small Viet Cong sapper team supported by a mortar crew attacked the base. When the all-clear siren rang out, we emerged from the bunker to a haze of black and gray smoke chocked with heavy fumes of Jp-4 as fires raged on in the distance. Like everything else that happened on our mission, nothing came without a degree of frustration."

As the men returned to the redoubt, they could see the F-4 Phantom II took a direct hit and was broken in two and was completely engulfed in flames.

"Son of a bitch!" exclaimed Wheeler.

Captain Swift recollected his description of the event:

"Of all the planes parked on that line of redoubts, Charlie had to hit that one. Luckily for us, Mason got some photos. But for the 497th Tactical Fighter Squadron, they would be short one less Phantom."

As the fire crews rushed over to put out the burning hulk of the destroyed fighter plane, General Harris walked past Swift and Mason and urged them to come with him.

"We had left Colonel Davis and his pilots there on the tarmac and followed General Harris back to the 12th Tactical Reconnaissance Squadron's mission briefing room. The guards that had previously been posted had since deployed elsewhere during the attack. Now it was just us. As we walked back inside the main room, Lieutenant Sparks could be seen preparing what looked like additional footage for us to see. It was then that a female Airman by the name of Lori Daniels appeared from out of the shadows of the projection screen. I am not certain if she had been there the whole time or if General Harris had intended for us to meet with her and not the pilots. She wore olive-drab green stateside USAF fatigues with blue patches and kept her strawberry blonde hair in a tight updo. I am not sure how that was regulation, but there you go."

Swift and Mason had followed the general back into the briefing room. He clearly had something to say.

"Captain Swift, I asked you and Lieutenant Mason to come back here in part as a professional courtesy. You see, back when I was at Strategic Air Command, I had a few instances like these that came across my desk. Normally, a pilot can get grounded over such things, but given my own experience over Germany, I'm inclined to look the other way. Officially, we're not supposed to talk about such things, but since you didn't bat an eye when I offered my opinion earlier, I feel that what I have to show you may be of interest to you," said Gen. Harris.

"Thank you, General. I appreciate your confidence," said Swift.

"This is Airman Lori Daniels. As you may be aware, the Australians do most of the Air Traffic Control at Tan Son Nhut. But for non-listed flights, we have our own ATC's. She is one of two Air Traffic Controllers who handles Company flights and anything else for Special Operations. She reports to me and to me alone on anything out of the ordinary. Based on my own experiences, I would say this qualifies," said General Harris.

"Is that a fact?" asked Swift.

"Yes, Sir, I was the ATC that night," she replied.

"My, that's quite an accent you have there. Where are you from?" asked Swift.

"Kenosha, Wisconsin, Sir," she replied.

"Wisconsin, huh? I suspected somewhere from the Great Lakes. I served with a guy from Milwaukee in Pleiku in 65. A good man who brought out the wounded onto the choppers," said Swift.

At that point, General Harris directed Lieutenant Sparks to cue up something on their projector.

"Sparks, let's dim the lights again and run that second reel," said Gen. Harris.

"Yes, Sir," replied Sparks.

"What you are about to see is the radar track recorded from the night of October 27th. Nobody outside this room has seen this. So I'll go ahead and turn this over to my ATC so she can describe what you are about to see," said General Harris.

As the projector ran, they could see the outline of Tan Son Nhut airspace with the troubled F-4 Phantom II appearing on the edge of the screen.

"For the record, we had no Special flights taking place that night. We were tipped off by the ATC from Biên Hòa on a secure channel that Black protocols were engaged. That's when I took over and started to record the radar track as it came in. What you see here is the local airspace covering the approach to Tan Son

Nhut. As you can see, Captain Wheeler's Phantom is here. Tan Son Nhut is in the center, and then this appeared," she explained.

"What's that second green blip on the edge of the screen?" asked Mason.

"We don't know what that was. You couldn't see it from the tower, but it appeared on radar. It was tailing the Phantom but managed to stay out of sight. From where I was in the tower, nobody could get a visual on it," said Daniels.

As the track of the F-4 lined up with the approach to Tan Son Nhut's runaways, the second blip disappeared.

"Hey, where did it go?" asked Swift.

"That's just it. It disappeared off the radar scope the minute the F-4 touched down. I notified General Harris the minute we stopped recording the radar track," explained Daniels.

"There's something else you should know," said Gen. Harris.

"What's that?" asked Mason.

"Lieutenant Sparks," beckoned Gen. Harris.

"All records of special flights are processed and then placed in a vault. Two nights ago, someone trashed the processing lab and broke into the vault. Fortunately, we had processed it earlier and had it under lock and key elsewhere," revealed Sparks.

"Did anyone see what happened?" asked Swift.

"Yes, please turn your attention to this short black and white reel of surveillance footage," instructed Gen. Harris

As Lieutenant Sparks rolled the small reel, they could see three shadowy male figures dressed in black breaking into the lab. They wore black field caps, black gloves, and dark sunglasses as they tore up the lab in search of the radar track.

"As you can see, someone came looking for this. I suspect they were not working for the Company, and they are not with you," said Gen. Harris.

A second later, one of the black figures waved his hand in front of the hidden camera before the footage went black.

"This recording survived because I took it directly to General Harris," said Daniels.

It was then that Swift looked over to his partner Mason and whispered to him.

"The Men in Black," said Swift.

"Are there any more radar returns that might have captured this encounter?" asked Mason.

"The Navy EC would have one, but that plane is attached to a carrier up at Yankee Station," she replied.

"Do you know which one?" asked Swift.

"As a matter of fact we do. It's the U.S.S. Oriskany. If you want to get out there, I would take a plane and fly out of here no later than 0600 hours to get up to Da Nang. It's a four-hour flight. From there, you'll need to catch a COD to take you the rest of the way to Yankee Station," suggested Gen. Harris.

"Is there any way we can get a copy of this radar track and the gun camera footage?" asked Mason.

"There are no other copies, and that's the way it's going to be. Lieutenant Sparks is packing up the actual footage and radar track for you as we speak. I'll assume it will make its way back to Langley. Once you leave this room, that footage will not exist, and I will deny any knowledge of its existence. Are we clear?"

"Crystal, thank you, Sir," replied Swift.

"You're welcome and good luck."

General Harris put out his cigar and left with Airman Daniels as Swift and Mason made their exit.

"Talk about strange shit! I had heard of some weird stories since I joined the Company, but nothing compared to this. Neither Fred nor I could wrap our heads around what we had seen or heard. It was getting late when Fred arranged to make the journey to Yankee Station in the morning. We went back into Saigon and had a late supper before returning to our hotel. Given what had happened at the American Embassy vault, we opted to keep the evidence we were entrusted with and placed it in the safe in Mason's room. It was a decision we would later regret."

CHAPTER VI
ENTER THE MAN IN BLACK

Late December, Kon Tum Province, 1964 in the Republic of Vietnam, the time was nearing 1620 hours on a dark overcast day. There, Captain Swift walked along the edge of a muddy rice paddy near the *Dak Ba* River. As a military advisor, he wore green tiger stripe jungle fatigues, a green beret, and carried a brand-new M-16 rifle that had just arrived in Vietnam. He was part of a twenty-four-man patrol with the 42nd ARVN Infantry Regiment. The South Vietnamese soldiers were led by twenty-three-year-old Lieutenant Tran Van Than. He stood at five-foot-five and sported an Australian-inspired olive drab green slouch bush hat. He wore an ivory-handled Colt 45 pistol at his waist and carried an M-1 Garand rifle. The rest of his troops wore steel helmets with camouflaged liners. They, too, carried M-1 rifles that were provided by the American Military Assistance Program to the Republic of Vietnam. They were near the end of their long daylight patrol when torrential rains left a seven-inch layer of mud to slog through as they neared the end of a muddy causeway.

A flash of white lightning lit up the darkened sky as scattered water droplets came down. The soldiers could see the droplets bounce off the rice paddy as they slogged ever closer to the end of their patrol. Across the way, they could see three Vietnamese farmers dressed in black, working the field. There was also a shirtless little boy in muddied shorts walking along the edge of the rice paddy next to a large water buffalo. This was a common sight out in the countryside. The scene was almost mundane when, unexpectedly, the monotony of the uneventful patrol came to a sudden and violent halt.

Nineteen-year-old Corporal Le Vinh Do walked behind his point man, Private Trang when he sunk his foot into the mud and heard an alarming click. His foot had stepped on something made of metal buried deep into the mud. He started to shout when the landmine exploded, tearing his leg from his body and ejecting him several feet into the air and down into the mud. The shrapnel wounded the two men closest to him. Everyone quickly got as low to the ground as possible, expecting any hiding Viet Cong to fire on them, but no shots were heard. Their medic "Doc" Bui Huong quickly leaped over to Corporal Do as he thrashed about and went into shock as he desperately reached for his missing limb.

"*Me! Me!*" he tearfully gasped.

Corporal Do struggled to speak as he started to cough up blood before succumbing to unintelligible moans of dire agony as he shook in convulsions. The color of blood spilled into the muddy paddy water as Doc Bui quickly administered morphine. Within seconds, Do calmed down but then began to lose consciousness. A moment later, he became still as he slipped into the abyss.

"Tell everyone to stay down," ordered Swift.

Lieutenant Tran Van Than wasted no time relaying orders in both Vietnamese and with hand signals. Medic "Doc" Bui Huong shook his head for no after finding no pulse before moving over to triage the wounds of the other two men seen bleeding in the mud that were blown back by the concussion of the explosion. It was then that Lieutenant Than noticed one of the farmers started to run away. It was a woman whose conical Non-La hat flew off her head as she scurried for cover towards the tree line.

"Get her!" ordered Than.

Private Thatch adjusted his gun site and fired just as two other of Lieutenant Than's troopers opened fire. One well-placed round quickly dispatched the Viet Cong guerilla in a sudden cloud of pink mist sending her down into the mud.

"What shit for luck!" griped Swift.

"They knew we were coming and planted that mine to kill my men," said Than.

"I'm sorry about Do. What was he trying to say?" asked Swift.

"He was calling out for his dead mother who was murdered in her village by the Viet Cong last month," wept Than.

"I'm sorry, Than. I should have known that," said Swift.

"No apology necessary. You haven't been with us long enough to know all of my men," replied Than.

"What does Doc Bui say?" asked Swift.

Lieutenant Than gave the nod to his medic, who replied his prognosis back to him in Vietnamese.

"He is applying a compress to Trang, but says he needs to be evacuated to the field hospital as soon as possible. Trinh has also been given morphine for his superficial wounds and will be okay," translated Than.

"All right, then, tag and bag our KIA and carry the wounded back across to the other side of the rice paddy for extraction," said Swift.

"Thank you, Captain. I will have my man radio in."

It would be another thirty minutes sitting in the wet mud before the sound of approaching helicopters could be heard in the distance. The ARVN soldiers looked up to the skies and started pointing at three black distant specs with expressions of relief as one of the soldiers popped open a blue smoke canister.

One by one, the twin-rotor U.S. Army CH-21C Shawnee *Flying Banana* as they were called lined up to set down on the small Landing Zone. Four of Lieutenant Than's men quickly loaded Do's body aboard the first chopper as the helmeted American door gunner holding an M-60 kept watch. Doc Bui jumped in next. Then four men assisted wounded Trang and Trinh climb aboard before lifting off as Private Thatch, and three other ARVN set up a small line to protect the LZ. The second Shawnee came in and set down and quickly loaded twelve of Lieutenant Than's troopers before taking off to join with the first chopper hovering above. As the third helicopter came into the LZ, an incoming mortar round exploded, sending shrapnel in all directions. Lieutenant Than ordered Thatch and his remaining men to get aboard the chopper before a second round came in that landed closer.

"They're adjusting fire!" shouted Swift.

"Okay, let's go!" replied Than.

The last of Lieutenant Than's men climbed aboard the banana-shaped heavy-lift helicopter. The radio operator and Captain Swift were the last three men to get to the side door of the helicopter right as a mortar round landed just feet away, nearly hitting the sitting chopper. Lieutenant Than hopped aboard the chopper behind Private Thatch as 7.62mm rounds could be heard whizzing all around them. Captain Swift was about to board the helicopter when he noticed something that unexpectedly caught his eye. It was as if he momentarily froze and looked up into the clouds as pings could be heard hitting the helicopter.

"We got to go, Captain!" shouted the door gunner.

It was then that Captain Swift noticed a blue-white light moving just above the gray clouds towards the direction of the LZ. For a moment, he seemed somewhat transfixed on the strange glow as the enemy fire started piercing the fuselage of the Shawnee, instantly wounding two ARVN soldiers sitting inside. The sudden screams of pain drew his attention and returned a sense of urgency of their needed extraction. Swift quickly climbed aboard the chopper as it lifted off the muddy ground while taking fire. Within seconds, the Shawnee regrouped with the other two helicopters that hovered overhead and turned towards the base, but not before Swift looked out the small round window as the door gunner fired back.

"What were you looking at, Captain?" asked Than.

"I'm not sure," replied Swift.

"I hope for the sake of my men; it was worth it. Just remember, once you leave Vietnam, we will still be here, fighting."

As the three CH-21C Shawnee choppers flew along the path of the *Dak Ba* River, Swift contemplated Lieutenant Than's scolding words. He thought about it as he stared at the wounded ARVN soldiers that moaned in agony aboard the chopper. Swift didn't know what happened in those last seconds on the ground. It was something odd that he had forgotten about that resurrected three years later to haunt his sleep. Whatever it was, it had him tossing and turning in his sleep until awoke in a cold sweat.

"Fuck!" he exclaimed.

Swift had woken up in his room in the Caravel Hotel in Saigon. He was nearly hyperventilating as he reached for his pistol and leaped out of bed. Swift needed to get some air and do so quickly to regain his bearings. He cast the sheer drapes aside and furiously opened the glass door before stepping out onto the balcony. The crisp night air and the sounds of motor scooters from the Saigon streets below helped him regain his sense of calm after that momentary distress. He still could not fathom why that particular memory unnerved his dreams. Swift had not thought about it in all that time but there it was.

"The memory of that fateful ARVN patrol kicked me out of bed in the middle of the night. I hadn't woken up in a cold sweat in some time before I returned here. I guess I am one of the lucky ones. After Operation Shiny Bayonet, I left Vietnam. The things I learned on that tour with Advisory Command had left a bitter taste in my mouth, and I wasn't down for a second helping. I don't want to say I lost faith, but from what I had seen made me question our real purpose in Vietnam. Sure, I could have shrugged it off and stuck around. Hell, they were going to promote me, but I opted out for a trip home and a more lucrative position with the Company. So much had happened between that time and where I was at that moment. I had almost forgotten about it. Like many vets that would follow, I just got busy."

Captain Swift collected his thoughts where he stood. But as he found his bearings, he realized he was standing out on his balcony in his boxer shorts holding a pistol. With his sense of order restored, Swift quietly stepped back to his room. Swift had barely taken two steps towards the light switch when he suddenly noticed there was an alarming figure of a man sitting five feet from him in the dark. Swift instantly aimed his pistol at the shadowy figure that held up his hand.

"Looking for this?" he asked.

Swift carefully turned on the light and could see an older American sitting across from him. He had a receding salt and pepper hairline and wore black fatigues as he sat there holding up a magazine clip. It was then that Swift realized that the clip belonged to his pistol.

"Who the fuck are you? And just how the hell did you get in here?" demanded Swift.

"You can call me Bob."

"Bob?"

"Ambiguous, am I not?"

"I suppose if you told me your name was Chester, it wouldn't have the same effect," said Swift.

"Probably not, now please put the gun down unless you plan to throw it at me. It won't do you any good since I took the round out of the chamber for my own personal safety," said Bob.

"Your safety?"

"Oh, yes, other people would like to not get shot around here too, you know," said Bob.

"Are you here to kill me?" asked Swift.

"Nah, if I wanted to kill you, that would've already happened, and then you and I would not be having this friendly conversation," said Bob.

"You call breaking into my room and scaring the shit out of me as the basis of a friendly conversation?" argued Swift.

"Okay, then, consider this a professional courtesy," replied Bob.

With caution, Swift carefully put the gun down on the table and put his undershirt on before sitting across from the mysterious Man in Black.

"We've been watching you for a while," said Bob.

"I am going to assume you are part of that Black Team I've been hearing about," assumed Swift.

"Most people mistake us for CIA. Of course, this makes our job easier when we have to come to Vietnam. Others say we are an urban myth. Some would go as far as to say we are the boogeymen that even the Spooks fear. Me, I'm like Johnny Cash, I am a Man in Black," chuckled Bob.

"I'm no Spook. I'm just a field analyst for the Company," replied Swift.

"Well, of course, you are! Keep on telling yourself that. I'll have you know you caught our attention out in the Sinai. You were one step ahead of Kasakov's team, and that really pissed him off to no end. I wish you could have seen the look on his face. Classic, I tell you! But it was your work with Operation Diamond that impressed me the most," said Bob.

"Can we cut the shit and tell me why we're having this friendly conversation?" asked Swift.

"Certainly!"

"If you're not CIA, then who do you work for?" asked Swift.

"That's way above your pay grade. If I told you, then I would have to kill you, and then where would all the fun be in that?" laughed Bob.

"Was it fun killing Colonel Linh?" asked Swift.

"Call that an unfortunate circumstance of a foregone occupational hazard," replied Bob.

Bob's casual demeanor filled an unsettling air about the room. Swift recalled Sanchez's description of a creepy white man that left them feeling unnerved.

"The photos that were slipped under my door last night, was that you?" asked Swift.

"You could say it came from an associate of mine," replied Bob.

"Are they real?" he asked.

"That's classified. The Tu-150 1A fighter recon variant did exist, but the GRU has done everything they could to make the project disappear. But if you must know, there were three prototypes, but the demands of the Soviet Military machine couldn't make it work, hence the project's failure. The first crashed on takeoff at a secret base near the Aral Sea. The second had a catastrophic failure at 85,000 feet over the Kamchatka Peninsula, killing both pilots. The third, well, let's just say it exists in the realm of imagination or whatever we want it to be," said Bob.

"And who are we?" asked Swift.

Bob just chuckled and grinned without replying as he cracked his knuckles and smiled.

"Trust me on this; you should sign off on the enemy helicopter story, take the photos, and leave Saigon with the story I have given you. There's nothing there to see at Dak To," warned Bob.

"If there's nothing to see there, then what the hell was that thing you stole out of the U.S. Embassy?" asked Swift.

"I didn't steal anything," laughed Bob.

"Then who did?" demanded Swift.

"You don't need to know, but I have to say I admire your tenacity. What took place at the US Embassy was part of a distraction. You work for the Company. You know the real reason why we are here in Vietnam; otherwise, you would have taken that promotion and become a Company Commander instead of being a glorified stolen technical readout expert," said Bob.

"I didn't expect to ever be back here, nor did I expect to be on some wild goose chase in the middle of a war zone," replied Swift.

"Then why not leave?" asked Bob.

Swift watched as Bob placed a white envelope on the table.

"What's that?" asked Swift.

"Call it an incentive. It's your ticket out of here. Diplomatic pre-paid priority tickets to Tokyo. From there, you and your partner will take a connecting flight to Sapporo," said Bob.

"What for?" asked Swift.

"I've arranged for a MIG-25 prototype to be flown by a yet to be named defector to Hokkaido. You'll be the first in the West to see it," explained Bob.

"MIG-25? I've never heard of it," said Swift.

"Oh, but you will, trust me on that. It's a high-altitude interceptor specifically designed to kill the A-12. I am giving you the opportunity of a lifetime. Don't look a gift horse in the mouth. All you have to do is let this one go. Accept the report. It was Kasakaov's team that flew those helicopters. They found nothing and left as you should while you still can," suggested Bob.

"And what if I don't?" asked Swift.

"You'll be making a big mistake. The Soviets let Hanoi know why you are here, and they've put a hefty price on your head. Unless you want to be a hero and rejoin the fight, you're just going to get you and your man Mason killed. Trust me; it's not worth it."

"So you are threatening me?" asked Swift.

"Not at all, I'm just here to offer you a way out. You see, I like you, Swift, even if that's not your real name."

"Smith was too common, so we changed it up a bit," replied Swift.

"Of course you did. It's what I would have done. Hell, you remind me of my younger self. You're the kind of guy who is going to see things to the end. And that's exactly why I can't let you throw your life away like this. You're a fine soldier, a tough Green Beret, and a true patriot. Your country would be proud of you if they only knew what you have done in service for the folks back home. But the reality is they're going never know especially since you started working for Langley. I know you'd like to think you're making a difference out here, but what you are dealing with is something I cannot explain to you. You just have to take my word on it and let it go. Close the case, go to Japan, and have fun tearing apart a brand new MIG. I'll even arrange for a night in a real geisha house in Kyoto if you'd like. I have connections you couldn't possibly dream of! All you have to do is file the report you've been given and let this go," pleaded Bob.

"You want me to put my name on a report that concludes enemy helicopters were the cause of the incidents that took place on October 27th? No one is going to believe that!" argued Swift.

"People will believe anything if you want them to. We do it all the time. You would be amazed at how much bullshit we've put out there that's been accepted as fact by a gullible public," replied Bob.

"Okay, Bob, if you claim to know me as you say you do, then you know I can't just walk away from this. Frankly, the more you entice me to walk away, the more I want to know what's out there," said Swift.

"I figured you would say that. All I can tell you is that you might not like what find there. Be that as it may, I have tried to reason with you, but you're stubborn like a hound on the trail. Fair enough. If you do not leave the country by sundown tomorrow, I can no longer guarantee your safety."

"Now, you're threatening me?" asked Swift.

"It's like I said before, call it a professional courtesy. But if you force me to resort to cliché's, then I'll say: You've been warned."

Just then, a sudden eruption of automatic weapons fire could be heard outside. In the split second that followed, Bob grabbed the magazine clip and tossed it to Swift. He caught it right as a loud explosion happened outside, instantly cutting the power and the lights.

"Everything went dark, and the shooting stopped. The lights would come back on, but just like that, Bob was gone."

A moment later, there was a knock at the door. Swift put the clip into his pistol and chambered a round before pointing it at the door.

"Hey Boss, are you all right?"

It was the familiar voice of his partner Fred Mason. Swift lowered his gun and opened the door to let Mason, who appeared with his sidearm.

"I thought heard voices just before the explosion. Was someone in here with you?" asked Mason.

"Yeah, I think I just met that guy that Sanchez described," said Swift.

"The creepy old Man in Black?" asked Mason.

"Yeah, the Men in Black really do exist, and I just had a conversation with one."

"How the hell did he get in here?" asked Mason.

"I have no idea. I had dead-bolted the door before I turned in for the night. I was having a heavy dream when I woke up in a cold sweat. I grabbed my gun and stepped outside onto the balcony. The next thing I knew, he was just sitting there, and he had already taken the clip out of my pistol."

"How did he do that?" asked Mason.

"Beats the hell out of me, he was in and out of here in the blink of an eye. One minute he was there, the next, he was gone, and there wasn't a damn thing I could do about it."

"Well, what did he want?" asked Mason.

Swift handed Mason the envelope containing the diplomatic pass tickets for Japan. Mason opened the white envelope and examined the tickets.

"What the hell is this?" asked Mason.

"It's a way out. He wants us to sign off on the enemy helicopter story and use these tickets to fly to Japan. He says there's going to be a brand new MIG defecting if we go there," revealed Swift.

"And what if we don't?"

"He implied a threat," replied Swift.

Mason merely shook his head as he walked over sat down on the bed by the wooden nightstand. He then reached for the phone and dialed the number for the front desk.

"What are you doing?" asked Swift.

"We're checking out," replied Mason.

Swift gave a slight nod in agreement. It was clear that the Caravel Hotel was no longer safe.

"It was just after 0100 hours when we quietly checked out of the Caravel Hotel. We had opted for the An Dao Inn on Nguyễn Huệ Street. Don't go looking for it. The VC burned it to the ground four months later during the 1968 Tet Offensive. We knew the An Dao had a safe in one of the rooms, and a night manager who went by the name Jimmy Tang who, for the right price, wouldn't ask any questions. We also knew that we had an early flight, so we checked our gear into our rooms and secured the evidence in Mason's room before heading to Tan Son Nhut Air Base to catch our 0600 flight to Da Nang."

"It had been a long day with little sleep. We looked like Voodoo zombies as we lumbered up to the small rear ramp of the unmarked

Company C-123. But once we were in the air, we would take advantage of the long flight and catch some Z's."

"As tired as I was, there was little rest for us, the aforementioned wicked. I kept thinking of that awful day on patrol with Advisory Command along the Dak Ba River. The stories collected from the 4th ID and the F-4 pilots possibly induced the memory of that tragic patrol. Or was it the accounts of one Johnny Sanchez and his childhood tale of bus trips with his maternal grandmother out to the Imperial Desert? And then there was the Man in Black known as Bob. He posed a specter of a figure with unnerving calm in the manner in which he spoke. I would have rather spent another night at Plei Me than be in a room with that man again if I could help it. I suspected it would not be the last I would see of him. Whatever truth he was hiding, it was clear that the closer we got to it, the more precarious this assignment would become. Perhaps we should have taken that trip to Japan. It would have been much easier, but it was too late now. As soon as the C-123 touched down at Da Nang, we would be on a course that would take us to into the darkness before we would see light again. I just could not have anticipated what would happen next."

CHAPTER VII
YANKEE STATION

Halloween, October 31st, 1967. The unmarked C-123 touched down at Da Nang Air Base just past 1000 hours. Fred Mason awoke first and looked out the small port window before waking up Swift. He could see it was sunny outside the plane. But as the plane turned onto the taxiway, he could make out the encroaching marine layer as the transport made its way on the tarmac.

"The events that took place the night before left us little doubt that the Men in Black were one step ahead of us. It was far too convenient for the Viet Cong to stage an attack that destroyed the very plane we needed to look at. For all we knew, the mortar crew might not have been the Viet Cong at all. It was, for this reason, we had called MAC-SOG and gave them explicit orders. Once the men of the 4th ID returned from their stay at Vung Tau, they were to be confined to the compound until our return. I'm sure it didn't go over very well with them, but it was for their own good. They just didn't know it yet."

As the loading ramp lowered, Swift and Mason arose from their seats. Mason had brought along his silver briefcase and waited to disembark. Swift had earlier informed the pilot that the plane was to stay there at Da Nang until their return from the USS Oriskany.

"We had a young guy named Hewitt who drove up in an unmarked Jeep to take us to where the COD was waiting for us. For those of you who don't know, COD stands for Carrier Onboard Delivery. In our case, it would be a twin-engine Navy Grumman C-1 Trader or the *Fuddy-Duddy* as they called it."

As the COD came into view, Swift and Mason's attention were drawn to a crowd around a U.S. Army UH-1 Huey across the way. They could see dozens of regular Army Soldiers and Marines gathered around a pair of young American women wearing powder blue knee-length uniform dresses that stepped out onto the tarmac.

"Now, there's an unusual sight!" pointed Swift.

"Who are those girls, and what are they doing here?" asked Mason.

"They call them Donut Dollies," replied Hewitt.

"Donut Dollies?" asked Swift.

"Yeah, they are American Red Cross volunteers. That's the fourth group of them I've seen pass through Da Nang since I got here. The last group handed out packs of Kool-Aid before boarding choppers bound for Chu Lai. Nice girls! Plucked them right out of college, I hear," explained Hewitt.

"What do they do?" asked Mason.

"They do what they can to bring cheer to the troops. They provide coffee and recreation activities for the troops. A taste of home, they call it. I believe they also visit hospitals to provide comfort for the dying and wounded, and you know that's got to be rough. Knowing that, I don't envy them one bit. They're brave girls to sign up for this shit and you got to love them," remarked Hewitt.

"Yeah, I bet," remarked Mason.

As Hewitt pulled the Jeep up on the tarmac, it came to a stop alongside the awaiting Navy COD C-1 Trader. Mason grabbed his silver briefcase and proceeded to board first. Captain Swift took one last look over his shoulder at the pretty Red Cross volunteers before boarding the plane. Where he and Mason were going, there would be no comfort in the middle of the Gulf of Tonkin, only death.

"There were no Donut Dollies when I was there in 64. I was unaware that the Red Cross even had such a program. I am sure they told them it would be a fun way to serve their country, and they probably believed it too. I just can't imagine what it would be like for them to be talking to some 19-year-old kid knowing that's as close to a woman he will ever get should he not return from his next patrol. I am sure that wasn't in the recruitment brochure. God bless them for trying."

"We had earlier told Hewitt we'd be back later on before boarding the awaiting COD, which had its engines running. A tall Petty Officer wearing a white flight helmet helped us board the plane and gave us headsets to wear to communicate on the bumpy ride to the fleet at Yankee Station. As we strapped in, we could see all the planes parked at Da Nang. There were scores of F-4's, F-102's, C-130's, and the occasional Navy A-3 Sky Warrior and one odd P-2 Neptune taxiing out on the runways past the crowded flight lines. We didn't know what was waiting for us as we lifted up into the clouds, but if earlier events were any indication, we knew that even in the middle of an American carrier battle group, there was nowhere safe."

"The facts still didn't add up. What bothered me the most was how Kasakov's team could have arrived at the impact site first. It made no sense. His team, like ours, was a reactionary one that would swoop in to recover wreckage or anything valuable after the fact and not beforehand. How would he have known the Soviet prototype would crash there ahead of time? That, too, was just another bullshit cover story to distract people from the truth. It seemed like someone was going out of their way to push a fake narrative for us to sign off on. No one in their right minds was going believe such nonsense about enemy helicopters in Vietnam much less, ones that could engage an F-4 Phantom at altitude. As soon as the fleet came into sight, it became clear to me that we were on a fool's errand. Something happened near Dak To. I wanted to know the truth, but at the same time, I wondered if we should have just taken that flight to Japan instead."

Before too long, the U.S.S. Oriskany with the number 34 painted on her deck came into view as the COD lined up to land.

"The Mighty O, they called her, the U.S.S. Oriskany. She was a WWII Essex-class aircraft carrier that saw some action in Korea and later in the film *The Bridges at Toko Ri* before receiving an upgraded angled flight deck. Having seen the film when I was a kid, I would never thought I would ever see this ship up close much less land on it. She was on her third cruise to the Gulf of Tonkin, but a year earlier in October 1966, a magnesium parachute flare accidentally shot off in the hangar bay that shot up five decks tragically killing forty-four men, many of them veteran pilots. After putting in for repairs, she returned to the scene of the crime at Yankee Station, where I Fred and I were about to set down."

The seconds seemed like an eternity as the Fuddy-Duddy raced up to the football field-sized angled deck that rolled in the Gulf of Tonkin. Just watching the approach to the carrier as it got ever closer started to make Mason feel a bit queasy. And then, in a sudden jolt, the plane's arresting hook was caught instantly, bringing the aircraft onto the deck and to a near sudden stop.

"Bumpy, huh?" asked the Petty Officer.

"I'll say!" exclaimed Mason.

"As soon as you guys step off, an Air Transfer Officer will escort you over to the Island to see the Captain," said the Petty Officer.

"Thanks!" replied Swift.

It was then that the rear side door latch opened as Swift and Mason removed their headsets. They then stepped off the plane and onto the noisy, bustling deck of the USS Oriskany. It was filled with the whistling sounds of jet engines and the thick smell of aviation fuel wafting through the salty sea air. Swift could see a helmeted man wearing a white sweatshirt indicating he was the Air Transfer Officer saluting him. He was one of the men in charge of handling anything to do with the COD awaiting them.

"This way, Sirs, the Captain is expecting you," directed the ATO.

Swift and Mason were escorted to the side door hatch of the Island, which is the aircraft control tower structure on the right side of the carrier. The hatch itself was under a large heeded warning painted in giant yellow letters that read Beware of Jet Engine Blasts Props and Rotors. They then followed the ATO through a sea of busy crewmen wearing yellow and green sweatshirts that were scurrying about the deck. The color-coded deckhands were moving a pair F-8E Crusaders off one of the large deck elevators. Swift and Mason could see others moving the COD off to the side as a pair of missile-laden A-4E Skyhawks moved to the forward steam catapults for launch. Once inside the hatch, they went through a dimly-lit narrow pipelined corridor that led into the bustling Command and Control Center, the nerve center of the Oriskany. Inside, the CIC was lit with the glow of radar consoles that reflected onto the faces of the enlisted operators that wore blue utility uniforms. They tracked all aircraft operations around the carrier and strike missions in the North as their officers in khaki uniforms plotted missions on the big boards. One could further see large lit up tactical display maps made of glass being updated by sailors wearing headsets over their blue covers that bore the ship's name in gold thread amidst the array of blinking lights of the communications equipment. From there, Swift and Mason would ascend up to the command bridge that overlooked the twin catapults leading to the bow of the ship and the gray horizon beyond.

It was thereupon entry that a young bridge Ensign announced to the benefit of those entering the bridge that the Captain was there:

"Captain on the Bridge!"

Swift and Mason could see Captain Holder. He wore a khaki naval uniform and a high relief Captain's cap adorned with a gold band, and the permagold visor or as many would refer to as the "scrambled eggs." The veteran captain sat on a mounted reclining chair that further gave him a commanding view overlooking his flight deck. One could see the weight of his command resting on his shoulders as he stared out towards the flight deck. For him, it was the last view he would see of his pilots that he would send off into the skies over North Vietnam, of which, some would never return.

"Permission to come aboard, Sir!" saluted Swift and Mason.

"Granted," replied Captain Holder.

"Sir, I'm Captain Swift, and this is Lieutenant Mason from the Special Operations Group. We carry orders from…"

Without allowing Swift to complete his introduction, Captain Holder cut him off with a stern commanding voice.

"You may hand them to my Executive Officer (XO)," replied Capt. Holder.

Mason quickly presented their orders and parameters of their mission to the Executive Officer, who briefly glanced at them before passing them over to his Captain. Swift and Mason stood there as Captain Holder glanced over their papers with a degree of suspicion to the sounds of whistling jet engines as a pair of A-4E Skyhawks rapidly thundered off the deck.

"Captain Swift," addressed Capt. Holder.

"Sir," said Swift.

"You could not have picked a worse time to come here. I have two strikes ready to commence. I'll need my E-1 up in the air," said Capt. Holder.

"We only need thirty minutes to talk to the Radar Intercept Controllers who were flying the night of the 27th, and then we'll be out of your way," said Swift.

"Captain Swift, I'll be frank with you so that we don't misunderstand each other. I don't like having Spooks on my ship. No good ever comes from it," said Capt. Holder.

"Sir, with all due respect, we're not Spooks. We just work for the Company as field analysts through MAC-SOG," replied Swift.

"You go on and keep telling yourselves that. The CIA comes aboard my ship all time, rarely paying me the courtesy of their intentions or what they are taking from my ship. After the bad month we've had losing an A-4 over Hanoi flown by the son of Admiral McCain and my other E-1 crashed near Da Nang killing all five men aboard, I'm in no mood for Spooks interfering with my operations. The sooner you conclude your business here, the sooner I want you off my ship. Is that clear?"

"Crystal, Sir," replied Swift.

"All right then, you have thirty minutes then get the hell off my ship," ordered Capt. Holder.

"Thank you, Sir," saluted Swift.

"I'll take you to them, follow me," said the XO.

Minutes later, the XO led Swift and Mason towards the E-1 Tracer that resembled the COD they had earlier flew in only this had a distinctive Radome attached to its roof which the crews called the "Stoof on the Roof." This plane belonged to VAW-111 Detachment 34 "Hunters," and it was seen being readied for flight on the aft elevator.

"Commander Floyd, this is Captain Swift and Lieutenant Mason. These two guys are here from MAC-SOG to ask you some questions about that night mission on the 27th. I'll leave you to it," said the XO.

"Army or CIA?" asked Floyd.

"We're field analysts here to find out what you tracked that night," replied Swift.

"We don't have much time. We have a mission in thirty minutes, but you can come on inside and talk to my Radar operators," said Floyd.

"Thank you," replied Swift.

The two men ducked their heads as they entered through the rear hatch of the E-1 Tracer and climbed into its cramped confines filled with electronic gear.

"This here is Lieutenant Milburn, and that's LTJG Van Buren who tracked that thing on the 27th," pointed Floyd.

"Hi there! What did you guys track that night?" asked Swift.

"Well, we saw some strange stuff," replied Van Buren.

"Strange, how?" asked Mason.

"We spent the last two days running diagnostics to make sure everything was working properly before we were checked to fly today," replied Van Buren.

"Did you, by chance, have a record of it?" asked Mason.

"Sure. That last guy from Langley told us to erase it, but we haven't gotten around to it. You want us to erase it now?" asked Milburn.

"No," replied Mason.

"All right then. Give us a second, and we'll play it back for you," said Milburn.

Mason nudged Swift at the mere mention of the second guy from Langley.

"When did that guy from Langley come by?" asked Mason.

"Earlier this morning around 0800 hours," replied Milburn.

"Did you get this guy's name or remembered what he looked like?" asked Swift.

"No, he was a tall non-descript looking white guy wearing black Ray-Ban sunglasses and a black uniform with no identifying unit patches. We just assumed you two were here to make sure we followed through," explained Van Buren.

Commander Floyd noticed the concerned look on Swift and Mason.

"Is there a problem?" asked Floyd.

"Yes, let the XO know that this plane must remain grounded until it has been inspected for explosive devices," said Swift.

"Are you suggesting that guy might have tampered with our plane?" asked Floyd.

"Affirmative, he's not with us! Have a crew run an inspection before your mission. Please direct me to the Marine Security Detachment," advised Swift.

"Right! I'll have them inspect this plane immediately," replied CDR. Floyd.

Commander Floyd quickly climbed out of the plane and stepped out onto the hangar deck to call Chief Petty officer in charge, CPO Arnold.

"Chief, Arnold!" cried Floyd.

Meanwhile, inside the E-1 Tracer, Van Buren sat down in his station and played the recorded radar track for Swift and Mason with Milburn seated next to him to observe as co-pilot Lieutenant Locke listened in.

"Here's the F-4, and then comes this bogey. Notice how it is appearing and disappearing on one part of the screen then another? Then it flies straight for the F-4 after making sharp ninety degree turns at supersonic speeds, then all of a sudden, BLAMO! This is where they merged, and then the bogey disappeared again," pointed Van Buren.

"Did anyone get a visual on it?" asked Mason.

"I think I might have when the call for air support came in but not the F-4. We were too far away to make out anything clearly," said Locke.

"What did you see?" asked Swift.

"Judging from the location of the river, it looked like someone fired a missile at something first, then something high up fired back. A second later, there was this sudden flash from an explosion. But I could be wrong," said Locke.

"Huh!" exclaimed Swift.

Mason seemed perplexed as he explored a theory.

"That doesn't make any sense! PBR boats don't carry missiles. Even if they did, why the boat would have fired up unless….."

"Someone else fired a rocket near the boat," concurred Swift.

Mason nods his head to concurrence with Swift's educated guess as to how or why a PBR boat would have fired a rocket at some unknown object high in the sky. Swift tried to rationalize this to himself:

"While I could not verbalize my summation in front of Milburn, troubling thoughts occupied my head. Someone must have deliberately baited that boat to draw the bogey's attention. But who would do that, and why? It wouldn't make sense for the North Vietnamese. Their ambitions are simple; force the Americans out and conquer the South. The chance that Colonel Linh had turned on General Kasakov, as titillating as it seemed, may not have been out of the realm of possibilities. Just how deep was the Soviet GRU with Hanoi? Were they even true partners at all? It all sounded too good to be true. Mason had earlier questioned if we were indeed chasing a Soviet Reconnaissance plane. By now, it was clear that the Prototype story was complete garbage designed to throw us off the trail of what really took place that night. What's more troubling, was the lengths someone was willing to go to push this narrative and where it would end."

"This is spooky," said Milburn.

"Is there any way we can have an original record of the encounter?" asked Mason.

"Sure, but we have to run our pre-flight checklist in ten minutes. The only way to do that is to pull the whole track array, and that takes ten minutes to unbolt and pull out of the plane. Any chance you guys can stick around until we get back in two hours?" asked Van Buren.

"We'll wait," replied Swift.

"Sorry to do that to you, but they don't want to ground us, and we're still ordered to go," said Milburn.

"Understood," replied Mason.

Once outside the hatch, Swift and Mason could see the elevator lift them to the flight deck. Commander Floyd was seen wearing his white flight helmet and dark Aviator sunglasses as he signed off on a clipboard held by Chief Arnold.

"Captain Swift. The Chief says his crew didn't find anything new. How about you?" asked Floyd.

"We found what we need, but your Radar Intercept Controllers tell me we'll have to wait until you return to pull it from the gear," replied Swift.

"Sorry about that, but that's the way it goes around here. We'll see you when we get back," said Floyd.

As Commander Floyd climbed into the cockpit of his E-1 Tracer and buckled into his seat, Chief Arnold offered Swift and Mason a better view.

"You might want to come with me to the catwalk so you can watch the launch," offered Arnold.

"Thank you!" replied Swift.

The two men were quickly led over to the narrow confines of the catwalk that lined the side of the ship. From there, they watched an assortment of men wearing blue and green sweatshirts move the E-1 Tracer to the catapult for launch.

"Watch this!" pointed Arnold.

From their vantage point, Swift and Mason could see green-shirted men stand at each corner of the E-1 with one man locking the front and back catapult latches to the nose gear. Once locked into position, a pair of men in white sweatshirts stood on one side of the E-1 as it prepared to launch while the one man in green got out of the way as Commander Floyd quickly checked his flaps and rudders before takeoff. Once signaled by the men in white, Floyd brought his two 9-cylinder radial piston 1,525 horsepower engines to maximum thrust for takeoff. At the thumb's forward signal, the E-1 Tracer was instantly hurled down the track of the steam catapult before lifting off the deck and into the air.

But no sooner than the plane cleared the deck, a flash of fire erupted from the starboard engine followed by a small explosion that violently sent the E-1 Tracer into sudden a hard dip below the horizon and into the sea as it rolled hard onto its back before breaking apart the fasteners connecting the plane to the Radome.

"Oh, shit!" exclaimed Arnold.

Swift and Mason turned to look at each other in shock and horror with suspicion that the Men in Black were behind this. What hidden truth was so profound that one would go as far as to sabotage the E-1? Within seconds, alarm horns erupted as the entire deck crew raced to the side to see what happened right as the call came over the 1MC:

"NOW HEAR THIS. AIRCRAFT IN THE WATER, PORT SIDE. RESCUE DIVERS TO YOUR STATIONS."

Swift and Mason could see the carrier was quickly changing course pulling hard to starboard to avoid steaming over the downed plane while the nearby destroyer USS Frank E. Evans changed course to assist. Moments later, a dark blue painted UH-2C Seasprite helicopter was quickly moved into position on the deck as its pilots promptly ran through their pre-flight checks. Once signaled by the deck officer, the pilots fired up the main rotor. Meanwhile, three Navy divers in their black wetsuits raced over carrying their black rubber flippers to the awaiting chopper and quickly threw their gear aboard before they sat at the edge of the open door. In a scene rehearsed many times, the rescue crew lifted off the carrier deck and made fast for the downed airplane.

The minutes that passed before the Seasprite could reach the stricken plane seemed like an eternity for those watching the rescue unfold. Swift and Mason could see that the plane was still half afloat. Everyone on the catwalk held their collective breaths until they could sight Lieutenant Locke surface with his yellow life vest then followed by Commander Floyd. By now, the rescue chopper was on scene, and the divers were in the water.

A minute later, one of the divers surfaced with one of the Radar

Intercept Controllers then the second. From a distance, they appeared unresponsive as they were quickly hoisted onto the chopper. Just then, a radio call came over Chief Arnold's headset.

"They are still breathing! They are going to make it!" announced Chief Arnold to the cheers of their shipmates.

But no sooner than the rescue chopper came around to land, the COD was lined up on the deck for launch and brought its engines to maximum power.

"Hey! Isn't that our ride back to Da Nang?" pointed Mason.

"Somebody, stop that plane!" shouted Swift.

Chief Arnold instantly radioed the Catapult Officers to stop the plane, but by then it was too late. The COD had hurled off the deck and into the clouds.

"Son of a bitch! I bet the culprit is on that plane!" shouted Swift.

"Agreed! We got to inform Captain Holder to arrest that man wherever he lands!" shouted Mason.

"No need, Sirs, look!" pointed Arnold.

It was then that they could see the angry XO and the Marine Gunnery Sergeant Newman walking towards them. They appeared from the Island with six large Marines in full tactical gear carrying M-14's and headed their way. Swift and Mason instantly climbed back up from the catwalk onto the flight deck to meet them. But as soon as they were within a few feet of them, the Marines drew their weapons and pointed them at Swift and Mason.

"We need to talk to Captain Holder ASAP!" said Swift.

"That's not going to happen," replied the XO.

"What do you mean?" protested Swift.

"You, Sir, were warned that you were already walking a very thin line here. The Captain has had enough of your CIA bullshit for one day and wants you off this ship!" said the XO.

"With all due respect, the saboteur just stole our ride, and we need to find him and have him arrested wherever he lands! It's pertinent to our mission," reasoned Mason.

"Well, that's not going to happen either. That SOB turned off his transponder, and we're not going to redirect a fighter halfway to Haiphong just to chase a stolen COD!" argued the XO.

"Then how are we going to get back to Da Nang?" asked Swift.

"That's your problem! You two caused enough trouble for one day. Gunny Newman here has been ordered to see you on your way. I sure hope you two can swim because it's a long way back to Da Nang!" scolded the XO.

"Sir, with all due respect, that's not how this works!" protested Mason.

"Gunny! Show these men how they are getting off this ship!" ordered the XO.

"With pleasure, Sir!" growled the mean-looking Gunnery Sergeant with his pistol drawn.

As the XO walked back to the Island, Gunny Newman and his Marines slowly stepped forward with their M-14 rifles pointed at Swift and Mason. They were making them step backwards towards the edge of the ship.

"Boss?" alerted Mason.

"No, they are seriously not going to...."

Just then, as the back heels of their boots neared the edge of the deck, a large elevator rose to the flight deck behind them. To their relief, they both turned their heads and discovered the Oriskany's second Seasprite ready to ferry them back to Da Nang.

"Ha! I had you there, didn't I, Captain?" laughed Newman.

"Yeah!" replied Swift.

Swift and Mason could see the entire grinning Marine detachment lower their weapons and chuckled among themselves.

"You know, Gunny, for a moment there, you sure did," replied Mason

"Mason, that's why we love the Marines!" chuckled Swift as he and Mason boarded the awaiting chopper.

"Yes, we sure do!"

CHAPTER VIII
MURDER IN III CORPS

The time was nearing 1600 hours as Swift and Mason touched down at Tan Son Nhut Air Base. The Company's C-123 that earlier flew into Da Nang had been swapped out with an available Air America Boeing 727-92C. It had been a long day for the two weary, sleep-deprived men who had embarked on that wild goose chase for any proof of what happened nights earlier. By now, Swift and Mason had agreed to extricate themselves from their dubious assignment in Vietnam. But, as their plane came to a stop, they looked out the window and found Lieutenant Madsen from MACV waiting for them. Fate, as it seemed, had other plans.

"Oh, what the hell does he want?" asked Mason.

"I don't know, but from the looks of it, we're not leaving for Japan just yet," replied Swift.

As soon as the cargo ramp was lowered, Swift and Mason walked down onto the tarmac wearing their gold-rimmed Ray-Ban sunglasses with Mason carrying his silver briefcase.

"What's up, Lieutenant?" asked Swift.

INCIDENT AT DAK TO

"I have a chopper waiting for you to take you straight away to Vung Tau," replied Madsen.

"For what?" asked Swift.

"Johnny Sanchez is missing," revealed Madsen.

"He was supposed to be at the MACV Compound under guard with the rest of his squad," said Swift.

"Well, that's not the case," replied Madsen.

"You have any idea where he might be?" asked Mason.

"CID found a body at Vung Tau Beach matching his description," replied Madsen.

"Take us to him!" ordered Swift.

"Right this way, Sir!" replied Madsen as he climbed back into the driver's seat of his Jeep.

Thirty minutes later, the U.S. Army UH-1 Huey carrying Swift, Mason, and Madsen passed over the white sandy beach. There on the ground, they could see an American MP with his M-16 slung on his back popping open a canister of green smoke to indicate where the chopper could set down. Upon touchdown, Swift and Mason stepped off the skid of the chopper and stepped onto the white beach sand. Right away, they headed straight over to the crime scene surrounded by a crowd of people near the water's edge.

The crime scene was circled by MPs. They kept back the scores of local Vietnamese and off-duty soldiers from getting too close. CID (Criminal Investigation Command) had just photographed the body that washed up on the shore. Swift quickly flashed his credentials to the MPs and walked up the drowned corpse.

"What happened here?" asked Swift.

"That depends on what you're doing in my crime scene," replied the CID Officer.

"I'm Captain Swift, and this is Lieutenant Mason from MAC-SOG," identified Swift.

"Well, Captain, this is what's left of Private Johnny Sanchez. On the surface, it looks like he had a bit to drink and drowned. But if you look closer at the bruises on his wrists and neck, I would say this was no accident," pointed the CID Officer.

"Let's roll him over and get a look," said Swift.

Mason grabbed Sanchez by his feet as Swift rolled over his shoulder to lay the body on his back. They could see the neck bruising more clearly.

"This man was murdered," observed Swift.

"But by whom and for what motive?" asked the CID Officer.

"I can't say," replied Swift.

"I was afraid you would say that," said the CID Officer.

"You're not going to find his killer. Make your report and relay it to a General Lowe at the Saigon Station. They will give you further instructions on how to file this and what to say to the man's family," ordered Swift.

"Just like that, huh?" asked the CID Officer.

"Sorry, but that's the way it has to be," replied Swift.

"Yes, Sir!"

Swift and Mason walked away from the crime scene and returned to their awaiting chopper.

"That's such a damn shame! All he wanted to do was serve his country only to be killed by his own countrymen," complained Mason.

"That's assuming Bob's associates are even Americans, much less humans," replied Swift.

"If the Men in Black are willing to kill the guys on the Oriskany and murder Johnny Sanchez, that means Private Coolidge is in danger," worried Mason.

"We got to find him before Bob and his associates get to him first," said Swift.

"I couldn't agree more," replied Mason as they walked up to the awaiting chopper that was powering back up for flight.

"Say, was it Sanchez?" asked Madsen.

"Yeah, get on the horn on the double. I need a twenty on the location of Private Alan Coolidge. We'll also need a fix on the rest of his squad from 2nd Battalion 12th Infantry 3rd Squad Charlie Company 4th ID. If he's not at the MACV Compound barracks, we'll need the MPs to go find him and hold him until we get there," ordered Swift.

"You got it, Captain!" acknowledged Madsen.

Thirty minutes later, their Huey was on final approach to the helipad by the Company hangar when the radio call came in.

"Say, Captain," said the Huey pilot over the headset.

"Go ahead," acknowledged Swift.

"MACV just radioed in. They got a fix on Coolidge," said the Huey pilot.

"Well, that's a relief!" exclaimed Mason.

"Where is he?" asked Swift.

"The MPs have him detained at the Trans America Terminal. He was trying to board a flight out of Saigon when they caught him. They're still holding up a 707 for him," relayed the Huey pilot.

"I'll have a Jeep standing by," said Madsen

"I don't have time for that! I need to get straight over to that terminal right away!" ordered Swift.

"Okay, you heard the man. Set her down by that 707 at the TWA terminal," ordered Madsen.

"Roger that!" acknowledged the Huey pilot.

Moments later, the UH-1 Huey sat down next to the awaiting TWA 707 that was surrounded by four Jeeps of MPs. Swift and Mason quickly removed their headsets before stepping foot onto the tarmac and raced inside the terminal. Once inside, they removed their sunglasses and looked for the MPs holding Coolidge. Several feet inside, they could see a pair of MPs standing near a corner guarding Coolidge, who was sitting by his olive green duffle bag in his Class A uniform looking out to the plane outside. Swift and Mason quickly flashed their ID to the MPs who let them approach Coolidge.

"Oh, man!" exclaimed Coolidge.

"Where did you think you were going?" asked Mason.

"My papers came in, but they told me I had to leave right away if I wanted to see my wife and my baby boy," explained Coolidge.

"Who told you that?" asked Swift.

"That creepy old white dude that talked to us, he said he was with you," replied Coolidge.

"He's not," replied Mason.

"Oh, man!" sweated Coolidge.

"Johnny Sanchez was found dead in Vung Tau today. Did you know about it?" asked Swift.

"No, Sir, I didn't."

Private Coolidge somberly removed his olive green side cap that bore a small crest of the 4th ID and shook his head.

"It don't mean a thing, it don't mean a thing," wept Coolidge.

A moment later, an MP stepped forward.

"Sir, the captain of the 707 wants to know how much longer before he can leave. What should I tell him?"

"Have him standby. This shouldn't take long," replied Swift.

"Thank you, Sir!"

"There's something you should know. We were threatened not to tell you what I am about to tell you now," revealed Coolidge.

"We're all ears," replied Mason.

"Those weird lights in the skies we saw four nights ago weren't the only times we had seen them," revealed Coolidge.

"Go on," urged Swift.

"We had seen them every night for the last three weeks around 0230 hours. It was only after one of them crashed in near Dak To that we were ordered to investigate," revealed Coolidge.

"Tell us about the Star of Bethlehem," urged Swift.

"That was some freaky ass shit. It gave me the heebie-jeebies. Yeah, we followed that thing for over three Klicks in the dark with it lighting up the way. Once we got there, we found dead VC on the ground with this weird blue shit burning everywhere. I ain't never seen anything like it. The next thing you know, a group of NVA came running at us, and we lit them up right as this weird fog rolled in. We cut the Dink-Slopes to pieces. The next thing you know, this weird old dude appeared out of nowhere, and then he was gone," revealed Coolidge.

"So your battalion commanders knew about those strange lights for weeks?" asked Swift.

"No, they were kept in the dark. Once we radioed in, we were passed over to another command calling the shots. That's how they sent in the MPs and those guys wearing black fatigues," explained Coolidge.

"Who called in the 1/9?" asked Mason.

"Our RTO, Billy Langford following standard operating procedures radioed in the location of the NVA tunnel on the channel we use. Sergeant Eldridge wasn't aware of it until The Chief was inbound. This got him in trouble with those CIA guys in black," said Coolidge.

"They're not CIA," remarked Mason.

"Then who were they?" asked Coolidge.

"It's better you don't ask that question. Your friend Johnny

Sanchez is dead, and you will be too if you don't get on that plane. Now get out of here and never speak of this again," ordered Swift.

"I can go and see my wife and baby boy?" asked Coolidge.

"That's right, my boss says you can go," replied Mason.

"Thank you, Sirs!" saluted Coolidge.

"Good luck to you, son," bid Swift.

Without delay, Private Coolidge grabbed his duffle bag and raced out the door to board the awaiting TWA 707 outside. A moment later, an MP stepped forward.

"All that drama and you're letting him go?" he asked.

"Yeah, we are done with him," replied Swift.

Swift and Mason sat down in the airport terminal seats and looked out the big glass window. They could see the TWA 707 close its doors as the ground crew removed the airstairs before the plane backed away to begin its taxi towards the runway. They sat there without saying a word until the 707 took off into the air bound for home.

"You think they won't get him?" asked Mason.

"It's hard to say. I believe if they wanted him dead, they would have already got him," replied Swift.

Just then, Lieutenant Madsen rushed into the terminal.

"What is it?" asked Mason.

"I just got word that someone released 4th ID from the MACV barracks an hour ago," revealed Madsen.

"Where are they now?" asked Swift.

"On the airbase side of Tan Son Nhut boarding a CH-47 bound for the field," revealed Madsen.

"Shit! We got to stop them!" exclaimed Swift.

Without delay, Swift and Mason quickly got up from their seats and raced back out onto the tarmac. They could see the UH-1 Huey had powered off its rotors and would take minutes before they could get airborne. Sensing the urgency, Swift commandeered one of the MPs Jeeps while Mason retrieved his silver briefcase. Mason then quickly jumped in as Swift turned the ignition switch and popped the Jeep into gear then sped off in the direction of the CH-47 pads.

Swift put the pedal to the metal as he sped across the taxiways. He nearly cut off a Vietnam Airlines DC-3 before making it over to the Airbase side of Tan Son Nhut. Once over the dividing line that separated the airbase from the international airport, Swift drove like a madman to avoid a pair of F-4 Phantoms, and an awaiting C-130 as a C-141 Starlifter came in for landing.

"Do you even know where you're going?" shouted Mason.

"Yeah, I'm sure the heavy-lift chopper flight line has to be around here somewhere!" replied Swift.

Swift made another sharp turn past another large cargo plane as they sped past sandbagged redoubts protecting a group of VNAF F-5 Tiger Jets. Then once clear of the F-5's, they spotted a dozen CH-47's with one readying for liftoff as the last of a troop of soldiers in full battle dress boarded the rear loading ramp of the Chinook.

"That's got to be them!" pointed Swift.

Captain Swift floored the accelerator to get to the chopper. They were within sight of the CH-47 Chinook when Swift made eye contact with Sergeant Eldridge right as the helicopter was about to lift off. Swift could see he had a sullen expression under his camouflage helmet liner. With a simple nod, Eldridge saluted Captain Swift as the CH-47 raised the ramp and began to lift off the tarmac. Once the Chinook dipped its nose, it took to the skies flying north as Swift brought the Jeep to a stop.

"Shit! We're too late," lamented Swift.

"What do we do now?" asked Mason.

Swift was about to reply to Mason when suddenly the Chinook exploded in mid-air! To their horror, they watched the fireball of debris fall to a field just outside of the base. Without delay, the base erupted in alarm sirens as firefighting crews and ambulances raced toward the scene.

"Oh God Almighty, nobody could have survived that! Time to Bug Out," remarked Swift.

"I could not agree more!"

As Swift and Mason quickly drove towards an exit and left the airbase for the busy Saigon streets at dusk.

"The Saigon sun was nearly set by the time we reached our part of Nguyễn Huệ Street where the An Dao Inn was located. And while Halloween would not be for another 23 hours back home, there was an unrelated street festival taking place here complete with firecrackers, drums, and marchers parading down the riverfront. You could see many beautiful Vietnamese girls in pretty *Ao Dais* alongside busy street vendors selling food as children ran about holding lit sparklers as if it were the 4th of July. We had no advance knowledge of this event which made moving through the crowds of colorful revelers in traditional Vietnamese costumes most cumbersome. All along, I had this horribly familiar sinking-gut feeling that I had not felt since the Siege of Plei Me. We were walking straight into an ambush and there was no avoiding it."

After sifting through the dense crowds, Swift and Mason, at last, made it inside the small amber-lit red-carpeted lobby of the An Dao Inn. No sooner than they walked towards the stairwell, the jovial manager, Jimmy Tang, stepped forward in a white see-through silk shirt covering black dress slacks and shoes to apologize humbly.

"I'm so sorry about the noise, Captain," said Tang.

"What the hell is going on?" asked Swift.

"I have no idea! They just assembled like a mob thirty minutes ago," replied Tang.

"That's odd," remarked Mason.

"Can I get you some beer, girls, Mary Jane, or anything not on our menu?" asked Tang.

"Thanks, Jimmy, but we got to get out of here as soon as we get our things," replied Swift.

"Jimmy Tang still A-Number-One, right?" asked Tang.

"Sure, Jimmy! You still A-Number-One!" replied Swift.

A moment later, Swift and Mason headed up the dimly fluorescent-lit staircase to the third floor of the five-story inn. Minutes later, they exited the third-floor stairwell entrance and proceeded towards their tandem rooms. As the two men pulled out their room keys, Swift turned to his partner.

"Give me a moment to freshen up, and I'll be over shortly," said Swift.

"You got it, Boss," replied Mason.

Both men unlocked the doors to their rooms and stepped inside and quickly closed the doors behind them. Once inside, Swift removed his olive drab cover and set it next to the small open sink. He then walked over to the closet, where he bent over and reached in to grab his black Bug-Out bag before returning to the sink. He sat it by his feet and took a small white towel and opened up the small spigot and immersed the towel in a small trickle of cold water then wiped his forehead with it.

Meanwhile, over in the next room, Mason had retrieved his black Bug-Out bag and sat it next to his silver briefcase as he knelt to open the safe. He made three turns to complete the combination lock sequence to open the safe. To his shock, the safe was empty. All the collected files and the F-4 gun camera footage were gone.

"Shit! Boss is not going to like that."

Suddenly, there were two loud knocks at the door.

"Speak of the devil," remarked Mason.

Fred Mason got up and walked over to the door to let Swift in. But to his shock, Swift wasn't there as he had expected. Instead, he was faced with a tall strange looking man with white alabaster skin. He wore black fatigues, black sunglasses, black gloves, a black cover, and had no face! He stood there, holding a Walther PPK pointed at Mason.

"Trick or Treat!"

In the blink of an eye, the Man in Black fired two rounds into

Mason at point blank range as he tried to slam the door shut before dropping flat on the floor. Meanwhile, Swift had just placed his cover on his head and grabbed his black Bug-Out bag when he heard what sounded like muffled gunshots and a thud coming from Mason's room. Sensing alarm, Swift instinctively drew his sidearm and chambered a round before racing over to Mason's room. Stepping into the hallway, he could see Mason's door was wide open. Pointing his gun at eye level, he carefully stepped inside and found Mason on the floor bleeding and pointing his finger. Two steps inside and Swift could see the tall strange looking Man in Black glaring right back at him as he held Mason's silver briefcase. The man leaped through the back wall as if disappearing into thin air.

"What the fuck!" exclaimed Swift.

"Don't just stand there, go after him!" muttered Mason as he lay there on the floor bleeding.

Without delay, Swift looked at the wall the Man in Black just leaped through and wondered if such a feat he just witnessed was even possible. A split second later, a woman's frightened scream could be heard from the room next door. Without hesitation, he chose to pursue the Man in Black.

"Here goes nothing!" remarked Swift.

Swift fearlessly charged at the same solid wall to replicate the Man in Black's seemingly impossible feat. With brute force, Swift crashed through the thin wall like an angry bull bursting through the next room in a cloud of plaster drywall and wooden splinters that sent him straight to the floor. As soon as he opened his eyes, Swift quickly got up and realized there was a naked American GI who was in the middle of having sex with a Vietnamese girl. She looked terrified as she just witnessed a Man in Black pass through the wall and through their room.

"Hey, Buddy! Can't you see I'm doing something here?" shouted the GI.

"Where did he go?" demanded Swift.

"Where did who go?" asked the GI.

Swift could see the frightened girl pull up a white sheet over her breasts to cover her naked body. Looking at Swift, she then pointed to the opened doorway. Swift quickly got off the floor, ignoring the fact he had hurt his shoulder in the process. The adrenaline of the moment fueled the chase out the door and to the stairwell. Swift stepped into the stairs, pointing his pistol towards the upper levels. No sooner than he could see the faceless man, three shots from the Walther PPK were fired at Swift. Having ducked for cover back into the stairwell, Swift extended his arm and fired two rounds back at the Man in Black, who by now had reached the roof of the five-story building.

Moments later, Swift had reached the top of the staircase with his pistol drawn. He could see the faceless man hopping aboard the open door of an awaiting black painted helicopter with Mason's silver briefcase. The intensity of the situation was nearly surpassed by the surreal nature of what Swift was witnessing. There, before him, was a uniquely modified UH-1, Huey, like none other he had ever seen before! It sported an odd round cover over the central axis of both the main rotor and the tail rotor that practically made no sounds! All one could hear was a muffled whoosh-whoosh sound reminiscent of a large moth flapping its wings as it passed over one's head.

The Man in Black made his timely escape aboard the chopper, but not before Swift fired a shot hitting the man in the back of the right thigh. No sooner than his bullet hit its mark, another Man in Black wearing dark sunglasses appeared in the doorway operating an M-60 machine gun. He fired a sudden violent burst of high-velocity machine-gun fire that sent Swift diving for cover back down into the stairwell to avoid being cut to pieces.

Swift had tumbled down to the fifth-floor stairwell basin so hard, he injured his injured shoulder again. A moment later, the M-60 fire ceased after shredding the top stairwell roof access port. Swift limped his way back up to the roof with his pistol drawn. But by then, it was too late. The modified black-painted Huey had already left the roof and disappeared into the Saigon night sky. Out of frustration, Swift shouted in rage and fired three more rounds at the chopper knowing there was no chance he would hit it.

"Dammit!"

The Man in Black had successfully made off with all the evidence Swift and Mason had collected effectively thwarting their mission. By no means was this over for Swift. There was no time to lament over this unforeseen setback. He knew that two floors down, Fred Mason was in a world of hurt and desperate need of medical attention. Ignoring his own injuries, Swift made his way back downstairs to Mason's room, which by now had attracted the attention of the startled guests and the beleaguered manager, Jimmy Tang. The Vietnamese prostitute had fled carrying her clothes down the stairwell. The American GI she was with was being questioned by two officers of the Vietnamese National Police. Jimmy Tang could be seen with blood on his hands and silk shirt helping Mason.

"What happened?" asked Tang.

"We were ambushed! Tell the police to clear the street because I am calling in a Medivac chopper," said Swift.

INCIDENT AT DAK TO

"Here, are you crazy?" asked Tang.

"Just do it!" commanded Swift.

Jimmy Tang quickly complied and translated Swift's demands to the Vietnamese National Police. It was then that Mason reached out to grip Swift's wrist as he gasped to speak.

"Stay with me, buddy! I'm calling for help!" assured Swift.

Fred Mason was still holding on as he lay there bleeding on the floor. Without delay, Swift quickly reached for the bedside phone and used the emergency number he had been given. By now, four other Policemen had arrived. Swift was going to need to move Mason and move him fast. Given his lack of Vietnamese language skills, he looked to a Police Sergeant and hoped for the best.

"Hey, do you speak English?" asked Swift.

"Yes, I do. My men are already clearing the street as we speak," replied the Policeman.

"Good, now make yourselves useful and help me get my man downstairs. You, you, and you two *nhanh lên* (hurry)!" ordered Swift.

The Vietnamese Policemen quickly jumped into action pulling the bedsheets and sliding them under Mason. Swift noticed the GI was still standing there after being question, which beckoned Swift to press him into service.

"Hey, you, I need some help here!"

"You got it, Captain!" replied the GI.

Moments later, Swift, Jimmy Tang, the GI, and the four Vietnamese National Policemen brought out Mason to the front of the hotel. Crowds of Vietnamese people stood back with the help of the local Police working crowd control. Several trees lined the riverbank so that a helicopter landing would be problematic at best. But given the situation, there would be no other viable choice to rush Mason to a field hospital in time.

"Say, do any of you guys have any smoke canisters?" asked Swift.

"I have a green canister," replied the Police Sergeant.

"Good! Puff smoke over in that clearing. Dust-Off is inbound!"

With no delay, the Vietnamese Police Sergeant retrieved a smoke canister from his squad car and opened it at the clearing as the unmistakable sound of the UH-1 Medivac chopper could be heard circling overhead. Swift walked over to the clearing and waved the big Huey with big red crosses painted on its sides and nose onto the small clearing at the edge of the riverbank of Nguyễn Huệ Street. With gentle ease, the pilot carefully maneuvered the chopper in and sat down with little room to spare. With urgency, Mason was quickly loaded aboard the helicopter with the help of the Vietnamese National Policemen. The two helmeted U.S. Army medics quickly got to work attaching an IV as Swift threw in their black Bug-Out bags and hopped aboard the unarmed Medivac chopper.

"Hey, Captain, you could have had us land on the roof!" complained the Dust-Off pilot.

"No time! The access way was just shredded by an M-60. It was easier to bring him downstairs," replied Swift.

"Fair enough!" said the Dust-Off pilot.

A moment later, the chopper lifted off and cleared the dense trees lining the riverbank of Nguyễn Huệ Street. All sounds muffled into Mason's dying heartbeat. For Swift, the seconds seemed like an eternity as the chopper raced through the amber-lit nighttime Saigon cityscape towards a landing pad at Tan Son Nhut Air Base where an ambulance awaited them.

"We're losing him!" shouted one Medic,

"Come on, Lieutenant, stay with us!" exclaimed the second Medic.

It was then that the 3rd Field Hospital came into view just down ways from Tan Son Nhut Air Base. With dire urgency, Swift tapped the pilot's shoulder.

"How long does it take for an ambulance to go from Tan Son Nhut to that hospital?" asked Swift.

"Five minutes," replied the Dust-Off pilot.

"We don't have five minutes! He'll be dead by then!" shouted Swift.

"Well, what the hell do you want me to do? There's a big Chinook sitting on the landing pad at 3rd Field Hospital, and that's the closest one to us," reasoned the Dust-Off pilot.

It was then as Swift overlooked a muddy racetrack adjacent to the hospital that he spotted a small clearing between two buildings within the hospital complex.

"Can you set her down there?" asked Swift.

"Are you crazy? That's a little hairy with all those telephone wires," replied the Dust-Off pilot.

"Hey buddy, you just pulled off a dangerous landing on the edge of the Nguyễn Huệ Street riverfront. Few guys I've ever flown with couldn't come close to doing what you just pulled," argued Swift.

"Yeah, if you put it that way, I guess I can do it. I might get a reprimand for it."

"Trust me; there will be no reprimands! This is a MAC-SOG Priority Medivac flight. The Company will have you covered," assured Swift.

"The Company, huh?" pondered the Dust-Off pilot.

"There's no time to lose," reasoned Swift.

"All right, Captain. If I crash this ship, this will be on you."

"Thank you," said Swift.

For the second time in one night, the skilled Huey pilot was faced with another dangerous night landing in a confined space. He made his final approach to the 3rd Field Hospital coming in low over the muddy adjacent racetrack. He hovered just over the telephone wires that lined both sides of the road separating the race track and the hospital complex. His small LZ was the small grass clearing within the surgical complex grounds unsuitable for such a feat, yet to his credit, he braved the narrow approach and went in any way.

Scores of U.S. Army Medical Personnel came outside to see if a Huey was indeed trying to make a near-impossible landing in that small clearing. To their awe, the meticulous Dust-Off pilot maneuvered into position with surgical precision then carefully set down vertically until he was on the ground with only a few feet to spare. By now, a medical team had raced up to the chopper with a wheeled gurney and wasted no time lifting Mason out of the chopper then straight away over into the hospital.

Exhausted and in pain, Swift watched the medics haul Mason away. As he reached back into the chopper to grab their Bug-Out bags, he could see the pool of blood that coated the inside of the helicopter. While he had seen spilled blood before, the sight and smell suddenly made him sick. Swift instantly vomited by the side of the Huey's skids after thanking the Medivac crew and headed inside.

There was nothing more Swift could do but wait in a small waiting room. It had a green couch spaced across from two brown leather chairs and a small table with a lamp that lit the room. Swift sat there playing the night's events over and over in his head with regret; he had not given enough credence to his gut intuition warning him of the ambush. The improvised street festival had proved to be a distraction intended to provide a false sense of security.

"Any way around it, the Men in Black had laid a perfect trap for us and we walked right into it. If Bob was able to slip into my room in the Caravel Hotel, I sure as hell should have known better. We should have gone to the MACV Compound instead of the An Dao Inn, where they reacquired us. Bob had earlier offered us a way out, but I was never the one to walk away from a fight. Private Coolidge had as good a reason as anybody to get out. It's hard to say what happened to Johnny Sanchez or what deal killed Sergeant Eldridge and his squad."

It wouldn't be until 2230 hours before Swift would hear of any word as to Mason's condition when Thirty-five-year old Dr. Townsend stepped into the waiting room.

"Captain Swift?"

"Yes?"

"Lieutenant Mason is going to make it, but for the time being, he remains in critical condition. We pulled two slugs out of him. They just missed the aorta, and he lost a lot of blood," revealed Dr. Townsend.

"Thank you, Doc. When can I see him?" asked Swift.

"He's in recovery for the time being. You can see him when he comes to," said Dr. Townsend.

"We work for MAC-SOG and this was an assassination attempt on my partner's life. I suspect there will be another attempt to kill him," said Swift.

"I was afraid you would say that," replied Dr. Townsend.

"Why's that?"

"Something peculiar happened during surgery," revealed Dr. Townsend.

"What do you mean?"

"I mean downright spooky. No sooner than I pulled those two slugs out and dumped them into the pan, they began to dissolve," revealed Dr. Townsend.

"Dissolve? You mean like the way an anti-acid tablet does once it's been dropped in a glass of water?" asked Swift.

"Precisely, within seconds, they were gone. They dissolved into thin air. I'll have you know this is my second tour, and I have seen all kinds of horror here, but I have never seen dissolving bullets before. What the hell are you guys involved with?"

"That's Classified," replied Swift.

"I get that. You should get some sleep. He's going to be out for a while," suggested Dr. Townsend.

"I will need to have my man guarded," said Swift.

"Understood, I'll have the MPs sent up here as soon as possible," replied Dr. Townsend.

Hours later, the time was nearing 0423 hours. A brunette nurse in a white hospital uniform dress walked into the waiting room. She could see Swift was sound asleep snoring on the couch with his feet up over the edge of the leather armrest with one hand gripping his chambered pistol. With great care, she gently placed her hand on his hand that held the loaded gun. Startled, Swift instantly awoke and grabbed her hand.

"Sorry, Captain! I didn't mean to startle you," she said.

"It's okay. Any word?" he asked.

"Lieutenant Mason is awake now. He is still in critical condition, but he is asking for you. Please follow me."

Moments later, Swift flashed his credentials to the posted MPs guarding Mason before entering the small room that was lit by a single lamp. Swift could see Mason still had an IV hooked up to him as he lay there in the hospital bed. Mason looked half asleep as he looked up to see Swift taking a seat alongside his bed.

"How are you doing, Fred?"

"Like some asshole double-tapped two slugs in me. Other than that, I feel like shit. I think I am going to have to sit the rest of this assignment out," replied Mason.

"I see they didn't kill your sense of humor," chuckled Swift.

"No, but they almost got me. They said I was dead on that table for a minute," said Mason.

"Well, you're here now," replied Swift.

"All I remember was I had just opened the safe and found it empty.

I was just about to tell you about it when I heard a knock at the door. I naturally thought you would be there being that you said you would be over in a few minutes, but instead, it was one of them," said Mason.

"The Men in Black?"

"Yeah, one of them. I opened the door, and here was this Man in Black pointing a PPK at me. He had pale white alabaster skin and not one remarkable feature I can describe about his face. It's like he was anyone, and yet, no one. It was like he had no face," described Mason.

"Did he say anything?" asked Swift.

"Trick or Treat. After that, he shot me," replied Mason.

"There's always a Joker every Halloween," remarked Swift.

"I'll say, and a damn-right spooky one to say the least!"

"You don't know the half of it. When I burst into your room, that Man in Black jumped through the wall into the next room as if it were thin air," revealed Swift.

"Whoa!" exclaimed Mason.

"Naturally, I followed him. Only, instead, I hurt my shoulder as I busted down the wall to pursue him. I managed to wound him on the roof, but then he had a modified black Huey waiting for him that made no sound. His M-60 gunner sent me diving for cover, so they got away. Later, the doctor told me the slugs he pulled out of you dissolved like water," revealed Swift.

"That's some spooky shit, Boss," remarked Mason.

"I agree," said Swift.

"There's something more I have to tell you," said Mason.

"What's that?" he asked.

"Before I came to, an unbelievably pretty blonde nurse smiled at me. I mean, this girl was beyond Playboy quality. She held my hand and then told me I had a visitor."

"Oh? Aside from being blonde, do you remember what this nurse looked like?" asked Swift.

"I don't know how to adequately describe her. She was kind of pale, yet, almost glowing. I mean, she was just indescribably beautiful. She reminded me of Chris Noel on some level. Man, I thought I was dreaming. I blinked my eye, and she was gone. The next thing I know there was for lack of a better word, an Angel sat by my bedside, talking to me," revealed Mason.

"An Angel?" asked Swift.

"You know I don't believe in that sort of stuff, but there it was. I don't know how else to describe this thin translucent being other than it was comprised of living light," described Mason.

"What did it say to you?" asked Swift.

"At first, I was not entirely sure, but somehow I just understood. The Angel spoke, but not in words. It spoke in images and thoughts if that makes any sense. I was led out of my hospital bed and into this dark misty place. Along the way, I saw Colonel Linh and Johnny Sanchez walking past me, but they didn't say anything. Then it was like stepping through a doorway and into this big lit aerospace factory. You could see these white-shirt wearing engineers working on this big plane that was bigger than a 707. I think I was at the Boeing plant up in Seattle, but I wasn't sure. I kept walking until I reached another door, and there I stepped into this house with children's toys scattered about. There was this pretty blonde woman who reminded me of Mamie Van Doren who asked if I would like something to eat. She seemed so familiar to me like I had spent a life with her, yet I've never met her. All I knew was that I had to go outside. But once I stepped through the door, the house was gone," described Mason.

"Where did it go?" asked Swift.

"I don't know. The Angel appeared again to tell me not to go further. It told me to go back through the oblique doorway that stood in nowhere. It was then that the Angel told me they had a message for you," said Mason.

"For me?"

"Yeah, I saw you out in the field at night. You were in tiger stripe carrying an M-16 up a ridge with three other guys. There, you would see an old Vietnamese man. He was kind of a tall and looked a little bit like Uncle Ho, but he's not from here," described Mason.

"What do you mean, not from here?" asked Swift.

"He just wasn't. I don't know how else to better extrapolate from the imagery I was shown to explain this to you. It was just so. And then there was Bob, just like you described him, sinister and up to no good. He was sitting on a hollowed termite log laughing his ass about something. I told the Angel I didn't understand. Then the Angel showed me Sergeant Thunderfoot pointing to this big spiral etched into a side of a cliff somewhere. He said Thunderfoot knows the answer. He's always known the answer."

"In other words, there's no Soviet wreck," remarked Swift.

"Oh, there's a wreck all right, but it's not Soviet, not even man-made or from this earth. You got to forgive me. I am very fatigued. Somebody shot me, you know," whispered Mason.

Mason yawned then closed his eyes falling soundly asleep just as a nurse returned to check on Mason.

"That's enough for now. He needs to rest," said the nurse.

"I understand. Say, do you know where I can find the pale blonde nurse who resembles Chris Noel that attended to him?" asked Swift.

"There are only five nurses on shift right now, and none of them are blonde or look like Chris Noel. We do have a few blonde nurses that will be coming in at 0600, but they're all tanned from R&R. Is there a particular nurse you were looking for?"

"No, I suppose not," replied Swift.

Just then, General Lowe and Bob Keene appeared in the doorway.

"Sir!" saluted Swift.

"How is Mason?" asked Gen. Lowe.

"He'll live, but he's more or less done here," replied Swift.

It was then that four Army Medics came in with a transfer gurney. Seeing what was happening, the nurse summoned Doctor Townsend. A moment later, he burst through the door.

"Excuse me, General, but what's going on here?" asked Dr. Townsend.

"We're moving him to a safer location," replied Gen. Lowe.

"You can't do that!" protested Dr. Townsend.

"We can and we will," replied Gen. Lowe.

"This is a matter of National Security," remarked Keene.

"Where are you taking my patient?" asked Dr. Townsend.

"That's on a need to know basis. Now, if you'll step aside, my men have to get this man to his plane. You too, Captain Swift," ordered Gen. Lowe.

Minutes later, Swift followed the medics who were carrying Mason out the back of the 3rd Field Hospital and loaded upon the back of a covered Duce and a Half truck bound for Tan Son Nhut Air Base. Once through the gates, they proceeded immediately to an awaiting U.S. Air Force C-141 Starlifter. As soon as the Duce and a half came to a stop, Swift jumped out of the truck as the medics carefully lifted Mason onto another gurney before they would make their way up the large loading ramp of the transport plane. Swift could see the C-141 Starlifter was a brightly-lit airborne hospital complete with medical bays and a dozen wounded soldiers with IV's attached to them. As the medics were about to step foot on the ramp that Mason came too and raised his left hand that was connected to an IV.

"Captain Swift?" summoned one Medic.

"Yeah!" he replied.

"Your man is asking for you," pointed the Medic.

The Medic pointed to Mason, who wanted to say something. Swift walked over and leaned into Mason.

"Say, Boss, you know I am not one to back away from a fight. I've been with you in harm's way before. But I thought about what I saw when I was under, and it had me thinking that I should probably call this quits. I might not get another chance if I don't," said Mason.

"What will you do?" asked Swift.

"I think I'll take my talents to that Boeing plant in Seattle and find that pretty wife I was shown," said Mason.

"Sounds like a pretty good deal to me," replied Swift.

"You know what else?"

"What's that?"

"It looks like I am going to Japan after all. Yokohama Naval Hospital, they say," said Mason.

"Well, I'll be damned!" exclaimed Swift.

"Boss, I just want to say it's been an honor and a pleasure working with you these past two years," said Mason as he gripped Swift's hand one last time.

"Likewise, amigo, good luck to you, Fred. Go get that life and that pretty wife. You've earned it," bid Swift.

"Thank you, boss. I could not have done it without you."

"Hooah," said Swift.

"Hooah."

Mason cracked one last smile and saluted Swift, before he nod his head to the Air Force Medics to carry up into the C-141. Swift stood alone on the tarmac and watched as the Loadmaster closed the rear cargo ramp doors as the C-141 fired up its four jet engines. But just as the whistling sound of the engines grew louder, Swift turned his head and looked to see Lieutenant Madsen driving up in an Army Jeep with General Lowe sitting in the passenger seat.

"Sir!" saluted Swift.

"Captain, you'll need to come with us. Operation Pleiades is now a go. You'll need some proper gear and weaponry for the field. Get in."

"Thank you, Sir. It's about fucking time!"

CHAPTER IX
THE CENTRAL HIGHLANDS

It was one hour later, at 0600 hours that Wednesday morning, November 1st, 1967, Captain Swift returned to the Company hangar at Tan Son Nhut Air Base. He drove in an unmarked Jeep wearing green tiger stripe fatigues and his Green Beret bearing the flash insignia of the 5th Special Forces. On his shoulder was the patch he had worn on his last tour with Advisory Command. He wore his sidearm on his gun belt and slung his black Bug-Out bag over his shoulder.

"The morning had finally come. I had just seen Mason leave Vietnam aboard a C-141 bound for Japan. I was now about to embark on the most critical leg of my mission, but I wouldn't be alone. ARVN Captain Ky would come along as my translator. To my surprise, 4th ID RTO Billy Langford was assigned to me. He somehow got sick from something he ate at Vung Tau and was sent to the 3rd Field Hospital to get his stomach pumped. Such dumb luck! He managed to miss his ride aboard that doomed chopper, sparing his life. I needed a radio operator for the field as well as someone who knew the terrain. I suppose he also wanted a little payback. I couldn't blame him. Part of me wanted some too."

Billy Langford stood there in full combat gear that included his steel helmet and camo liner, flack vest with his PRC-10 radio pack strapped to his back and an M-16 slung on his shoulder and rolled-up sleeves. He stood alongside Captain Nguyen Ky, who also wore Tiger stripe fatigues with a slouched bush hat carrying an M-16 and a sidearm on his belt. Swift could see they had been waiting for him at the base of the cargo ramp of the unmarked Company C-123 that would take them to the starting point of their intended objective in the Central Highlands. Once Swift's Jeep came to a stop, Langford came to full attention and saluted Captain Swift.

"Sir! Specialist 4th Class Billy Langford reporting for RTO duty!"

"At ease, Billy, glad to see you're still alive," replied Swift.

"Me too, Sir, whoever thought a plate of poorly cooked prawns would save my life," replied Langford.

"You're fit for duty, right?" asked Swift.

"I'm ready to rock and roll, Sir!" he replied.

"All right, then," replied Swift.

"Captain Ky," addressed Swift.

"It is good to see you again," smiled Ky.

"Likewise, you look a bit cheerful today," said Swift.

"I am a new father. My wife gave birth to a baby boy yesterday," revealed Ky.

"Well, congratulations, Captain Ky!"

"Thank you. I am sorry to hear about Lieutenant Mason. It is most unfortunate," said Ky.

"He got hit hard, but he is on his way to a good hospital out of the war zone," explained Swift.

"That is good to hear," said Ky.

Swift shook Captain Ky's hand then turned his attention back to Langford.

"As for you, have they told you about this mission?" asked Swift.

"Not much, Sir, you're going to need an RTO to go into Dak To. My whole squad, save Coolidge, is gone. I was offered this opportunity, so I took it. I figured you could use the help. Besides, you're not the only one who needs answers," said Langford.

"Thank you, Billy. Let's get rolling," said Swift.

It was then that the Company pilot came into the cargo hold.

"What's the word?" asked Swift.

"The mechanics say it's going to be another hour before we get the avionics in order, so I'm going to have to ask you to hold tight for the time being," said the pilot.

Captain Swift noticed one of the Company Hueys was being prepped for flight across the way; this gave him an idea.

"Hold that thought," said Swift.

"Where you going?" asked Ky.

"I got to go spring someone out of jail. I'll be back in an hour," replied Swift.

"Eh?"

"Just don't take off without me!" waved Swift.

Twenty-five minutes later, at the USARV Stockade at Long Binh, two MPs stood atop the twenty-foot high wooden guard tower. The tower stood just outside the ten-foot-high double chain-link fences wrapped in concertina razor wire to prevent escape. The tower was accessible by a single wooden ladder that reached up to its center floor. There within the sandbagged lined shack at the top were two helmeted MPs on watch who shared a Marlboro cigarette as they watched a flight of four Hueys flying towards the base down the way. It was then that they noticed one of the choppers suddenly broke formation and changed course heading their way with the intent to land.

"Oh shit! It's that crazy Captain again!" cried one MP.

"Call the Warden!"

Just like the time before, the UH-1 sat down right in front of the stockade entrance. Captain Swift quickly disembarked from the helicopter and stepped onto the red clay earth. He could see two MPs carrying their M-16's racing towards him.

"Say, Captain, what do you want me to do?" asked the pilot.

"Keep the engines running," instructed Swift.

"You got it!" acknowledged the pilot.

The MPs ducked their heads as they carefully approached Swift to avoid the spinning rotor blades of the Huey.

"Sir, you can't land here!" protested one MP.

"Sure I can, I have priority," argued Swift.

"Sir, if you want to argue about it, you can take it up with the Warden," replied the MP.

"Fair enough, take me to him!" replied Swift.

"Have it your way, Sir, follow me!" replied the MP.

Moments later, Swift was led into the main administration building, where he was led into the Warden's wood-paneled office. A minute later, a Major who was a little older than Swift stepped in and closed the door behind him.

"That's one hell of a dramatic entrance you made there, Captain. I am going to assume this must be very important to pull a stunt like that," said the Warden.

"I apologize, but there's no time to waste," said Swift as he presented his orders to the Warden.

"I'll need Sergeant Wayne Thunderfoot released to me immediately," said Swift.

"But according to his paperwork, he's awaiting court-martial," replied the Warden.

"Courts adjourned," replied Swift.

The Warden looked back at Swift with wide eyes as he looked up from reading the orders held in his hands. The Warden shook his head then reached for the black rotary phone that sat on his desk and dialed.

"This is the Warden. I need Thunderfoot up front and center with his gear and weapons returned to him on the double. That's an order."

The Warden placed the phone down and nodded his head to Swift.

"All right, Captain. He's all yours, but let me ask you one question: why is he so vital to National Security?" asked the Warden.

"Only he knows, and that is why I need him," replied Swift.

"I sure hope he's worth it," said the Warden.

"We'll soon find out. Thank you for your cooperation," saluted Swift before exiting the Warden's office.

Captain Swift walked over to the entrance of the stockade where he could see Sergeant Thunderfoot being given back his U.S. Army issue M-7 bayonet and his Colt 45 pistol of which he quickly holstered before noticing Captain Swift.

"I suppose I have you to thank for my freedom?" asked Thunderfoot.

"I don't know about freedom. Last I checked you're still in Vietnam, right?"

"Yeah, I suppose so. Where's your partner?" asked Thunderfoot.

"He's strapped aboard a flying air hospital with a breathing tube on his way to Japan," replied Swift.

"Sorry to hear that," replied Thunderfoot.

"All charges against you have been dropped, but you're assigned to me for the duration of my mission," said Swift.

"What mission?" asked Thunderfoot.

"I'll explain it to you on the chopper. We got a plane to catch," ordered Swift.

"Sure beats sticking around here," said Thunderfoot.

"I thought you would agree."

A half-hour later, Captain Ky checked his wristwatch anxiously as the Company pilot did his last pre-flight walk around. It was then that Billy Langford heard the sound of an incoming chopper.

"Hey, I think that's Captain Swift!" alerted Langford.

"It's about time," remarked Ky.

"I'll go ahead and start her up," said the pilot.

The Company chopper sat down exactly where it had taken off from an hour earlier. Billy Langford could see Captain Swift stepping off the helicopter with Sergeant Thunderfoot in tow.

"Holy shit!" exclaimed Langford.

"Who is that?" asked Ky.

"That's The Chief!" replied Langford.

"The Chief?"

Captain Ky watched Captain Swift, and Sergeant Thunderfoot made their way up the cargo ramp into the plane.

"Captain Ky, this is the Air Cavalry's most feared Tunnel Rat, Sergeant Thunderfoot. He'll be coming with us," said Swift.

"I see," replied Ky.

"Hey, Chief, good to see you again!" greeted Langford.

"Have we met before?"

"No, but I was with the 4th ID at Dak To when you got into that scuffle," said Langford.

"Fair enough," replied Thunderfoot.

Sergeant Thunderfoot said nothing as he gripped Langford's hand in acknowledgment before taking a cargo net seat. The C-123 then powered up its twin engines as the cargo ramp slowly raised before closing shut.

"It had been a long twenty-four hours with little sleep, much less, something to eat. I had managed to spring The Chief out of the LBJ Ranch, but given the task ahead of us, I wasn't doing him any favors. As our plane taxied down the runway, I sat down in my seat contemplating our next move. We were a step closer to our objective, but a world apart from the truth that awaited us at Dak To. To get there, we would have to catch a chopper out of Camp Radcliff at An Khe. By now, I had the makings of a small team with the help of Captain Ky, Billy Langford, and Sergeant Thunderfoot to lead the way. Little was said on the flight there, but as soon as we arrived, Charlie had other plans."

Hours later, the Company C-123 dropped out of the clouds and came in for its final approach to the airstrip at Camp Radcliff. Captain Swift looked out the small window as the plane crossed over the varying terrain along the Song Ba River and rounded the Hon Cong Mountain to line up with the narrow runaway. He could further see the vast hillside terrain that constituted the world's largest heliport known as "The Golf Course" which was home to the 1st Air Cavalry Division.

"Camp Radcliff, by An Khe Village, this was where we were to catch the next leg of our journey. From the air, it looked so peaceful. It was hard to believe three years earlier, this was a triple canopy rainforest lined by an old abandoned French airstrip at the base of the Hon Cong Mountain. Now, it's the world's largest heliport and home to three helicopter aviation battalions. From our altitude, it looked like a peaceful suburban housing tract under construction. As you got closer, you could see near the top of the Hon Cong Mountain just below the Signal Corps station. It loomed over the large division base camp with a one-hundred-foot gold kite shield patch bearing a single black diagonal stripe running across from top left to lower right. It also bore at its top-right corner the black silhouette of a horse head facing left that harkened back to the days of when the Cavalry rode horses a century earlier. This visible patch on the side of the mountain made sure that everyone knew that the 1st Air Cavalry Division was there. Believe you me, from what I heard of the nightly mortar attacks, Charlie made sure they knew they weren't all too happy about it either."

As their plane touched down on the asphalt runway, Swift could see an awaiting USAF C-130 transport waiting to use the single runway and a twin-engine U.S. Army OV-1 Mohawk taxiing just behind him. Just beyond the red clay embankments that lined the runway was the massive Division base camp. It was larger than he remembered. The base had been undergoing major construction since he had last passed through there on his way to catch the "Freedom Bird" in Pleiku, December 1965. And while it was not Plei Me, the unsettling unknown he had encountered as an Advisor seemed all around him as he looked at the shadow of the Hon Cong Mountain. No sooner than the rear cargo doors of the C-123 opened, a large green Duce and a Half truck pulled up behind the plane.

"Hey, is there a Captain Swift onboard?" hailed the truck driver.

"Yeah!" acknowledged Swift.

"I'm Specialist 4th Class Tommy Biggs 15th Trans Battalion. Division HQ requested me to drive you around while on base," saluted Biggs.

"Is that so?" asked Swift.

"Yes, and oh, Sir, there's a black crate in the back marked for Swift and Mason. I have been ordered to give you this key to the padlock," said Biggs.

Captain Swift took the key and went around the back of the truck and climbed aboard. He quickly found the black crate with a white tag marked Swift / Mason and unlocked the silver Masterson padlock and flipped open the metal latch. Inside the container was a field kit for two complete with two of everything needed for the field. It contained steel pot helmets with camo liners, web gear, flak jackets, canteens, C-rations, M-7 bayonets; a pair of brand new M-16's wrapped in plastic and spare ammunition magazines.

"They thought of everything," said Swift.

"What's that, Captain?" asked Biggs.

"Nothing," replied Swift.

"Oh, that reminds me, the Provost Marshall wants a word with you about the prisoner," mentioned Biggs.

"What prisoner?" asked Swift.

"The one we're holding at the Division Stockade," replied Biggs.

"Captain, I just got out of the Stockade. Like hell, if I'm going step another foot in one!" protested Thunderfoot.

"It's okay, Chief. He's not talking about you," said Swift.

"Good!"

"I'm still going to need guys to stick with me. So let's mount up and get to it," said Swift as he hopped into the passenger side of the truck's cab.

Ten minutes later, Specialist Biggs drove the Army Duce and a Half truck up the dusty red clay road just past a small clearing. It featured a pair of flag poles with one bearing the American Flag

INCIDENT AT DAK TO

and the other of the Republic of Vietnam with a view of the mountains and the infamous Yang Mang Pass that lead to Pleiku. Several feet away from the two flagpoles stood a one-story museum of captured Viet Cong and NVA weapons. But it was the one-story wooden building just past the water well and down by the museum where they were headed. The path took them to the small stockade that was set up to hold captured prisoners awaiting transfer. The main building was no larger than two mobile homes put together. It served mostly for the MPs manning the small stockade for both administration and interrogation purposes. Behind the building was an open area lined barbed wire lined yard behind it. There, one could see three rail-thin emaciated-looking Viet Cong prisoners in filthy black pajamas watching every move with fearful eyes from behind the barbed wire fence as Captain Swift, Billy Langford, and Captain Ky quickly got out of the large truck and while Thunderfoot and Biggs stayed with the Duce and a Half.

Once they stepped through the door, they found themselves in a small administration office that was lined with cheap wood grain paneling, which was typical in many U.S. Army administrative buildings throughout Vietnam. As they walked inside, they could see a four foot high wooden counter that served as the front desk and four smaller desks with electric metal desk fans, typewriters, stacks of reports, and black rotary phones. In the back were metal file cabinets upon which five black MP helmets sat next to the weapons locker and a rack that held a dozen M-16 rifles. Above it was a 1967 pin-up calendar featuring a girl holding a surfboard. There was a narrow hallway that led to the Provost Marshall's office near the interrogation rooms towards the back where prisoners were held. The small building was staffed by a dozen MPs and their Provost Marshall.

"Can I help you, Captain?" asked Duty Sergeant.

"I'm Captain Swift from MAC-SOG. I was told you had a prisoner for me."

The Duty Sergeant gulped and then looked over nervously to his superior. It was then that the Provost Marshall stepped out from his small office and up to the front desk.

"You just missed him," revealed the Provost Marshall.

"What?" exclaimed Swift.

"Three guys in black fatigues just took him less than three minutes ago," explained Duty Sergeant.

It was then that the loud *whup-whup-whup* sound of a nearby UH-1 Huey could be heard as it shook the small wooden building. Swift instinctively bolted outside only to see the black painted UH-1 Huey lifting off one hundred feet away from him. The black chopper resembled the ones the CIA used, but he could tell it wasn't theirs as the UH-1 lifted over the nearby trees before rounding the Division Stockade. Captain Swift could see what looked like a Vietnamese national on board as the chopper made its pass. To Swift, it seemed deliberate move so he could see the faceless Men in Black waving to him with a one-fingered salute behind their black sunglasses before closing the chopper door as they flew away over the Green Line towards Pleiku.

"What was that about?" asked Ky.

"You don't want to know," replied Swift.

Once again, Captain Swift discovered the elusive Men in Black were one step ahead of him and that they wanted Swift to know it. Having drawn first blood with Mason, Swift walked back inside with a sense of pure indignation.

"All right, can someone tell me who they took away?" asked Swift.

"An elderly Vietnamese National. No identification papers or nothing," replied the Provost Marshall.

"Did he talk with the other prisoners?" asked Ky.

"They stayed clear of him. They seemed to be afraid of him for some reason," said the Duty Sergeant.

"Why was he being held?" asked Swift.

"He was found early this morning having crossed a minefield near the aviation fuel dump near the maintenance area. We detained him on the charge of being a suspected saboteur," replied the Duty Sergeant.

"Suspected Saboteur, huh? Did you guys take any photos of him?" asked Swift.

"Yes, but the Spooks confiscated them," replied Duty Sergeant.

"Uh, Sir, if I may?" interrupted Cpl. Kline.

"Yes, Corporal?" acknowledged Swift.

"They didn't confiscate the one we took when we took him into custody," said Cpl. Kline.

"Let me see," said Swift.

Corporal Kline walked forward and placed the small black and white photograph on the countertop of the front desk and slid it forward to Swift. Billy Langford's eyes opened wide with alarm.

"What's wrong?" asked Langford.

"That's him! That's the freaky old man we ran into out in the field," exclaimed Billy.

"Our ARVN translator Lieutenant Lâm couldn't get a word out of him, and then the Spooks came in and grabbed him. Lâm's pretty freaked out about it too," revealed the Provost Marshall.

"Freaked out?" asked Swift.

"Yes, I don't know what the prisoner said to him, but Lâm is shaken up," said the Provost Marshall.

"May I speak with Lâm?" asked Ky.

"Sure, he's sitting by himself in interrogation room #2. Perhaps you can make sense out of him. Corporal Kline will show you where it's at," said the Provost Marshall.

Swift then turned to speak.

"Billy, I need you to wait outside with The Chief. Captain Ky, you're with me," ordered Swift.

"Yes, Sir," acknowledged Langford.

Moments later, Swift and Captain Ky entered the small wood-paneled interrogation room. There they found Lieutenant Do Lâm wearing the same green tiger stripe camouflage as Captain Ky slumped over the simple wooden table with his hands and fingers clutching his temples. Lieutenant Lâm quickly became startled then came to attention and saluted Captain Ky.

"At ease, soldier. Please sit," instructed Swift.

Lieutenant Lâm quickly complied and sat back down as Swift and Captain Ky sat on the two folding chairs across from him. The young Vietnamese Officer billowed with sweat and anxiety as Swift looked to Captain Ky to begin questioning him in Vietnamese.

After a couple of tense exchanges, it wasn't long before Captain Ky got up from his chair and reached across the table and slapped Lieutenant Lâm hard across the face, nearly knocking him from his chair before speaking again in English.

"Hey! What was that for?" demanded Swift.

"Tell him! Tell him what you just told me!" ordered Ky.

"That was no man. That was a demon!" said Lâm.

"A demon?" asked Swift.

"Yes!" answered Lâm.

"Are you trying to tell me that old man wasn't human?" asked Swift.

"Yes! He is an imposter. I tell you, he's not human!" answered Lâm.

"How is that possible?" demanded Swift.

"He says the man didn't speak with words but got into his head somehow and spoke," explained Ky.

"He looks like any southern villager of the Central Highlands, but I know he was not from Vietnam. He is not from this world. I have no other way to explain it to you," pleaded Lâm.

"What did he tell you?" asked Swift.

"He said they were coming for him and he had to go," answered Lâm.

"What did he mean by they?" asked Ky.

"I don't know," replied Lâm.

"You said he had to go. Go where?" asked Swift.

"A dark place with glowing blue lights," stuttered Lâm.

"Did he tell you where that was?" asked Swift.

"No, before I could get him to say more, three men dressed in black uniforms came in," said Lâm.

"Can you describe them to me?" asked Swift.

"One was an older American in his fifties. The other two, I can't remember. I think they were demons too," said Lâm.

"Like the old man?" asked Swift.

"No, they were different and a bit scary. It was like they had no faces, but I can't remember what they looked like. All I remember is they told me to forget I had seen them. But how could I forget? I heard of such stories of demons in the countryside, but until now, I have never encountered one before."

"All right, that's enough for me. Let's go," said Swift.

"Agreed, that will be all Lieutenant," said Ky.

Swift and Captain Ky got up from their seats and left Lieutenant Lâm where he sat. As they exited the building and made their way to the Duce and a Half truck, Swift asked Captain Ky for his thoughts as he adjusted his slouch hat.

"Do you believe him?" asked Swift.

"I've heard the same strange tales, but believed it was nonsense to distract us from the communists seeking to undermine and destroy the South. Now, I am not so sure," answered Ky.

Twenty minutes later, Specialist Biggs drove the team in the Duce and a Half along a row of trees and company areas to a series of one-story buildings that served as the Division Command HQ that was in the Southwest corner of the base at the end of a dirt road that circled the base. The Command HQ building was one small prefabricated metal-sided building with a simple screen door connected to two Quonset buildings on either side that would form the letter H if seen from the air. Outside there was a small parking lot with several Jeeps parked there facing a lone metal flagpole waving Old Glory and the flag of the 1st Air Cavalry Division. It was here that Captain Swift got out and walked down the small cement pathway that led into the Headquarters.

Once inside, he was saluted by a young duty officer who quickly led Swift down a small narrow corridor to the large cigar and cigarette smoke-filled war room lined with maps and a large table that contained a raised relief map of the area surrounding Dak To. This was where the Division Commander, Lieutenant-General John Tolson, and his staff officers were planning a large-scale air assault into the same area of operation of Swift's classified mission. Captain Swift was led over to where General Tolson stood as he was conferring with another General to positions on the map. Captain Swift saluted before presenting his orders to the General Tolson. He didn't look up but instead put his hand up to hear a Lt. Colonel's radio conversation.

"Say again, Little Bird?"

"We're taking heavy fire from a big gun South West of Hill 823!" radioed the chopper.

The sounds of alarms from the helicopter could be heard through the desperate radio transmissions.

"We're hit! We're going down!" radioed the chopper before

cutting out to heavy static.

"Little Bird, do you copy? Little Bird?"

"Dammit!" grunted Gen. Tolson.

"We lost him," lamented the Lt. Col.

"All right then, pull our ships out of the AO (Area of Operations). I'm shutting it down for the night. Nobody goes there until we go in large at dawn," ordered Gen. Tolson.

Captain Swift recollected:

"General Tolson was a tall, robust man with salt and pepper hair who had seen action in WWII and Korea. I could tell he was having a bad day as he wiped his brow in frustration. I am sure my presence didn't help in that matter."

"Sorry to intrude, General, Sir, but I have a MAC-SOG priority mission," said Swift.

General Tolson looked over Swift's orders and sighed before handing it back to him.

"Did Saigon send you or did Langley?" asked Gen. Tolson.

"Both," replied Swift.

"You could not have picked a worse time to show up here," said Gen. Tolson.

"That's what people keep telling me," replied Swift.

"Look, I just lost three ships today and some good men near Hill 823. You want to go three klicks east of Hill 875? Are you crazy? That whole valley is crawling NVA from Hill 1338 all the way to the Cambodian border! I'm not risking any more lives today until we go in with force."

"What are you calling this?" asked Swift.

"We're calling this Operation Macarthur. The 173rd Airborne will move in from the North while 4th ID comes in from the east. 12th and 8th Cav will swoop in close to your objective. As a courtesy, you're welcome to ride along with the Cavalry at dawn when we make our air assault," offered Gen. Tolson.

"Sorry, but that won't do," replied Swift.

"Look, it's a take it or leave it offer. I'd love to accommodate you, but that's the way it's got to be. Now, if you will excuse me, I have to coordinate with 4th ID," said Gen. Tolson.

"General, with all due respect, my mission is time-sensitive. I may not have until dawn," argued Swift.

"Sorry, but my answer is still no. There's nothing more I can do, Captain. Right now, my crews are readying for tomorrow's air assault," replied Gen. Tolson.

"Well then, is it possible to send a telex from atop the mountain signal station?" asked Swift.

"You can don a flack vest and take a twenty-minute ride up the mountain, wait another hour for the next chopper going up, or you can follow me to my office. I believe we have the same black box. We had this installed about a month ago after Colonel Maples got killed going up the mountain by a sapper. They're both hooked up to the same Company relay atop the Hon Cong Mountain," revealed Gen. Tolson.

"Thank you, Sir."

"It's the least I can do for one of Colonel Wallace's men. Step inside here. Use the Crypto unlock, then close it up and shut the door when you're done," said Gen. Tolson.

The General looked the other way as he opened the door to his private office and stepped away. Captain Swift closed the office door behind him and stepped around the large desk where he could see a black vinyl cover over a machine that sat to the side. Swift quickly removed the cover and could see it was a black Telex case used by the CIA. Swift sat down in the office chair that wheeled atop a clear hard plastic floor mat and quickly entered the combination to open the box. Once unlocked, he switched the power on and began to type the following coded message:

TELEX ACTIVE:

SENDER: CONDOR - RECEIVE: KURIOT

(Central Intelligence Agency Technical Services Division Langley)

MISSION COMPROMISED

FRATBOY DOWN

KEY ASSETS LOST

EYES KIA

GRID UNREACHABLE

MISSION FAILURE

REQ RTB (Return to CIA HQ, Langley, VA).

A moment later, he received the following reply:

TELEX REPLY: COMPLETE:

SENDER: KURIOT - RECEIVE: CONDOR

RESOLUTE NEGATIVE

NEW DIRECTIVE

PROCEED TO MAIN ROTOR IMMEDIATELY

COALESCE WITH LANCER

RESUME OBJECTIVE

END TELEX

"Lancer? Colonel Wallace? You've got to be shitting me!" exclaimed Swift.

Astonished, Captain Swift powered down the telex. He then locked the device and covered it before leaving the general's office with the door closed. Swift quietly exited the Division HQ without saying a word and walked back to the waiting Duce and a Half.

"Got what you need there, Captain?" asked Biggs.

"Not sure yet, ever heard of the Main Rotor?" asked Swift.

"Yeah, it's a local restaurant just outside the camp near the edge of the village. Why do you ask?" asked Biggs.

"I need to meet someone there right away. Can you take us there?" asked Swift.

"Anytime, anywhere, Captain. Hop aboard!"

Twenty minutes later, the U.S. Army Duce and a Half truck pulled up to the Main Rotor Restaurant. It was a strange sight sitting just before the bridge leaving An Khe Village. The restaurant consisted of a large square one-story building that could comfortably seat over one hundred people. It had a slanted art trapezoid art deco façade rooftop that led to its high chimney-like steeple at its corner entrance that displayed the name Main Rotor at the top and Restaurant An Khe. It was in reference to the U.S. Army helicopters which were the dominant aircraft of 1st Air Cavalry Division Basecamp nearby written in bright red bold lettering. There was a white awning that welcomed guests from out of the sun or rain that led you to its wooden French bay window doors that were flanked by art deco rectangle pastel-painted shapes that lined the restaurant's façade.

"I had no idea this was here," remarked Thunderfoot.

"Neither did I," said Swift.

"Captain Swift, I have important business at the local ARVN station down the road. I shall meet you by the highway gate in two hours," said Ky.

"Very well, do what you have to do. We'll rendezvous then," agreed Swift.

"Say, uh, you might want to leave your helmet, flack vest, and rifles with me. You can keep the side arms, but they don't want rifles inside the restaurant unless you're an MP," advised Biggs.

"He's right. Billy, leave your gear with Biggs,"

Captain Swift unslung his M-16 and handed it over to Biggs for safekeeping. Billy Langford already had his radio pack in the back of the Duce and a Half and complied with Biggs's suggestion. Billy removed his camo-lined helmet and flack vest then handed over his M-16 as Thunderfoot followed Captain Swift inside. Specialist Biggs stayed behind with his Duce and a Half truck while Swift, Langford, and Thunderfoot proceeded to walk over from the small dirt parking area to the white awning that framed the entrance. Once inside, they could see how spacious it was with its high ceilings and hanging fans. There were around thirty or so diners seated at that time, with dozens of Vietnamese waiters attended to them. There were over a dozen U.S. Army Soldiers, including two Warrant Officers, five USAF Airmen, a small group of Australians wearing olive drab slouch hats, and a small number of Vietnamese locals. But it was off to an isolated corner that Swift could see Wallace wearing his Green Beret with his Colonel's rank pinned to his 5th Special Forces flash seated alone enjoying his meal in a wooden booth as Swift and his team walked over to join him.

"Glad you could make it," said Col. Wallace.

"Thank you, Colonel," replied Swift.

"Gentlemen, please sit," said Col. Wallace.

Captain Swift could see Colonel Wallace was eating a plate of cooked prawns and rice. The sight of such made Billy Langford uneasy.

"What's the matter, soldier?" asked Col. Wallace.

"Prawns, Sir. I just got out of the hospital for food poisoning I contracted in Vung Tau," explained Langford.

"That's all right, son. My man Thieu will fix you up a burger and fries if you'd like. I had them flown in," said Col. Wallace.

"Thank you, Sir. I appreciated it," replied Langford.

"How about you, Sergeant?" asked Col. Wallace.

"I'll have what the locals over there are having. Best to eat what they eat before I enter a tunnel," said Thunderfoot.

"That's smart," replied Col. Wallace.

Captain Swift just nods his head in agreement as the Colonel waved over to his Vietnamese waiter dressed in white to bring over two more plates and a hamburger for their queasy RTO.

"Let's eat before we get down to brass tacks," suggested Col. Wallace.

Captain Swift later recalled:

"Twenty minutes later, we finished our meals and pushed our plates to the side as the Vietnamese waiters came by to clear the table. It was then that Colonel was ready to talk business. And by the look of things, he was not happy with the mess he inherited."

"Gentlemen, as you might have guessed, I'm now overseeing this final phase of Operation Pleiades. General Lowe has been recalled to the Pentagon, and it's a good thing, given his mismanagement. Now that I have been privy to the full parameters of your mission, I have to say that this is one big cluster-fuck to add to the stack of bullshit piling up here in Vietnam and I am not too happy about it," remarked Col. Wallace.

"It nearly got my man Mason killed," replied Swift.

"How is he, by the way?"

"He's going to make it and plans to get out of this line of work after he gets stateside," replied Swift.

"That's good to hear. A talented kid like him has a bright future ahead of him," said Col. Wallace.

"Unlike us, right?" remarked Swift.

"You and me, my friend, we're fucked. Do these two have any idea what they are getting themselves into?" asked Col. Wallace.

"Sir, I have a unique understanding of the situation," replied

Thunderfoot.

"And what say you, Billy?" asked Col. Wallace.

"Sir, with the exception of Private Coolidge and myself, our squad was murdered for something we weren't supposed to see. I need to know why and the only way is to help the Captain get to the bottom of this. It's the least I can do," replied Langford.

"Well, son, I admire your determination," said Col. Wallace.

"Thank you, Sir."

"Well, Jay, I have some unpleasant news for you. That F-4 crew you interviewed was killed last night by a SAM up north. The two Radar Intercept Controllers you met that was plucked out of that E-1 Tracer died in their hospital beds at Subic Bay. Now, if that wasn't tragic enough, that poor ATC girl Daniels you met from Tan Son Nhut Air Base was found dead this morning. It's clear someone doesn't want any knowledge of this operation to exist. For that reason, I am having Coolidge and his wife 'Sheep-dipped' upon arrival in Alameda for their own good," revealed Col. Wallace.

Captain Swift sighed and shook his head in disbelief upon hearing this grim news.

"Sir, are you aware of the existence of rogue operatives known the Men in Black?" asked Swift.

"Never really heard of them until now outside of a rumor I heard in New Mexico back in the 1950s. I recall a couple of G-Men in dark suits came to talk to us in an assembly area and oddly enough, I don't remember a damn thing about it. From what I can tell you, they're likely an elite group of Spooks made up of ex-military who answer to no one. They're killing good men, including Special Operators who came here to fight for their country contrary to our war effort. And for what, just to cover up some black ops bullshit? Boy, I'll tell you what, I don't know what they're up to, but they're really pissing me off!"

"Well, Sir, I have a problem. General Tolson just informed me he grounded all combat flights, including Special Ops, until 0600 tomorrow when the Air Cavalry goes in heavy. Three full NVA regiments have moved into my AO."

"Oh, it's worse than that!" said Col. Wallace.

"How so?" asked Swift.

"As you know, the crash site was overrun by enemy troops three nights ago and then strangely abandoned. Now the area is surrounded by enemy troops in greater numbers. The 173rd Airborne is trying to make a push towards the site from the north, but 4th ID is bogged down in the east while the NVA is pouring in reinforcements. It seems Hanoi wants this thing even though I doubt they even know what the hell they are looking for. In any case, nobody believes that enemy helicopter cover story anymore," said Col. Wallace.

"I had my doubts early on. It sounded a bit too convenient," replied Swift.

"Thankfully, I am here to help. Now to get to the crash site, you will have to fly through a hornet's nest of hardened NVA soldiers who are trying to beat you there. They're expecting us to go in big, but what they are not expecting is a single chopper to go in and recover what's there provided there's anything there worth recovering. For all you know, they probably already picked it clean. The only way we'll know is for someone to go there before the shit hits the fan at 0530 hours," explained Col. Wallace.

"On the other hand, they abandoned the site for reasons unknown, yet have not lost interest in it. General Tolson said I could ride in with them, but not before his big predawn air assault due to the large influx of enemy forces in the area of operations. I need to get there before they do if I am to complete this mission," said Swift.

"Are you shitting me after what we went through at Plei Me? You should know me by now. I've already arranged for you and your team to fly out there in two hours on a bogus air certification flight. It's the only way I could get a chopper flight past Tolson short of the base perimeter CAP to lift off. Tolson plans to use every ship he has to hit the area between Hill 875 and Hill 823. So what you'll need to do is go over to the far corner of the Golf Course to the 15th Trans Battalion Maintenance Area and ask for Warrant Officer Edvard Severson, better known as Crazy Eddy. He's the only Huey pilot I know who can pull this off," said Col. Wallace.

"Crazy Eddy?" asked Swift.

"Boy, I feel better already," remarked Thunderfoot.

"To paraphrase a young UPI reporter I met through Charlie Beckwith named Joe Galloway, Crazy Eddy is part of a special breed of God's Own Lunatics, and God love him, he works for me," praised Col. Wallace.

Sergeant Thunderfoot couldn't help but smile upon hearing the Colonel's enthusiastic praise of this peculiar Huey pilot.

"Crazy Eddy will get you in and out of there before the shit hits the fan at dawn. I won't kid you guys, this may very well be a one-way mission, but that's what we get paid for, right?" asked Col. Wallace.

"Yes, Sir," replied Swift.

"Crazy Eddy will claim to have a sudden mechanical problem along the way and will set down at the nearby Special Forces camp to await your extraction call. Squawk 'Pulsar,' and we'll come to get you. Key twice if for any reason you cannot speak. Leave whatever you don't need and destroy any documents you may still have pertaining to this mission. Until then, I wish you good luck, Godspeed, and God Bless America."

Colonel Wallace got up from his seat as Captain Swift, Thunderfoot, and Langford all stood up and saluted and remained standing until the Colonel exited the restaurant. It was then as the men sat back down in their booth that Swift looked at the time on his wristwatch.

"We still have an hour and a half to kill before we reconnect with Captain Ky," said Swift.

"In that case, there's something you should see," said Thunderfoot.

"What's that?" asked Swift.

"I would explain it to you, but you would think I was crazy," replied Thunderfoot.

"You want to talk about crazy? I just got into a close-quarter gun battle with a faceless assassin in the middle of the night inside my Saigon hotel room. He jumped through a solid masonry wall without so much as breaking a flake of paint. It was as if the wall didn't exist before he flew away aboard a black helicopter that made no sounds. So you go on right ahead and tell me what's crazy," challenged Swift.

"All right then, follow me," said Thunderfoot.

"Where are we going?" asked Langford.

"To Sin City," replied Thunderfoot.

"Sin City, what's that?" asked Langford.

"Billy, you're about to find out!" replied Swift.

Minutes later, Specialist Biggs brought the Deuce and a Half to a stop. Ahead was a fifty-foot dirt path that led to what could be best be described as a small segregated block of single-story pastel pink-painted buildings with a single u-bend avenue of dirt running through the course of it. They comprised the bars and brothels set up for the U.S. Army, which otherwise became known to those based at Camp Radcliff as Disneyland.

"This is as far as I am allowed to drive. They don't allow vehicles or weapons beyond this point," explained Biggs.

"That's alright. I figured as such," replied Swift as he exited the Deuce and a Half.

"This way," said Thunderfoot.

The three men walked up to the dirt path to the wide dusty avenue that wrapped around the city square block, passing other U.S. Army soldiers strolling along the way. The trio walked past sex parlors, and colorful painted bars with names like The California Bar, The Olympia Restaurant, The New York Bar, The Twist, Paradise, and the Washington Bar. Captain Swift later recalled:

"Sin City they called it. It was a pastel-pink painted twenty-five-acre sprawl where the men of the 1st Air Cavalry would go to blow off steam. There, they could shoot some beers, get a little boom-boom, and perhaps avoid the Clap. That, and a load of embarrassing questions on the return home to their wives and girlfriends provided Jodie hadn't snatched from them. It was a haven away from the suicide bar bombings committed by the Viet Cong at An Khe Village and nearby Qui Nhon. A place where the grunts, pilots, and air maintenance crews could all relax and yes, fraternize with the local female population. Believe you me, there were plenty of pretty Vietnamese girls to look at and some homely ones too. There were scores of them wearing skin-tight Capri pants or fitted mini dresses standing at the doorways to lure the horny and lonely that stepped through their doors. I could see that young Billy Langford was enjoying the sights, whereas The Chief seemed relatively unfazed. Poor Billy looked like a kid in a candy store chomping at the bit in the sight of the Highland girls whose eyes projected their best attempt of that age-old sophisticated come-hither look. Who knows what the going rate was at that time. Chances were they didn't take MPC's (Military Payment Certificates). Then again, how the hell would I know? I never had any time when I was with Advisory Command, and right now, the clock was ticking. We sure as hell weren't there for R&R, nor did we have time to waste. The Chief had led us to the far end of the dirt avenue to a sun-faded yellow single-story building named The Topeka Bar. He had something to show us, and I'll admit after what I had been through, I was curious to see what it was."

Sergeant Thunderfoot stepped inside the concrete floor of the open doorway of The Topeka Bar, followed by Captain Swift and Billy Langford. The inside was painted a deep aquamarine blue and had several small wooden tables with matching chairs. There was one standing woodgrain bar that had six red leather-covered bar stools. Sitting at the end of the bar wearing a skin-tight black Ao Dai was the meanest looking Mama-san in her forties whose cat-painted eyes watched their every move. Bartending was an older Vietnamese male who wore a white shirt and moved with a limp. There were several mini-skirted bar girls there sporting big bouffant hairdos that famed actress Raquel Welch sported when she toured Vietnam that year. Captain Swift took note of these details as he sat down and let Thunderfoot talk with the Mama-san, who nodded her head once, the bartender placed a tattered leather

INCIDENT AT DAK TO

book wrapped in a faded bar rag on the table that had been kept behind the bar. Thunderfoot grabbed the book and brought it over to the table as a pair of bar girls brought the men bottled beers before being waved off.

"What's this?" asked Swift.

"Something I found in one of the tunnels at the start of my second tour," replied Thunderfoot as he slid the book across the small table to Swift.

"That looks like Japanese writing," observed Langford.

"You're right," agreed Swift.

"I had this translated by a Japanese-American friend at Pleiku. There are a couple of entries in French and Vietnamese. This has changed hands a few times. I keep it stashed here with Madame Nhi. Once you read it, you'll understand why," said Thunderfoot.

Captain Swift opened the tattered leather book and started flipping through the pages.

"I see the date. Is this really from 1944?" asked Swift.

"Wasn't that during the time of the Japanese Occupation?" asked Langford?

"That's what Paul Tamae, says," replied Thunderfoot.

"Okay then, let's see what you have here," replied Swift.

Captain Swift began to read the scribbled translation and quickly became engrossed in the harrowing account of events that took place in nearby Pleiku. This was the personal journal of one Captain Shindo of the Imperial Japanese Army Airforce of what was now regarded as The Lost Sentai.

CHAPTER X
THE LOST SENTAI

Pleiku Airfield May 1944. The time was nearing 1000 hours. It was here under a crystal blue sky that the Vichy French tricolor flag waved in the late morning breeze. The solitary flagpole stood in the center of a small group of white tents situated one-hundred feet from the deserted flight line. Off to the side was a large grassy assembly area where twenty unarmed Colonial French soldiers dressed in khaki shorts, tunics, and white *"Kepi"* hats stood at attention. Across from them were two green Mitsubishi half-ton trucks that carried a platoon of helmeted soldiers of the Imperial Japanese Army who had assembled in full battle gear complete with their Type 99 Arisaka Rifles with fixed bayonets. They stood behind two officers that wore holstered pistols, and Samurai inspired Gunto Swords off their brown leather belts. The French and the Japanese stood motionless until the uncomfortable silence was broken by the distant drone of incoming airplanes.

Inside the command tent was thirty-six-year-old Captain Jean-Paul Aumont, who was writing his final duty log before turning Pleiku Airfield over to the Imperial Japanese Army. A career officer, Captain Aumont, had been stationed in French Indochina before the French Capitulation to the Nazi Reich. He had no love for the

Vichy Government, who he viewed as collaborators, but was powerless to oppose them so far away from France. The status quo up north in the Colonial capital of Hanoi continued its indifference to the occupation forces of Japan, who left them in charge of maintaining civilian order throughout the countryside. He saw it as a Devil's Alliance. Captain Aumont could do little more than play his part. It was a role he disliked, for he had seen the Japanese troops carry out brutal civilian reprisals in Saigon in retaliation for attacks on their forces that he hoped he would never see again. With the Japanese Occupation of Indochina now in its third year, the prospect of such atrocities was always near.

Such trepidation worried Captain Aumont every time he encountered the Japanese Occupiers that superseded his authority. With his few planes destroyed, the handover of the airfield was inevitable. Until that point, the Japanese mostly stuck close to the coast to maintain their naval bases and the air corridor that stretched to the oil fields in Burma. But now, the Japanese were encroaching into the interior. As far as Aumont could see, no good could come from it.

Colonel Yoshida's men had been waiting across the field from them for over an hour. He could be best described in Western terms as being a short and stocky forty-year-old bald man with a thick black mustache who liked to grip the hilt of his sword. Colonel Yoshida made Captain Aumont feel uneasy. It seemed like Colonel Yoshida watched him like a predator waiting to pounce. His lack of French and limited English did not help matters. He looked like the kind of man he envisioned carrying out massacres such as the one at Nanking. Captain Aumont hoped that the incoming squadron would be tired from their long flight from Haining Island, China, to keep the handover ceremony from being lengthy. In any case, he would carry out his orders and make his encounter with the Imperial Japanese Army as brief as possible.

Moments later, Captain Aumont wiped his brow and checked his silver pocket watch, noting the time before closing his log entry. A moment later he heard his trusted second in command, Lieutenant Jouvet call:

"Mon Capitaine!"

"Oui," acknowledged Aumont.

The thin, twenty-five-year-old Lieutenant removed his white Kepi hat and ducked his head as he entered the small command tent then quickly came to attention.

"They're here," reported Jouvet.

"Very well, let's get this over with," replied Aumont.

Without delay, Captain Aumont closed his log and then rose from his small desk donning his white Kepi hat before exiting the tent for the bright blue sky that awaited him outside. Captain Aumont squint his eyes as he walked into the bright morning daylight. He looked off into the distance observing the fluffy white cumulus clouds that dramatically ringed the rim of the mountains surrounding the small French airfield as he awaited the incoming planes of the 59th Sentai of the Imperial Japanese Army.

"Over there, Captain!" pointed Jouvet.

The Lieutenant handed his superior his set of binoculars to view the incoming squadron. Captain Aumont auspiciously looked up to the sky through the binoculars and could see thirteen specs in the sky approaching the airfield. Moments later, the planes became visible to the naked eye. He could see a green camouflaged twin-engine Mitsubishi Ki-67 bomber with the Rising Sun on its wings. It was flanked by a dozen smaller green painted Nakajima Ki-43

Hayabusa fighter planes with yellow lightning bolts painted on their tails as they came in for their final approach. One by one, they set down on the small asphalt airstrip. A cacophony of loud piston engine sounds quickly muted as the planes taxied towards the small camp before turning to form a single flight line.

"Most impressive, is it not?" asked Col. Yoshida.

Captain Aumont gave a simple nod in acknowledgment, daring not to engage the grinning sword-bearing officer. Lieutenant Jouvet stood alongside his superior marveling at the Japanese fighter planes.

"Magnifique!" expressed Jouvet.

"Oui, c'est magnifique! If only we had such advanced fighter planes. Our country would not be under the Nazi boot," lamented Aumont.

It was then that they took notice of the lead pilot as he slid open his glass canopy while he cut his engine to power it down as he parked into place. The pilot quickly stood up from his small seat and removed his goggles and his brown leather flight helmet. He then donned his brown *Sen-bou* cap bearing the single gold star emblem of the Imperial Japanese Army before reaching to retrieve his ornate gold hilted *Gunto* sword that had been carefully stowed inside his cramped cockpit. Only commanding officers carry such swords indicating to the French that he was likely the squadron commander.

Captain Aumont and Lieutenant Jouvet watched as the presumed IJA Air Group Commander climbed out of his cockpit and onto the wing before stepping onto the wet grassy field. Meanwhile, over to the left of the other fighters, the Ki-67 bomber parked a ways from the fighters. They could see the plane was carrying the mechanics, tools, and supplies. The men aboard the bomber wasted no time unloading their gear before they saluted the squadron leader who walked right past them.

"That must be him," pointed Jouvet.

"Oui, that must be Captain Shindo," observed Aumont.

Captain Shindo saluted Colonel Yoshida and walked towards Captain Aumont with another pilot presumed to be his executive officer. They came within three paces of Aumont and Jouvet before saluting their outgoing French counterparts.

"Bienvenue, Captain Shindo, welcome to Pleiku," greeted Aumont.

"Merci beaucoup Capitaine Aumont," replied Shindo.

Captain Aumont appeared momentarily flattered at Shindo's attempt to reply to his greeting in French.

"I am Captain Shindo. This is my 1st Officer, 2nd Lt. Kuwahara, and this is Colonel Yoshida, who I see you have already met. Please forgive me, but I do not speak enough Francais for meaningful conversation. May we converse in English?" asked Shindo.

"Of course, but first, we must conclude our business here and formally hand over control of this airfield as ordered by the Vichy Government in Paris," explained Aumont.

2nd Lt. Kuwahara could be seen whispering translations to Colonel Yoshida, who spoke limited English and no French. With a careful nod, Captain Aumont signaled his bugler to play the French National anthem, La Marseillaise, as the French Tricolor flag was ceremoniously lowered. Captain Aumont and Lieutenant Jouvet stoically stood at attention saluting their flag while their men somberly sang La Marseillaise at Pleiku Airfield for the last time. Once the flag was lowered and folded, Sergeant Batiste called out the command to come about-face to begin the march towards Pleiku City. Captain Aumont and Lieutenant Jouvet were to drive there with Colonel Yoshida's armed escort. But first, the flag bearing the Rising Sun was raised as both Imperial Japanese Soldiers, and Airmen alike sang the Kimigaiyo – the Japanese national anthem before raising their arms in the air to give out three loud cheers of Banzai! Banzai! Banzai! Upon their conclusion, Captain Aumont spoke directly with Captain Shindo in English before driving away in his two-seat Peugeot.

"Capitaine, Pleiku Airfield is now yours. Everything you need is here in the camp as dictated by the terms of Tripartite Pact. Vichy France is still a vassal state of the German Reich. Thus, I am ordered to comply with its terms," said Aumont.

"Merci, Captain Aumont," thanked Shindo.

"Before I leave, I must offer you a word of advice," said Aumont.

"Eh?" exclaimed Shindo.

"Never leave beyond the perimeter at night. The Viet Minh hate you as much as they hate us. If you must fly at night, do not fly Northwest of Pleiku City. I cannot explain what strange things my men have seen in the night sky or beyond the tree line, but I will tell you they died looking for it. I strongly advise against it. If you live long enough to return home to Japan, forget what you have seen here, and speak nothing of it for it may give you terrible nightmares as it has given me. It is the best I can offer. Now, it is time for me to leave; thus, I wish you luck and bid you adieu."

"Hai," saluted Shindo.

Captain Aumont made a quick salute and abruptly joined the small caravan of French and Japanese military vehicles awaiting him that would drive away to Pleiku City and sped away.

"Well, that was odd," said Kuwahara.

"Indeed, he seemed to want to get away in a big hurry," replied Shindo.

"Sir, Lieutenant Ono just received a radio transmission from Saigon informing us we have a flight of Type 100 bombers that need our fighter screen," reported Kuwahara.

"So much for getting acquainted with our new home or getting any rest after our long flight. Inform the squadron that we will have a mission briefing at 1600 hours," said Shindo.

"Hai!" replied Kuwahara.

Later that afternoon at 1600 hours, 4:00 pm local time, the pilots and ground crew all sat around in two rows of wooden canvas-covered folding chairs in front of the Command Tent. Two large standing boards were brought out. One board displayed the map of French Indochina with their area of operations circled in red. The other board showed the mission sortie assignments. Captain Shindo walked over to the board in his brown flight suit carrying a small black and white candy-striped cane, which he used as a pointer for the briefing.

"Minna-san(everyone) wa. I know that you are all tired from this morning, but we have a job to do. Third Army Air Division Command has instructed us to perform the following missions from this airfield positioned here in the Central Highlands of Indochina. Our mission here is simple: Provide fighter escort for our bombers that constitute the Southern Air Corridor. We are to collect all scheduled inbound flights of Army Type 100 Heavy

Bombers ferrying oil from Burma from all points southwest of Qui Nhon and provide them fighter cover to our base in Da Nang. In the mornings, we shall escort the bombers returning from all points north to their southern collection points near our base at Cam Rahn Bay. To accomplish this, we shall be flying at minimum two sorties per day or as needed. Eat and rest when you can because we are going to be busy."

"Our squadron will be divided into two groups. If you look at the map, we are here. The 51st Sentai is to the south of us at Cam Rahn, and the 63rd Sentai is to the north of us at Da Nang. Due to long-range attacks by American A-26 attack aircraft, the Southern Air Corridor for this region has been moved inland. Our remaining fighters left at Hainan are being redeployed to Formosa, so what we have here is what we must work with. Lieutenant Yamashita's men will guard the airfield. Sergeant Kagawa and his men will rearm, refuel, and maintain our planes. Sergeant Matsuda will pull volunteers to help him with kitchen duty. Since we do not have our full squadron here, I expect no complaints. I must further warn you not to venture beyond the perimeter. The French have alerted us to the presence of the Viet Minh partisans operating in this area. Be on the lookout, particularly at night, and when in contact with locals. We are in hostile territory. I would have liked for all of us to have some rest and a good meal before we get to work, but Third Air Army Group commanders in Saigon are already putting us to work two days ahead of schedule. We will not have much time to get to know the local terrain, so study your maps diligently."

"So, getting back to our first mission, we are expecting a flight of a dozen Army Type 100 bombers just north of the area near Biên Hòa. We should collect them at dusk. Visibility, for the most part, should be good; however, once we are near Da Nang, we may encounter some weather, including some rain, so pay close attention to our navigator. I will personally lead tonight's mission as part of the night group. The night group will consist of the following pilots: Warrant Officers Genda, Yasuda, Takizawa, Suzuki, and Hasebe. The rest of you are on the day group. You may get some rest tonight for tomorrow at 0600 hours you fly with 2nd Lt. Kuwahara and every morning mission scheduled. Lieutenant Ono's Hiryū (Ki-67 Flying Dragon) and his crew will serve as our command and control plane and navigator for night missions, so listen carefully for any calls from him. I will also remind you to pay close attention to your wingman and your distance to the bombers. Being laden with oil, I needn't remind you that these planes are flying petrol bombs that can take out the entire sortie with one incendiary round from an American fighter. I don't want to lose any planes or men because of sloppiness or inattention. I cannot emphasize enough how imperative ferrying oil is to our war effort. Those we love are counting on us to ensure they reach the refineries Kagoshima. The American fighters are getting closer and in greater numbers. Our challenges will be great, but they must be met, and we shall meet them!"

Two hours later, a flash and puff of smoke erupted from the port eighteen-cylinder radial Ha-104 engine of the Ki-67 as it came to life. The ground crew led by Sergeant Kagawa waved to Lieutenant Ono to fire up his starboard engine as Captain Shindo looked on from the cockpit of his Ki-43 Peregrine Falcon with his canopy open. One by one, the sounds of magnetos hummed as engines roared to life. With his throttle up, Captain Shindo taxied his plane out towards the asphalt runway before taking to the skies into a setting sun. The night group of the 59th Sentai was expected to be in the air for a five to six-hour night sortie. Captain Shindo would later write about it in his mission log:

"Thursday, May 18th, 1944. After a brief rest and mission briefing, the night group took to the air at 1800 hours. We flew with a heading pointing due south. We rendevous with the dozen Type 100 bombers ferrying oil ninety-three minutes into the flight without incident. We encountered a small headwind on the return north, which forced us to set down and refuel at Da Nang before returning to Pleiku, adding an extra hour to our long mission."

"Friday, May 19th, 1944. 2nd Lt. Kuwahara's day group flew at 0600 hours northeast to escort nine Type 100 bombers from the collection point. They were near Cam Rahn when Warrant Officer Ishii's Hayabusa experienced a hydraulic leak forcing him to make a landing at our base there. The rest of the day group returned to base at Pleiku by 1230 hours. The night group departed Pleiku by 1800 hours. Eleven Army Type 100 bombers were escorted from the southern collection point to the northern handoff. It should be noted for the record that Warrant Officer Takizawa spotted a bright light at twenty-thousand feet, sixty nautical miles away near the area of Dak To, but did not engage. The strange light flew parallel with our formation and was visible for ten minutes before it disappeared. No identification could be made."

For the next three weeks, Captain Shindo and the night group of the 59th Sentai would observe the nightly appearance of the mysterious light in the night skies in the direction of Dak To. It would appear for ten minutes at twenty-thousand feet and would keep matching course and speed with the formation before disappearing. The occurrence became so routine, Captain Shindo stopped mentioning it in his logs until this entry:

"Wednesday, June 7th, 1944. The morning group recovered three surviving Army Type 100 bombers from a flight of ten planes. Three American A-26 attack aircraft engaged the 51st Sentai at the loss of two fighters, seven bombers, and fifty-eight airmen. What a terrible day! All planes from the day group returned safely to

Pleiku. The night group collected eleven Type 100 bombers, which we successfully escorted north over the Highlands to our base in Da Nang. Our nightly friend appeared on the return from twenty-five thousand feet and descended to twenty-thousand feet flying a parallel course to our formation. The object appears as bright as the moon and is observed as an oval. No other details could be extrapolated. The object closed the distance with our formation to ten nautical miles before making a sharp ninety-degree course correction at a rapidly accelerated rate. Lieutenant Ono reported that the radar and navigational equipment of our command plane briefly disengaged during contact. Neither Lieutenant Ono nor Avionics Specialist, Onda had any definitive explanation as to why the equipment worked once the object disappeared. My men are becoming nervous."

"Tuesday, June 13th, 1944. The day group's mission was canceled due to another American A-26 attack near the coast of Thailand that wiped out an entire flight of twelve Navy GM4 bombers ferrying oil before they reached their fighter escorts. The attacks are becoming more frequent, and we are suffering greater losses. There is the talk of returning to the more direct route cutting across Laos, but Tokyo insists that the Southern Air Corridor remain as it is. We expect a shift in operations tonight. So far, the night group has not lost any planes to enemy fighters, but our nightly friend has not been sighted since June 7th. We take comfort in knowing the unknown object has not posed a threat or has interfered with our mission."

"Friday, June 30th, 1944. There were no day missions today, but several sets of footprints were found along our northern perimeter, where sections of barbed wire were cut. Sergeant Matsuda put two men on report for this dereliction of duty. We believe the Viet Minh are planning an attack on our base. Thus, we have doubled our guard and lookouts for saboteurs. Meanwhile, the number of night missions has increased but without our nightly friend. The day group has been pressed into flying nights. 2nd Lieutenant Kuwahara nor his pilots have yet to see it. I have no way to explain what we have seen; thus, I have ordered my men to not speak of it outside of the night group."

"Monday, July 3rd, 1944. The attack we had been expecting on Pleiku Airfield had come. The attack occurred at dawn at 0530 hours. Mortar fire destroyed one Ki-43 with a direct hit instantly killing OR-3 Jun Fukushi and severely wounding OR-2 Masaki Ito, who was preparing Warrant Officer Tama's Hayabusa for flight. An adjacent Ki-43 assigned to Warrant Officer Ishii was damaged in the mortar attack. The damage came to the control surfaces of the wing of the plane rendering it inoperable pending repairs. Security Chief Sergeant Matsuda reported that three of his men were killed in action, and another two were wounded. They repelled a dozen Viet Minh partisans dressed in black armed with captured French MAS-36 rifles who were killed attempting to capture our Type 92 machine gun on our eastern flank. The entire pre-dawn attack lasted fifteen minutes before the Viet Minh withdrew into the tree line and disappeared. Colonel Yoshida believes this was a probing attack suggesting a larger attack is imminent. The looming tension is high, and we have two sorties tonight. May the silent Buddhas and Gods of War favor us!"

Captain Shindo could not have anticipated the events that took place two weeks later.

"Thursday, July 20th, 1944. 2nd Lieutenant Kuwahara flew the first sortie before dusk at 1600hrs to collect Navy flight 317. Upon reaching the collection point, a GM4 bomber was sighted in flames and soon exploded midair killing its crew. The 51st Sentai had engaged American A-26 attack aircraft near the Thailand coastline at the cost of two fighters. Only five GM4's of the twelve that refueled in Saigon made it to Da Nang. The first Sortie would wait for navigational aid from Lieutenant Ono's Hiryū bomber to return home with us to our base at Pleiku. The second sortie of the night left at 1900 hours with one plane short. We collected the nine Army Type 100 bombers north of Cam Rahn. What happened next is difficult to describe. I have no way to explain to the 3rd Air Division Command what transpired as were nearing thirty-six nautical miles southwest of Da Nang. Had this not been wartime, I am certain I would have been removed from my command and flown on a one way trip to a Tokyo sanitarium or military prison. Of my years in combat, I have never seen anything more frightening."

It was a starry, moonless night that July 20th, 1944. Captain Shindo and the 59th Sentai escorting Army Flight 1272 were nearing their planned course correction for their final at Da Nang. The sortie had been rather uneventful up until this point. But like the war itself, things turned for the worse as the radio crackled with life.

"Prepare for final course correction," radioed Ono.

"New heading, make Course for zero-three-five, begin descent and level at five-thousand feet," radioed Maeda.

"Lead, acknowledged," replied the lead Type 100 bomber pilot.

Meanwhile, onboard Lieutenant Ono's Ki-67, radar operator Maeda noticed something at the edge of his small screen.

"Sir! I have three aircraft coming in from the coast at fifteen-thousand feet," alerted Maeda.

"Are they changing course?" asked Ono.

"Hai! They are on an intercept course. Estimated time three minutes!" radioed Maeda.

"Alarm! Our secret is out. Incoming fighters are coming in from the south-east! At fifteen-thousand feet," alerted Ono.

"Acknowledged, maintaining formation. All gunners, standby," radioed the lead bomber pilot Capt. Matsuyama.

"Baka!" exclaimed Yasuda.

"How the hell are we supposed to see them?" asked Yaneda.

"When you see the red tracer fire, you'll know," replied Capt. Matsuyama.

"Pay attention!" scolded Shindo.

"Sorry, Sir," replied Yaneda.

"All Falcons, assume fan formation. Prepare to engage!" radioed Shindo.

As the Army Type 100 tightened their diamond formation, The 59th Sentai led by Captain Shindo spread out like an arched staircase with Shindo and Lieutenant Ono flying above the bombers. Warrant Officer Yaneda was flying below them when suddenly red tracer fire erupted, instantly setting the middle plane on fire.

"There they are!" said Shindo.

"Komei's plane is hit!" observed Lieutenant Ono before the bomber exploded in a bright fireball.

In the bursts of fire on a second bomber, the enemy aircraft appeared in the dark.

"It's radar-equipped F6F Hellcats painted black!" cried out WO Suzuki.

"Do what you can to steer them away from the bombers!" ordered Shindo.

The 59th Sentai quickly broke formation and began to engage with three Peregrine Falcons for each Hellcat as the surviving bomber's gunners fired green tracer rounds back. Suddenly, a call came from Warrant Officer Hasebe.

"I'm hit!" he shouted.

Just then, Warrant Officer Hasebe's plane was fired on again, hitting his fuel tank, killing him instantly.

"This is madness!" remarked Lieutenant Ono, who was now taking evasive action.

"Genda! Cover Ono!" ordered Shindo.

"Hai!" acknowledged Genda.

An American Hellcat swooped in from a dive to fire on a third bomber scoring a direct hit that sent the plane into a fiery nosedive before exploding. At that same moment, Captain Shindo found a Hellcat in his sights. He dove in, right behind him, and pulled up to give chase. The Hellcat pulled up into a tight turn, which lined up in Shindo's gunsight. Without hesitation, Shindo squeezed the trigger, opening up his machine guns in a burst of green tracer fire. His first burst missed, but then he pulled on the stick to tighten the ascending turn and fired a second burst hitting the enemy fighter.

"Gotenda(got you)!" exclaimed Shindo as the Hellcat pulled out of the fight with a trail of smoke as it arched into the night sky. He could see by the appearance of a white chute that the American pilot had bailed out just in time before his fighter crashed. But there was no time to savor his first aerial victory at night over the skies of Indochina. Captain Shindo now found a Hellcat on his tail firing 50 caliber incendiary rounds at him!

INCIDENT AT DAK TO

"I have one on my tail!" radioed Shindo.

"I'm coming in to assist," radioed Ishii.

As a fourth Army Type 100 bomber burst into flames, the American F-6F Hellcat kept firing intermittent bursts of fire at Shindo's plane. Captain Shindo pulled hard on his stick to outmaneuver his attacker in a scissor-like turn as WO Ishii lined up a potential kill when suddenly the entire night sky turned brilliantly white.

"What the hell is that?" exclaimed Matsuyama.

"I don't know! Radar is out!" radioed Maeda.

"Navigation and compass, too!" added Ono.

It was then that Captain Shindo's attacker broke off his attack as two smaller white oval orbs gave chase to the Hellcats as they quickly went to maximum throttle for the coast.

"Captain!" radioed Ishii.

"Do you see that?" radioed Ono.

"Look at the size of that thing!" radioed Ishii.

Captain Shindo looked up and saw to his disbelief a sizeable white object the size of Tokyo's Korakuen Stadium hovering above the raging air battle at sixteen-thousand feet! The massive craft appeared as bright as a full moon and looked like a giant walnut dwarfing the belligerent planes, which were now breaking off the fight. The remaining two Hellcats quickly fled for the coast before the massive craft changed course and slowly turned towards the area of Dak To before disappearing into the night sky.

"It was the strangest thing I had ever seen! No sooner than the

Americans broke off their attack, two smaller objects gave chase before disappearing. The large craft looked like a walnut with what looked like small windows at its center and no visible means of propulsion. As soon as it moved away towards Dak To, our crude radar and navigational instruments resumed service."

"I don't know how else to describe what took place next. We continued with our mission, but I have no recollection of any radio transmissions between Lieutenant Ono, I, or any of the bomber pilots. We landed at Da Nang under heavy guard. We were then whisked away to a hangar for a mission debriefing. 3rd Air Division commanders at Da Nang were not happy with our reports. For some unexplained reason, we were individually taken to small interrogation rooms. There, we were met by three men dressed in black double-breasted business suits and matching fedora hats. They did not identify themselves, nor did they appear to be Kempeitai. I assumed the one that spoke was Japanese. At least he appeared so. The taller one appeared to be a Westerner. At first, I assumed him to be a German Agent of the Nazi Reich, but that too was not so clear. There was a third Man in Black whose mere presence made me most uncomfortable. No matter how much I tried, I could not see his face. It was like he did not have one. Most disturbing, I cannot recall what was discussed or a description of the black plane they left Da Nang in. I don't remember hearing a sound as the Kempeitai ordered us to look away."

It was then that Captain Swift abruptly closed Shindo's journal shut. He took a deep breath, then looked up and recalled his strange encounter with the Man in Black who called himself Bob. The third man described in Captain Shindo's journal matched the description of the man who shot Fred Mason at point-blank range before escaping into the night aboard a silent chopper.

"Holy shit!" exclaimed Swift.

"I don't get it, what is it?" asked Langford.

"It's right there in Shindo's journal. The faceless Man in Black," pointed Thunderfoot.

"Disturbingly so," concurred Swift.

"Just after I was brought into the LBJ Ranch, I was interrogated by two men dressed in black fatigues and covers. One was an older American in his fifties who was slightly balding and called himself Bob. The other man was like a blur. I couldn't see his face and don't remember shit. All I knew was they weren't Intelligence officers, nor were they CIA. I sure as hell wasn't going trust anybody after that," said Thunderfoot.

"Can you trust me?" asked Swift.

"I don't think I have a choice," replied Thunderfoot.

"This is getting creepier by the moment," remarked Langford.

"Any time you want to back out of this, you can always return to the line with 4th ID," said Swift.

"No, Sir, you need me for this mission, and I'm your man," said Billy.

"Okay, then," replied Swift.

"You might want to continue reading on," suggested Thunderfoot as he reached over and reopened the tattered journal and nudged Swift to continue reading.

"The terrifying encounter left both pilots and crews shaken. We were ordered not to speak of the incident. Until further investigation, the Southern Air Corridor was closed."

Hours later, the 59th Sentai was permitted to fly back to Pleiku Airfield. It had been a terrible night for the Air Army Forces of Imperial Japan. The mission had cost the life of WO. Hasebe and twenty-four men aboard the four Type 100 bombers that was lost in the aerial battle. It was clear to the 3rd Air Army Division Command that the Americans now had the range and knew when and where the slow-moving oil-laden bombers would be. With the addition of long-range radar-equipped F-6F Hellcat night fighters, the night no longer offered passage through the skies of Indochina to the Okinawan Island Chain. The mounting loss of life and viable aircraft to ferry oil was determined to be unsustainable. Thus, the decision was made to close the Southern Air Corridor.

"We returned to Pleiku Airfield around 0230 hours. It had been a rotten night, but our troubles were far from over. As we lined up in the night sky for our final approach, we took small arms fire that punctured the fuselage and wings of our planes. Luckily, the self-sealing fuel tanks held up in part because we were low on fuel. But this did not help Warrant Officer Yaneda. We had no way to know he was in trouble until our ground crew found him still strapped inside his cockpit, drowning in his blood. A single round pierced his main artery. It was clear that between the American air attacks and the increasing attacks of the Viet Minh, our days here in Pleiku are numbered. I recall looking up to the stars as my men carried Yaneda's body from his plane and seeing a tiny moving star high above. I screamed and demanded to know what did they want? The star disappeared to the moans of my grieving pilots. We had lost a friend, and now we have a memorial service to plan while we await orders that will determine our fates."

The following day, the Southern Air Corridor remained closed after much deliberation by the military government of Hideki Tojo. A direct overland test flight of three Type 100 bombers from Burma to Hanoi ended in disaster. Allied fighters from Southern

China intercepted the flight thus, the task of ferrying oil was returned to the Imperial Japanese Navy. All squadrons assigned to bomber escort duty were ordered to stand down.

Meanwhile, back at Pleiku Airfield, a brass bugle was played as the Rising Sun flag was lowered for the night. 2nd Lieutenant Kuwahara stood alongside Captain Shindo and the junior officers in Salute as Sergeant Matsuda led a six-man detail that fired three volleys from their Arisaka rifles in memory of their fallen men. The Japanese death toll at Pleiku Airfield was mounting. It now included WO Yaneda, WO Hasebe, Corporal Yoda, OR-3 Fukushi, OR-2 Tanaka, OR-2 Ozawa. As of that morning, another of Yamashita's men was killed by a Viet Minh sniper at dawn. Private (OR-1) Akamatsu was found dead with a single bullet wound to his head while manning at his post. Sadly it would not be their last.

Later that evening, near 2300 hours, Corporal Yakusho, OR-3 Kanai, and OR-2 Jojima manned Post #23. It was a small bunker in the northeast post along the perimeter wire of the airfield. Up until this point, it had been an uneventful evening as nineteen-year-old Pvt. Jojima anxiously operated the Type 92 machine gun. Corporal Yakusho had just awoken from a small nap and noticed sweat dripping off the back flap of Jojima's IJA regulation *Sen-bou* cap he wore under his steel pot helmet.

"What's Jojima so nervous about?" asked Yakusho.

"I don't feel good about tonight," replied Jojima.

"You say that every night," remarked Kanai.

"I can't distinguish shadows in the tree line. For all I know, the Viet Minh could be right in front of us watching," complained Jojima.

"Baka!" laughed Yakusho as he stood up and exited the sandbagged bunker.

"Where are you going?" asked Kanai.

"Relax, I'm going to take a piss," replied Yakusho.

Corporal Yakusho had left wearing only his back flapped Sen-bou cap and no helmet. He slung his Arisaka rifle on his back as he walked over to a fence post the lined the razor wire of the perimeter. There, he quietly unlatched his breeches and began to relieve himself when he noticed the wire from the fence post, and the posts along the way had been cut again.

"Shit!" he exclaimed as he ran back to the bunker.

"What is it?" asked Kanai.

"The wire has been cut!" he replied.

Corporal Yakusho unslung his Arisaka rifle and placed it against the sandbag wall of the bunker then reached for the small hand crank telephone. With three swift cranks, he picked up the black handset receiver and called the other posts.

"Post #23 calling Post #22, check the wire!" he called.

"Post #22 acknowledged! The wire is cut here too!"

"Damn!" exclaimed Yakusho.

"Hey! There's something out there," reported Jojima.

Corporal Yakusho looked out of the bunker and spotted a strange white glow emerging in the distance. He put down the receiver and passed the phone to Kanai.

"Call Sergeant Matsuda," ordered Yahusho as he reached for his rifle and made for the bunker exit.

"Where are you going?" asked Kanai.

"Out there, I have to know what that is," he replied.

"What do we do?" asked Jojima.

"Stay at your post or come with me!"

As Kanai cranked the telephone, Jojima grabbed his rifle and followed Yakusho into the brush beyond the cut perimeter wire. Just then, the phone rang.

"Post 23!" he answered.

"This is Sergeant Matsuda, what is going on?"

"A large section of the wire has been cut," replied Kanai.

"We're sending a squad over now," said Matsuda.

Kani quickly hung the hand receiver and immediately manned the Type 92 machine gun ready to fire. But as he looked out the bunker, he could see an eerie white mist envelop the silhouettes of Corporal Yakusho and Private Jojima as they cautiously moved towards the glowing white light beyond the trees. A moment later, they disappeared without a trace.

Just then, Sergeant Matsuda arrived with a twelve-man squad of Imperial Japanese Soldiers. They were in full battle dress carrying Arisaka rifles with fixed bayonets. They immediately took up firing positions on the ground around the sandbagged bunker of Post #23.

"Where the hell is Corporal Yakusho?" demanded Matsuda.

"Corporal Yakusho and Private Jojima went to investigate a strange white glowing light," answered Kanai.

"What light?" asked Matsuda?

"The one out there!" pointed Kanai.

By the time Matsuda turned to look for it, the light had disappeared, leaving only ground mist in its wake. Sergeant Matsuda stepped outside the bunker and kept his head low as he reached for a pair of binoculars and looked into the misty tree line.

"What's out there?" asked Ogawa.

"Two of our men are out there. I want you, Toshima, and Hamada to go find them!" ordered Sergeant Matsuda.

"Hai!" they acknowledged.

The three-man team got up and moved from tree to tree into the dark misty tree line as the rest of the squad anxiously awaited their return. Moments later, several muzzle flashes and sounds of gunfire erupted, then silence. Kanai nervously looked to Sgt. Matsuda for leadership. A moment later, a whistle blew from the within the tree line followed by muzzle flashes and the sounds of rushing men.

"UTE (Fire)!" commanded Matsuda, who instantly took a round in his shoulder that sent him flat on his back.

Kanai could see what looked like a wave of one hundred Viet Minh partisans rushing towards him. Without hesitation, he squeezed the trigger of the Type 92 machine gun and opened fire on the multitudes of attackers. Kanai screamed in fury as he mowed down the Viet Minh, who raced through the cut perimeter wire, killing dozens of them until a bullet nicked his helmet, which made him duck low. A second later, a grenade landed at his feet, he instinctively threw outside the bunker, killing two Viet Minh who were about to storm his position. Matsuda, while wounded, reached for his pistol and fired upon the attackers who came within five feet of him as they overwhelmed the remainder of his squad. Just as the Viet Minh soldiers sought to bayonet Matsuda's remaining overwhelmed men, reinforcements came! Captain Shindo appeared out of nowhere with Gunto sword in hand. He quickly dispatched a Viet Minh attacker who was an inch of bayonetting one of Matsuda's wounded men. The enemy soldier's head was sliced with a single diagonal upward thrust sending it flying to the ground. To Kanai's relief, Captain Shindo had also brought a dozen of his men and another two squads of ground troops Colonel Yoshida had stationed there to help. Within moments, the battle had ceased. There were bodies of Viet Minh insurgent fighters all about the perimeter of Post #23. The Japanese had narrowly repelled the Viet Minh attack, but it came at the cost of eight of Matsuda's men with Corporal Yakusho and Private Jojima reported as missing.

The very next day, Captain Shindo rode as a passenger in the seat green two-seat Kurogane Type 95 car with its canvas top conspicuously set up. OR-3 Oneda drove past the sentry gates and past the scores of rice paddies that led to Pleiku City. It was there on the outskirts that they noticed an abandoned French Military Cemetery just off the dusty road. For Shindo, something was unsettling about it, but its reason escaped him. For the moment, such ponder would have to wait as Oneda honked his horn, yelling at a barefoot Vietnamese boy pulling a large water buffalo across the road.

'What a country,' he thought.

The momentary delay would allow him to see pretty Vietnamese girls in their white Ao Dai walking by to school and scores of peasants pulling ox carts to the crowded outdoor market. Having meandered through dense street traffic of bicycles and oxen, Oneda had made into the large open square. From there, they drove to the white-pillared French Colonial building, which served the last vestige of the French Colonial Authority in the region.

OR-3 Oneda quickly pulled the Kurogane Type 95 car right up to the white building and brought the vehicle to a stop. Captain Shindo stepped out and adjusted his khaki *Sen-bou* cap bearing the insignia of the Imperial Japanese Army as he walked up the steps leading to the entrance. They could see the French Tri-Color had replaced the Vichy French flag. It was clear that things had changed.

A moment later, after walking up to the front desk, a young French Corporal led Oneda and Captain Shindo to a small office that had a large open window looking out to the city square. There sat Captain Aumont, who quickly rose to greet his unexpected visitors.

"Captain Shindo, to what do I owe this unexpected pleasure?" asked Aumont.

"I need to talk to you," replied Shindo.

"Very well, how may I help you?" asked Aumont as he casually sat back at his desk.

"When we first met, you gave us an ominous warning of things you could not explain," said Shindo.

"I see," sighed Aumont.

"We have encountered them in the air, and now we have men missing on the ground," revealed Shindo.

It was then that the sounds of whistles and shouting could be heard from the city square. Captain Aumont and Captain Shindo both stood up to see what was happening outside their window. There they could see Imperial Japanese Army troops rounding up civilians. A moment later, Colonel Yoshida could be seen brandishing his Gunto sword pointing at one young Vietnamese man in his thirties. He looked like a farmer wearing black pajamas and sandals. Two of Yoshida's men had tied his hands behind his back then forced him on his knees before a frightened crowd of onlookers. Without any words, Yoshida drew his sword and dispatched the poor farmer to the horror of all to see!

"This is what happens when you kill our men!" shouted one Japanese soldier through a megaphone.

Captain Shindo shook his head and sighed in disapproval.

"Can't you do anything to stop these barbaric civilian reprisals?" asked Aumont.

"He is my superior," replied Shindo.

"Is this how you conduct yourselves as an Occupying Army?" demanded Aumont.

"I cannot endorse what just happened, yet I am powerless to stop him," lamented Shindo.

"Sooner or later, we shall all pay for our sins. The question is, when and how?" said Aumont.

"I know the Viet Minh are not responsible for what happened this morning. Colonel Yoshida believes otherwise. Something is happening to my men, and only you understand what I am dealing with," said Shindo.

"What would you have me do? The Vichy Government has just capitulated to the Allies. Until a new government in Paris forms, the French Colonial Authority here in Indochina remains beholden to your Occupation Forces. Like you, I am powerless to stop what is happening," lamented Aumont.

"My men are frightened by what they have seen," revealed Shindo.

"I've told you once before; I can't explain it to you. But if you must know the truth, then I will advise you to go to the French Military cemetery outside Pleiku City. Find the grave of Private Jacques Clement. Trust only those closest to you. Your answer lies buried there."

Later, Captain Shindo and his driver OR-3 Oneda drove the Kurogane Type 95 car down the dusty back road at dusk. Sergeant Matsuda and several of his men followed close by in a large Mitsubishi truck as they pulled into the black iron gate of the French Military Cemetery outside Pleiku City. As soon as the Japanese vehicles stopped, the men got out carrying lanterns, shovels, and their Arisaka rifles on their backs.

Thirty minutes would pass before the grave of Private Jacques Clement was located just as the sun sunk below the horizon. Captain Shindo, once alerted, walked over to the grave as one group provided cover from the Viet Minh, and another began to dig. Minutes would pass as three soldiers dug deep into the clay. They had dug down six feet before a shovel hit something buried deep in the ground.

"Sir! I think found it!" said one soldier.

Captain Shindo looked down as the soldiers kept digging. It was then that a strange blue-white glow started to appear from beneath the ground, making them nervous.

"Something's not right," observed Matsuda.

"What do you see?" asked Shindo.

"The coffin is another few inches deep, but the ground is getting warm," revealed one soldier.

It was then that the blue-white glow became more intense. Suddenly, a deep ringing sound deafened their ears, causing them pain!

"*Yame* (Stop)!" ordered Shindo.

The three exhausted sweat covered soldiers quickly climbed out of the grave as the heat became intense. Everyone was keeling over as they tried to cover their ears.

"What is happening?" cried Oneda.

"I don't know!" shouted another.

It was then that the dirt on the coffin began to rumble as the ringing became more deafening. The coffin began to shake violently to the horror of the Japanese Soldiers.

"Cover it up quickly!" ordered Shindo.

Everyone quickly grabbed a shovel and began shoveling dirt back into the grave. As dirt quickly filled the grave, the glowing light slowly disappeared. The ringing in their ears also subsided. Without hesitation, then men promptly fled the cemetery. They climbed into their vehicles and sped away back to Pleiku Airfield.

By the next morning, Shindo had sent out a couple of men to inspect the gravesite. To their horror, the grave was found to be empty, and the headstone of Jacques Clement was nowhere to be found.

CHAPTER XI
THE POINT OF NO RETURN

Captain Swift abruptly closed the tattered journal and wished to read no more. The account of what took place in those very same highlands twenty-three years earlier had unsettled him in a way that recalled that strange incident he experienced with the 42nd ARVN Infantry Regiment while in Advisory Command. An event, Swift strangely had trouble remembering much beyond what took place after they had lifted off the rice paddy. For this reason, he kept it to himself.

"Are you alright, Captain?" asked Langford.

"Yeah," replied Swift.

Captain Swift slid the tattered journal across the table back to Sergeant Thunderfoot.

"Quite a read, don't you think?" asked Thunderfoot.

"I see why you keep it hidden here," replied Swift.

"What's in it?" asked Billy.

"The stuff of nightmares," replied Swift.

It was then that Swift looked down at his wristwatch and noted the time.

"I believe we ought to be going now," said Swift.

"Agreed," said Thunderfoot.

The three men got up out of the booth. Thunderfoot returned the tattered journal to the mean-looking Mama-san in the black silk Ao Dai for safekeeping before exiting the Topeka Bar. Once outside, the three men donned their gold-rimmed military issue Ray-Ban sunglasses as they walked out into the bright sun and down the wide dusty alleyway of Sin City. Once they reached the concrete barriers built to prevent vehicle passage, they could see Specialist Tommy Biggs smoking a cigarette as he leaned against the shaded side of his Duce and a Half utility truck. Having noticed the three men heading his way, he quickly took the cigarette out of his mouth and threw it away before climbing into the truck's cab.

"Where we headed, Captain?" asked Biggs.

"We need to go to the 15th Trans Battalion's Maintenance Area," replied Swift.

"Hey, that's my neck of the woods!" exclaimed Biggs.

"Good, then you'll have no trouble finding it," said Swift.

"You got it, Sir!"

With no delay, Specialist Biggs turned on the ignition. Captain Swift then climbed into the passenger seat up front while Billy Langford and Sergeant Thunderfoot climbed into the back. Once aboard, Billy tapped the side of the cab twice, indicating to Biggs to speed away. All Billy could do was hold on and look out the back of the truck as the brightly colored cat houses of Sin City faded from view.

"I hope you got an eyeful," said Thunderfoot.

"I have this bad feeling, that might have been my last chance to look at the pretty girls there," said Langford.

"Don't think of it that way," said Thunderfoot.

"Huh?"

"Where we are going, you'll see some pretty girls. The only difference is, they'll be trying to kill you," laughed Thunderfoot.

"Thanks, I feel better already."

The Duce and a Half rounded a dusty bend in the road past a large white wooden sign bearing two gold black horse patches of the First Air Cavalry Division that read in big, bold red letters: Welcome to Camp Radcliff home of the First Air Cavalry (Airmobile) Division. Upon approach to the rear gate, a fifteen-foot-high wooden guard tower with sandbags covering the top of the elevated platform came into view as the MPs waved them on through. The dusty road rounded another bend that was lined with a large earthwork topped with sandbags. Behind those sandbags was a battery of three 105mm howitzers manned by a shirtless sunburned crew in the afternoon sun readying for their next fire mission. They continued up a slow grade incline featuring a few original trees left over from the rainforest that was cleared away by the defoliant Agent Orange which was used to construct the base leaving much of the mountain base barren with only sporadic trees throughout the camp.

Specialist Biggs continued to drive up the road that hugged the lower edge of the vast rolling hillside shadowed by the looming Hon Cong Mountain that overlooked the Division base camp. This bumpy patch of deforested land was commonly known as the "Golf Course," which was at that time the world's largest heliport.

There, they could see scores of UH-1 Huey helicopters of the 227th and 229th Aviation battalions being readied for tomorrow's big operation, including the Armed Rocket Artillery of the 2/20th battery. They could further see the large heavy-lift Ch-47 Chinook's of the 228th Aviation battalion was being paired with artillery pieces and jeeps. The Air Cavalry was going in big. The question in Swift's mind was, could he reach his objective and complete his mission before they arrived.

Captain Swift wouldn't have time to concern himself with such things as the Duce and a Half crossed a berm in the road. Beyond it lay two long lines of Hueys facing each other which were in need of servicing. Specialist Biggs drove to the end of the way just passed a Quonset hut hangar where a sign read 15th Trans Bn Maintenance Area.

"This is it," said Biggs.

As Captain Swift opened the door and hopped out of the Deuce and a Half, he could see a small mobile radio mounted on a miniature two-wheeled trailer hitch manned by two Army Specialists.

"I need to find Warrant Officer Edward Seversen," said Swift.

"Check with those guys. They would know who is on duty or who's in the air," said Biggs.

Billy Langford climbed out of the back of the Duce and a Half with Sergeant Thunderfoot. Billy had never been to Camp Radcliff before and was curious about the black covered surface that covered the ground.

"Hey, what's that smelly black stuff?" he asked.

"Penne' Prime," replied Biggs.

"Penne' what?" asked Langford.

"It's a mixture of oil and JP-4 used to keep the dust down. Whatever you do, don't lie down in it. That shit is hard to get off you," replied Biggs.

"Thanks for the warning," said Langford.

Captain Swift looked over to Thunderfoot and beckoned his assistance.

"Help me pull out that black crate," said Swift.

"What's in it?" he asked.

"Captain Ky and Billy have what they need for the field. You and I don't. This was left for Mason and me. Everything we will need is in that crate, so gear up," said Swift.

Sergeant Thunderfoot opened the crate and pulled out a flak vest, then grabbed an M-16 and unwrapped it before handing it to Captain Swift. He reached for the spare magazine clips and passed them around before handing out the four C-ration cartons and water canteens.

"Each one of you take C-rations and put it in your pack and grab a full canteen. I would also take the spare mags," said Swift.

Sergeant Thunderfoot next picked up a helmet then put it back in the crate, instead he opted for a black bandana that he tied over his head.

"You want any of this?" asked Thunderfoot.

"I don't need the flak vest," replied Swift.

INCIDENT AT DAK TO

"Well, Captain, I believe this is where we part ways," said Biggs.

"Thank you for all your help," said Swift.

"You're welcome and good luck, Captain," replied Biggs.

Specialist Biggs saluted Captain Swift and climbed back into the Deuce and a Half and drove away. It was then that they noticed Captain Ky sitting alone in a lawn chair with his M-16 under an old parachute suspended by three tree branches.

"I was wondering when you would get here," said Ky.

"Let's just say I had to gather some valuable Intel while we waited for our ride. Speaking of which, I need to find our pilot," said Swift.

"What do we do?" asked Billy.

"Why don't you and The Chief relax on those lawn chairs with Captain Ky while I get a twenty on our pilot," suggested Swift.

"Fair enough, come along, Billy," said Thunderfoot.

Captain Swift walked over to the two radiomen that were monitoring operations.

"Can I help you, Captain?" asked Specialist Gonzales.

"I'm looking for Warrant Officer Edvard Severson," said Swift.

"He's doing a hot recovery. Should be back soon any minute," replied Gonzales.

"I'm going to need a better answer, Specialist. I have a priority mission," said Swift.

"Yes, Sir!"

Specialist Gonzales nudged his partner Sp4 James who sat on a small folding chair to make a radio call.

"Base to Pappa-Goose. Pappa Goose, come in, over," radioed SP4 James.

"Pappa-Goose, copy," crackled the radio.

"What's your status?"

"We're inbound crossing the Song Ba Car Wash. You should see us shortly," crackled the radio.

"There you go, Captain. They should come in visual range over there," said Gonzales.

Just then, a loud distant rumbling of a large heavy-lift helicopter could be heard approaching. It was then that the large twin-engine CH-54 Tarhe "Sky Crane" appeared rounding the treetops of the Green Line perimeter with a downed UH-1 Huey suspended by cables. More remarkably, a man was standing on top of the Huey's main rotor blade holding onto the wire with one hand. Everyone got on their feet as the CH-54 came into position to lower the disabled Huey. Captain Swift recalled this moment:

"Crazy Eddy, they called him. He was definitely as Colonel Wallace had described him as being one of God's Own Lunatics. He came in like some Hollywood Action Hero standing tall and looking fearless with his big Cheshire Cat grin, but this was no movie set. This was Vietnam, where the absurd and surreal often met. I think Fred Mason would have got a kick out of this guy. I could tell right away he was one character and one my life and that of my men would come to depend on."

The downed UH-1 was lowered onto the ground and guided by two men. Once the skids touched terra firma, Warrant Officer Severson gave a hand signal to the crane tether operator sitting in the rear third seat bubble to release the cables. Once that was done, the uniquely shaped Sky Crane flew away. No sooner than the cables dropped and hit the ground, Severson climbed down onto the ground and walked towards a large oil drum filled with water. He then removed his gold-rimmed Ray-Ban aviator glasses and his cover that bore his pilots wings and dunked his head into the water and then refreshingly shook it off as Captain Swift waited to speak with him.

"That was some Hollywood entrance," said Swift.

"Well, they don't call it a hot recovery for nothing! Can I help you with something?" he asked.

"Are you Warrant Officer Edvard Severson?"

"According to this here name patch, I am," replied Severson.

"Colonel Wallace at MAC-SOG sent me."

"Wallace, huh?" asked Severson.

"Is there a place we can talk in private?" asked Swift.

"Sure, follow me."

Warrant Officer Severson donned his cover back on his head and led Captain Swift to a wrecked Huey, which they boarded and closed the sliding doors.

"How can I help you, Captain?" he asked.

"I have a priority mission that requires your help off the books," said Swift.

"That might be tricky with the base on lockdown. Where do you need to go?"

"I need an insertion point within five klicks of Hill 875," said Swift.

"That puts us at Dak To. Some pretty hairy stuff has been happening there lately. You do know the Cavalry is going in big tomorrow, right?"

"I don't have time for the Cavalry. I need you to fly me and my small team past three NVA regiments, get in there before dark and get out of there before all hell breaks loose at dawn," said Swift.

"That sounds like an insane FUBAR mission, and I'm just the kind of guy to do it," declared Severson.

"So how do we go about this?" asked Swift.

"Nothing's set in stone here. Short of stealing a chopper, I will have to pull some bullshit airworthiness certification flight number on my supervisor. It's the only way I can get a Slick (UH-1) out of here that's not flying the perimeter CAP and avoid a court-martial. How soon do you need to go?"

"As soon as you are ready, I'm already burning daylight," said Swift.

"Look, I've been out in the field all day, so give me thirty minutes to get things in order and wolf down some chow. In the meantime, you and your men stay close, and I'll see what I can do."

Twenty minutes later, Warrant Officer Severson appeared after having eaten and changed into fresh fatigues. Captain Swift got up from the lawn chair he had been sitting in and slung his M-16 over his shoulder before walking over to Severson to have a word with him.

"So here's what we're going to do. We're going to fly out on that stripped-down slick over there, but I have to sign out for it first. So what I want you and your crew to do is sneak over to that other chopper parked next to it and close the doors. Wait until after I've signed off on it, then when I have the Slick up to full power; you guys sneak over and climb aboard as indiscreetly as you can."

"I think we can manage that," replied Swift.

"All right then, my supervisor will be here in a few minutes, so get your team in position now."

"You got it," replied Swift.

As Edvard Severson walked over to his supervisor, Captain Swift and his team grabbed their gear. They quietly walked out onto the Penne Prime covered ground and quietly climbed aboard a UH-1 Huey with mounted .50 caliber guns of the 1/9 Cavalry then slid the side doors shut.

"I'm glad we're going on this Slick. She's armed to the teeth," said Billy.

"We're not flying this Slick," said Swift.

"What?"

"We're taking the one next to us," said Swift.

"But that has no guns!" argued Billy.

"The whole aviation battalion has been grounded until tomorrow's air assault. Only perimeter CAP's and Air Certification flights are allowed, so that's what we are doing," explained Swift.

"Hey, Captain, I think he is done," said Thunderfoot.

Captain Swift poked his head out the door window and could see Severson was climbing into the pilot's seat and starting her main rotor. After an initial whine from its turboshaft engine, it would be minutes before the rotor blades reached their full power. Its sound could be easily distinguished by the unique Whup-whup-whup it made. The time had come to make their move. Sliding the side door open, they climbed out to sneak over to the adjoining chopper. At that moment, Sergeant Thunderfoot looked down and made a heavy sigh of profound resignation. His reputation, having preceded him, spurned Captain Swift's curiosity to ask him if such stories of his wartime conduct as a feared Tunnel Rat were true.

"Sergeant, before we go, I've heard people talk, and I got to ask you, is it true?"

"What is?"

"I heard you've taken trophies?" asked Swift.

"Captain, people will believe whatever they want to believe in this f-d-up war. Only those who have lived it will truly know. But truth be known, the only trophy I've ever taken was that Japanese journal I showed you. I did so because I recognized it was something that didn't belong here, and that's the way it has to be," replied Thunderfoot.

"Fair enough," said Swift.

It was then that Captain Swift could see Severson waving his hand to them to get moving.

"All right, let's go!" said Swift.

"It's about time," said Ky.

Billy loaded his PRC-10 radio backpack onto the helicopter then climbed aboard with his M-16, followed by Thunderfoot and Captain Ky. Severson waved his hand for Swift to jump into the co-pilot's seat. Captain Swift unslung his M-16 and climbed aboard. Having stowed his weapon and buckled in, he instinctively donned a pilot's helmet that had a built-in headset.

"Can you hear me?" asked Severson.

"Yeah!" replied Swift.

"Good. Here we go!"

Warrant Officer Severson pulled on his stick and brought the UH-1 Huey up into the air and started making for the Green Line before gaining altitude. Captain Swift looked back to see Thunderfoot, Captain Ky, and Billy Langford seated as Crazy Eddy banked the chopper. Looking down, he could see the ground crews making final preparations for the air assault on Dak To. Like many of sky troopers that later boarded Hueys that would take them to the battle, Swift would take one last look at the giant 1st Air Cavalry patch that was plastered on the side of the Hon Cong Mountain. For all he knew, it would likely be the last time he would ever see it.

"I didn't know it then. But this was the last time I would come in contact with the real war that was taking place in Vietnam. You could just feel it. Even Captain Ky had a deep sense of foreboding as he stared out the door. He seemed fixated on the sunset as if he were looking at the sun for the last time. Perhaps he knew this was not going to end well. As far as I could tell, The Chief had no reservations of what was about to go down as he sharpened his bayonet. Billy Langford on the other hand fell fast to sleep. In hindsight, I'd say Billy had the right idea."

One hour later, the helicopter started taking ground fire, instantly startling Billy Langford.

"Oh shit!" he exclaimed.

A bullet round pierced the inside of the helicopter inches from where Billy sat. Then another, soon, the chopper was being fired from several directions.

"Fuck!" screamed Langford.

Panicked, Langford reactively reached for his M-16, couldn't load a mag. Sergeant Thunderfoot calmly took his rifle and returned fire.

"Calm down!" shouted Severson.

Billy Langford could see Severson point to a small white sticker pasted to the back of his flight helmet that read:

STOP SCREAMING – I'M SCARED TOO!

Billy Langford quickly got a hold of himself to Thunderfoot's sense of amusement.

"Hey, kid," shouted Severson.

"Yeah!" replied Langford.

"Make yourself useful and open that big wooden crate in front of you."

Billy slid over to the crate and flipped open the metal latch. He then opened the lid. To his surprise, he found the container with a case of glass peanut butter jars inside.

"Peanut butter, what the hell am I supposed to do with that? Throw peanut butter at the enemy? We're supposed to be fighting them, not feeding them!" protested Langford.

"Look closer," pointed Thunderfoot.

It was then that he noticed packed inside the glass jars were live grenades with the pins pulled.

"Holy shit!" exclaimed Langford.

"Ha! I haven't seen anything like that since my first tour," laughed Thunderfoot.

"Carefully reach in and grab one and throw it down to Charlie. He'll appreciate it," laughed Severson.

Crazy Eddy chuckled with amusement as he banked the chopper to make a run at the Viet Cong firing at them as Billy quickly took the glass jars and threw them down to the enemy. He could see two quick explosions killing one Viet Cong who pointed a rifle at him.

"That's a neat trick," said Ky.

"That's a leftover from the guys of 65," revealed Severson.

"Leftover?" asked Swift.

"Yeah, the 15th Trans battalion didn't have much to fight with back with on those early Air Certification flights, so they devised this idea for when things got hairy. They stopped after a Slick made a hard landing and cooked off an entire crate blowing up the chopper and killing the crew. Like I told you before, I had a trick up my sleeve," said Severson.

Minutes later, Severson spotted a clearing.

"Say, Captain; there's a clearing up ahead that would put you just over five klicks. What do you say?" he asked.

"That will do," replied Swift.

"All right, I'm taking her in," said Severson.

Seversen came into a wide patch of elephant grass just beyond the tree line. He brought his Huey to hover three feet from the ground.

"This is it. Everybody out of the chopper!" ordered Swift.

Captain Ky grabbed his M-16 and hopped out of the hovering helicopter as did Thunderfoot. Billy Langford had to hand his PRC-10 radio backpack do The Chief before jumping out of the chopper with his M-16.

"Just remember to squawk PULSAR for extraction or key twice if you can't talk. I will be nearby at the SF camp on the other side of the mountain with a mechanical problem waiting for your call," said Severson.

"Thank you," replied Swift.

"Remember, if I don't hear from you by 0530 hours, I never heard of you," warned Severson.

"Roger that," acknowledged Swift.

The team quickly immersed into the thick elephant grass down below. A moment later, Edvard Severson flew away into the early evening sky. Captain Swift quickly turned to his team and pulled out a small map as Thunderfoot passed him his L-shaped night flashlight. Swift promptly turned on the flashlight, which had a red gel to diffuse light.

"We have to proceed in this direction through those trees over there to get to the tunnel complex near the base of that mountain. We have LRRP (Long Range Ranger Patrol) teams in the field. We have to avoid our people at all costs, so stay out of sight if we encounter them. The same could be said of any VC we run into. Remember, we're not here to fight the war. We're here to find out what's buried somewhere near the base of that mountain. So Billy, if you remember a better way to get there, you let us know," said

Swift.

"You got it, Captain," he replied.

"You too, Chief," said Swift.

"Call me Wayne or call me Thunderfoot. I get tired of being called Chief. It sounds kinda racist, you know," said Thunderfoot.

"Fair enough, Sergeant Thunderfoot," replied Swift.

Captain Ky smiled as he chambered a round in his M-16.

"Locked and loaded," said Ky.

"Good, let's move out," said Swift.

"We made our way through the thick elephant grass and deep into the bush. Our objective, while being not so distant, proved to be daunting, given the terrain. The first hour seemed uneventful, yet never for a second could any of us shake that unmistakable feeling of being watched."

Sergeant Thunderfoot was few feet ahead of the team walking point when he put his left hand up, signaling to stop.

"What is it?" whispered Swift.

"Something close," said Thunderfoot.

Sergeant Thunderfoot looked up and scanned the skies in the opening in the trees. He then pointed his finger upward to the sky.

"What do you see?" whispered Langford.

Captain Swift stood right next to Thunderfoot and looked up. They spotted two black silhouettes of UH-1 helicopters passing overhead that made no sounds.

"What was that?" whispered Ky.

"The Men in Black," replied Swift.

"Do you think they spotted us?" whispered Langford.

"No, they don't see you if you're not moving. Just don't ask me how I know that. I just don't have any adequate ways to explain it to you," replied Thunderfoot.

"Are you okay?" asked Swift.

"Yeah, I think I'll stay on point," said Thunderfoot.

"All right then, let's keep moving," said Swift.

Thirty minutes later, something caught the eye of Sergeant Thunderfoot. He instantly stopped and raised his M-16 to near eye level. Sensing something up ahead in the dark, dense bush, he quietly got behind a tree and gave another hand signal. Captain Swift quietly walked up to him and crouched down to sneak a peek at what was up ahead. It was then the two men noticed a faint flashing red glow one hundred feet up ahead.

"There's a flashing red light up ahead," whispered Thunderfoot.

Captain Swift waved for Billy to come forward.

"Is that the light you saw?" whispered Swift.

"No, it was a bright blue-white light," replied Langford.

"What do you think it is?" whispered Thunderfoot.

"I think it's a downed chopper," replied Swift.

It was then that Captain Swift and his small team could see shadows of a dozen Viet Cong guerillas taking up a perimeter around what appeared to be a downed helicopter.

"What do you want to do?" whispered Ky.

"I need to get a better look at that chopper. What do you say?" whispered Swift.

Captain Swift turned his head and noticed Thunderfoot's M-16 was left propped up against the tree.

"Where did he go?" whispered Swift.

A second later, Thunderfoot crashed through the thick brush and tumbled to the ground as he grappled a Viet Cong Guerilla. They were locked in a death grip as they rolled on the ground and into the stump of a fallen tree. With his left arm wrapped around the neck of the Viet Cong, they could see his right arm raised holding his bayonet then savagely plunging it into his chest as he struggled to fight Thunderfoot off. The Guerilla's throat had already been slit, yet he kicked his legs to fight back until he could kick no more. A moment later, the Viet Cong insurgent was dead.

"Fuck!" exclaimed Langford.

"Quiet!" whispered Swift.

"Sorry, he was about to get the drop on us," said Thunderfoot.

"They're going to wonder where their man went," remarked Ky.

"All right, there's eleven of them and only four of us. Billy, leave the radio here and hide it. Lose the flak vest and stay close to me. Thunderfoot, you, and Captain Ky will make a stealth approach from those two points. One-shot, one-kill," ordered Swift.

Billy quickly removed his flak vest as they proceeded to make their stealthy approach. As they got closer to the red flashing glow beyond the trees, the sounds of a running creek could be heard.

"Psst," whispered Swift.

He quietly pointed to Captain Ky and then to the sounds of the creek below.

Captain Ky picked up a large rock and threw it in the direction of the stream. The sound of the rock hitting other stones in the creek bed drew the attention of five Viet Cong Guerillas who withdrew from the downed chopper to investigate, leaving two Viet Cong that climbed into the helicopter and their four remaining comrades guarding the perimeter. Captain Swift slung his rifle on his back and then pulled out his Colt.45 pistol. He then snuck up on an unsuspecting Viet Cong Guerilla; he could see Captain Ky flank further to the right then making a faint whistle that drew the attention of a Viet Cong fighter. Clad in black, the Viet Cong gripped his AK-47 and took five paces into the brush when Captain Ky tackled him. Noticing his comrade disappearing into the bush, he chambered a round into his Kalashnikov rifle when out of nowhere; he was struck in the head by Swift.

It was then that he noticed another Viet Cong Guerilla being yanked off his feet from behind. Sergeant Thunderfoot had taken a jungle vine and lassoed his neck before stringing him up from a tree, but not before he made a shout that alerted his comrades. It was then that the remaining two Viet Cong Guerillas emerged from the chopper with their AK-47's in hand. With no time to spare, Billy fired a round that pierced the man's skull, dropping him back into the helicopter. In that same instant, Billy looked up and could see a pretty female fighter under her bamboo hat who had her AK-47 zeroed in on him as he squeezed the trigger twice. She managed to fire her weapon right as Billy fired back. The two exchanged fire so fast; he was briefly blinded by the muzzle flash. A second later, he could see her slumped over the open side door as the last black pajama-clad fighter made a break for the trees but then was cut down in the abdomen by a machete wielded by Captain Ky.

Billy appeared dazed by what had just happened as he walked up to the downed chopper and looked at the dead girl. Her long black braid ran the length of her back to her ammunition belts on her waist as she lay slumped over with her hands open, and her Kalashnikov dangled by her strap.

"Are you okay, Billy?" asked Swift.

"Yeah, I thought I would never have to do that. Usually, I am with the LT calling in fire missions. I have never fired my rifle in anger until now," said Langford.

"It was your life or hers, it happens to the best of us," replied Swift.

"A second later, she would have cut you to pieces," said Thunderfoot.

"He's right," said Ky.

"You see Billy, I told you there would be pretty Vietnamese girls trying to kill you," laughed Thunderfoot.

"Daum!" sighed Langford.

"All right, let's get a look at this thing before the rest return," said Swift.

It was then that the sounds of distant 5.56 caliber single shots exchanged with automatic fire from 7.62 mm rounds of the AK 47's. This could only mean a LRRP team was nearby engaging the remaining Viet Cong by the creek below. Sensing that the Army Rangers were nearby, Swift wasted no time getting to the chopper. It was then that the team noticed the big red star and bold red numbers painted on its side. They could tell that this was no downed American chopper. It was a Soviet Mi-2 helicopter painted in a Southeast Asian camouflage scheme.

"Dude!" exclaimed Langford.

"You were never meant to see this," said Swift.

"I had heard rumors, but I didn't want to believe it was true until now," said Thunderfoot.

"Those Russian bastards have been aiding the North the whole time!" said Ky.

"Shall I call it in?" asked Langford.

"Negative, that's not our mission," said Swift.

Swift quickly climbed inside and discovered the Russian pilots and their side gunners were dead. It was then that he heard Vietnamese and noticed there was a severely injured North Vietnamese Officer strapped into the back seat. It was then that Swift called for Captain Ky to translate.

"There's an NVA officer still alive," said Swift.

Captain Ky climbed in and began to interrogate him in Vietnamese. He angrily repeated the same questions and became quickly agitated as the NVA officer kept shaking his head and spitting up blood in the flickering red light.

"What's he saying?" asked Swift.

"He is not making sense! He keeps repeating the same thing about men with no faces and to get away from here," replied Ky.

As Swift moved in closer, the NVA officer opened his bloodied eyes and looked directly at him.

"Swift," whispered the NVA officer.

A second later, he closed his eyes, clenched his teeth and braced for something. It was then that Swift noticed he was sitting on a bomb.

"Everybody, get the fuck out of the chopper, NOW!"

Without delay, they made their escape from the downed Soviet helicopter and ran for cover.

"What's going on?" asked Langford.

"FIRE IN THE HOLE!" shouted Thunderfoot.

A split second later, the Soviet helicopter blew up in a massive explosion. The shockwave knocked all four of them to the ground as they narrowly escaped the sudden fireball that rocked the jungle. Moments later, the wreck was reduced to a smoldering burning hulk. Billy Langford sat up and then picked up his M-16 before uncovering his PRC-10 radio pack.

"You okay, Billy?" asked Swift.

"I think so," he replied.

It was then that Captain Ky put his hand on Swift's shoulder.

"How did he know your name?" asked Ky.

"He didn't. The Men in Black told him. They knew we were coming and planted the bomb," revealed Swift.

"You mean to tell me that was deliberate?" asked Langford.

"They knew we were coming," said Thunderfoot.

"How do you know that?" asked Swift.

"I just do," replied Thunderfoot.

"We best get the hell out of here before we run afoul of any more Viet Cong. We also have to avoid running smack into one of the four NVA regiments headed this way or our own LRRP teams. So let's pick up the pace and get moving," said Swift.

"We were four men against four entire regiments of NVA with no support until dawn. We would have to do it alone before the shit storm would hit Dak To. Somewhere out there was the Man in Black known as Bob and his faceless accomplices. My worst suspicions were being confirmed, and my belief in God and everything I was taught back home was severely tested. I'm glad Mason got out in time."

Swift's four-man team continued towards their objective. But as they got deeper into the bush, the way to the tunnel complex near Hill 875 became unclear. Sensing doubt, Captain Swift stopped to check his compass and map. He then noticed his compass spun clockwise then counterclockwise in rapid succession.

"Shit," said Swift.

Captain Ky looked at the compass and discovered the same phenomena.

"That's odd. It has to be in that direction," said Ky.

It was then that distant blue-white glow could be seen in the upper tree line.

"Perhaps not," said Swift.

Captain Ky and Sergeant Thunderfoot's eyes collectively opened wide as Billy took notice of the strange distant, slow-moving light that illuminated the top tree branches. It was as if someone had lit a bright illumination flare and somehow made it move sideways.

"There it is, the Star of Bethlehem!" exclaimed Langford.

"Well, I'll be damned," said Swift.

"Trust me, Captain, we already are," remarked Ky.

The team continued to keep a steady pace with the slow-moving light as it brought them closer to the plain of Hill 875. It was remarkable that within one hundred meters of the undefinable object, the sounds of the hostile wilderness fell silent. Not one sound could be heard from any bird, monkey, tiger, or mosquito. At best, one could get an unnerving sense of foreboding accompanied by a subtle fluttering sensation in their eardrums as they got nearer.

The time was now fast approaching 2330 hours. The strange slow-moving light that hugged the treetops began to descend into the bush and dipped out of sight. It was then that Swift noticed the ground had somehow been disturbed. Clumps of dirt had been kicked up, indicating he was close to the crash site as they began to move uphill. The closer they got, the more they noticed the grasses and bushes seemed devoid of moisture despite having rained. All plant life appeared dried and dead. It was then that Thunderfoot tapped Swift on the shoulder.

"This is it. Five meters past that earth mound is the crash site, and to the right of it lies the entrance to the tunnel complex," said Thunderfoot.

"You have anything to add, Billy?" asked Swift.

"We came in from over there and cut down Charlie that stood on the edge of that earth mound. I can't remember what happened after that."

"All right, note the time 2335 hours, follow me," said Swift.

The four men cautiously approached the earth mound with their M-16's drawn. Swift carefully got down on the ground and peeked over the edge of the mound. He could see it was a significant impact crater with burned rock exposed and charred debris. Seeing that there was no one around, he stood up and walked into the crater. From his black bag he wore on his back, he pulled out the small Geiger counter that belonged to Fred Mason and switched the battery-operated device to on. The team could hear crackling sounds from the Geiger counter as Swift held it close to the charred debris. Captain Ky bent down and carefully looked at a particular piece of charred debris and was about to touch it when Swift waved his hand to advise him not to.

"What is this?" asked Ky.

"I was told this was a Soviet prototype," replied Swift.

"Is this a…?"

"Captain," whispered Thunderfoot.

The Chief pointed to a faint blue-white glow coming from the entrance of the tunnel complex that was partially buried and covered with a thatched covering and bamboo frame.

"Okay, you and Captain Ky come with me. Billy, keep the radio on and hold on to my rifle. There's a spider hole over there. Hide in it until we return. Squawk PULSAR if we are not out by 0500 hours or key twice if you run into any trouble. You got it?"

"Got it!" replied Langford.

Sergeant Thunderfoot unslung his M-16 and handed it to Billy then chambered his Colt .45 pistol before going in.

"Captain, there is a four-foot drop at the entrance. At three paces, there's a one-foot punji stake trap before the second four foot drop.

So pay close attention when you get down there. I will go in first to show you the way," said Thunderfoot.

"Thank you. You ready, Captain?" asked Swift.

"After you, Captain," replied Ky.

As Billy Langford got down into the spider hole, the rest of the team lifted the thatched latch of the tunnel entrance. Sergeant Thunderfoot climbed down first and drew his bayonet. He then bent down and carefully lifted the straw covering of the punji stake trap before turning back to wave the two Captains. Swift climbed down next, followed by Captain Ky, avoiding the exposed trap. They could see amber lantern light emanating from the open doorway to the next lower level chamber that descended ten feet down the narrowly hand-carved A-framed tunnel. Crouching down, the two captains followed the experienced tunnel rat, who led the way into the next chamber. Once inside, they could see the chamber was tall enough to stand in. There were several cots, chairs, and a Viet Cong flag lined up against the earthen walls.

"Smells like a cross between blood and vomit in here," said Swift.

"This was a hospital," remarked Thunderfoot.

"Well, that explains the smell," replied Swift.

"There's another ten-foot tunnel way that leads to another chamber. Beyond that, there are two lower chambers. You should find what you are looking for down there," said Thunderfoot.

"You're not coming?" asked Ky.

Thunderfoot shook his head to indicate no.

"Okay, then, you cover us here," said Swift.

"Captain, look at your watch," pointed Ky.

Swift looked down at his wristwatch and noticed the time was 0100 hours.

"That's impossible! We just got here," exclaimed Swift.

"Then we have no time to waste," said Ky.

The two men entered the tunnel way to the next descending chamber. They were more than a third of the way down when they noticed a strange heat and a faint blue light that offset the amber glow of the Viet Cong lanterns that lit the tunnel. The two were within several feet of the chamber entrance when Captain Ky stopped and seemed to have trouble breathing.

"Are you okay?" asked Swift.

"No, something is not right," replied Ky.

"Either wait here or turn back," suggested Swift.

"Give me a moment, and I will catch up with you," said Ky.

"Okay, then."

Swift gripped the pistol in his hand as he made his stealthy approach. As he crept up to the entrance, he could feel the heat coming at him in subtle waves. Swift pointed his weapon and entered the chamber. Inside, he could see several North Vietnamese and Viet Cong bodies lying on the ground, and one North Vietnamese officer slumped dead in his seat. In the middle of the room was a large folding table that had several strange glowing blue-white lit connecting spars with tiny translucent fiber like cables sticking out. It was then that he noticed among the dead were three Soviet GRU officers with one lying on his back, still breathing as he held a 9mm Makarov pistol in his hand. Swift carefully approached the disheveled Soviet GRU officer with his Colt .45 pistol pointed toward him when he recognized him.

"Sergei, is that you?"

"Captain Jay Swift, we meet at last," said Kasakov.

"You're not supposed to be here," said Swift.

"I know, but I had to see it for myself. You can put the gun down. It's not meant for you," replied Kasakov.

"What are those things?" asked Swift.

General Kasakov struggled to reach for a handheld Geiger counter; he had turned the sound down. Captain Swift slid it to the ailing man who revealed the red needle had crossed the red line as its small speaker crackled revealing the high radioactivity in the tunnel chamber.

"The recoverable parts of the wreckage were brought underground here. There's more in the next chamber."

"Are they man-made?" asked Swift.

"Nyet," he replied.

"What?"

"They are strange things, exotic things, and fantastic things that come from outer space that are way beyond our understanding. They contain things you could not believe!" revealed Kasakov.

"Hanoi seems to believe enough to send in three regiments," said Swift.

"Listen to me; this alien technology wields vast immense power too complex for us to reverse engineer. Hanoi wouldn't know what to do with it. Neither Moscow nor Washington should have it," warned Kasakov.

"The Kremlin would not be pleased to hear this," replied Swift.

"You and I serve two opposing countries, yet we serve the same masters. What has been recovered here must not fall into the hands of our governments. It's too dangerous," said Kasakov.

"If you did tell Moscow, what would be your conclusion?" asked Swift.

"We are not meant to have this," said Kasakov.

It was then that Captain Ky revealed his presence in the chamber entrance.

"Saigon must know!"

Captain Ky turned around and raced out of the tunnel chamber.

"No!" choked Kasakov.

Swift quickly exited the chamber to give chase as General Kasakov went into a violent seizure before shooting himself in the head. Meanwhile, Captain Ky passed Thunderfoot repeating:

"Saigon must know!"

Captain Ky quickly climbed out of the tunnel complex entrance and raced over to Billy Langford's spider hole.

"Do I call for the extraction?" asked Langford?

"No, I need you to transmit to frequency 31709. Hand me the handset," ordered Ky.

"31709," repeated Billy as he handed the handset to Ky.

"Saigon must know!" said Ky.

"No, they don't," said an older audible American Male voice.

Captain Ky's eyes opened wide then spat out blood as the Man in Black appeared having pulled a large knife from out of Captain Ky's back. Billy quickly reached for his M-16. Bob had kicked Billy knocking him to the ground. Thunderfoot had raced up to the man, and the two exchanged fists. The Man in Black got in a punch while Thunderfoot struck the man's jaw knocking him off balance. Thunderfoot reached for his Colt.45 and pointed at Bob. Thunderfoot angrily glared at The Man in Black with deep-seated prejudice. Enraged, his finger was on the trigger when suddenly a familiar yet unknown voice echoed his name.

"Wah-ne!"

Thunderfoot noticed a bright white light unexpectedly appeared behind him.

"What the fuck!" exclaimed Thunderfoot.

"You might want to take a look," said Bob.

Thunderfoot slowly turned his head around with his pistol still pointed at Bob. To his shock, he could see a familiar yet antiquated United States Marine in full WWII combat gear with a slung M-1 Carbine and a large radio pack strapped to his back, staring at him.

"Dad?"

"Son, I don't have much time, but I wanted to see you and tell you how proud I am of you. I love you, but I have to warn you are in grave danger," said Lance Corporal Thunderfoot.

"Danger?"

"Let him explain first," said Lance Corporal Thunderfoot.

"Yeah, Bob, explain!" demanded Swift.

Thunderfoot's father smiled then disappeared into a haze of white mist. It was then that the old Vietnamese man appeared in his place just as Swift pointed his pistol at the mysterious Man in Black he had met in Saigon.

"It's good to see you, Jay," said Bob.

"I wish I could say the same," replied Swift.

"You know this prick?" asked Thunderfoot.

"Not by choice," replied Swift.

"On the contrary, this choice has always been yours," said Bob.

Bob slowly adjusted his black jungle tunic with an unnerving grin as he sat down on a tree stump.

"Have you looked at the time?" asked Bob.

Swift carefully looked at his wristwatch while keeping his pistol pointed at Bob's head. He could see the time had advanced to 0430 hours.

"How is that possible?" asked Swift.

"You still don't get it, don't you?" said Bob.

"So this was all just a cruel illusion?" asked Thunderfoot.

"Not entirely. The old man thought you would appreciate a familiar face," said Bob.

"I never met my father. He was killed in Saipan before I was born. How is that possible?"

"He knew that and meant you no harm," replied Bob.

"A lot of people are dead because of what's here, and you were behind their deaths, weren't you?" accused Swift.

"Not entirely. I assure you I had nothing to do with that boat story. The incident never happened as they told you. The CIA in Saigon came up with the particulars to lure you in; otherwise, they would have made an effort to recover the bodies and declared them KIA," revealed Bob.

"But why kill Colonel Linh, the F-4 pilots, the E1-Hawkeye crew, Private. Johnny Sanchez, that poor ATC, the 4th ID squad, and Captain Ky? And why did you try to kill my partner?"

"Hey, it was nothing personal," replied Bob.

"Give me one reason why I shouldn't kill you?" threatened Swift.

"Because you'll never know the truth if you do," replied Bob.

"And just what is the truth?" asked Swift.

"It's above your pay grade," laughed Bob.

"Now you're fucking with me. I have Top Secret Clearance," protested Swift.

"You're going to need Majestic 12 or higher to even begin to have that conversation and we don't have time for that," said Bob.

"What do you mean?" asked Swift.

"At exactly 0530 hours, a black C-130 is going to drop a Daisy Cutter right on top of this position," laughed Bob.

"That will obliterate the entire crash site and the entire tunnel complex," said Swift.

"Correctomundo!" laughed Bob.

"So what's so damn funny?" demanded Swift.

"Warrant Officer Severson isn't coming," replied Bob.

"What?" exclaimed Swift.

"Don't worry. We saw to that when he stepped away from his chopper at the Special Forces camp. But since you are going to die anyway, and mind you I do feel really bad about that because you have so much potential, I'm going to let you in on a little secret."

"A lot of people are going to die once the Cavalry arrives. So pretty please, get to the fucking point!" demanded Swift.

"Hydro-Benzoin! Yup, that's what did it!" said Bob.

"Huh?" exclaimed Swift.

"Once it made contact with the Pularium leaking from the Phyron Injector Core, it spread to the Phased Reactor Pod, then it was all she wrote," revealed Bob.

"What the hell is Pularium?" asked Swift.

"It's an exo-element found throughout the deep corners of the Galaxy. Normally, their Immersion Field Coil Projector can handle such minor collisions. And by all means, it should have survived bumping into that Phantom. But, like all things biomechanical, they break down just like a regular airframes built right here on earth. I'll tell you, such technology is a marvel to endear! Fascinating stuff I bet nobody here could have ever thought of! I'd love to explain their engineering further, but there's three entire NVA regiments headed this way and my ride is here," explained Bob.

It was then that two near-silent black-painted modified UH-1 Hueys appeared just above the trees.

"What the fuck!" exclaimed Langford.

"Kasakov's team did their best to recover what they could, but the radiation proved too much for them. That's why Charlie is too afraid to come near it," said Bob.

"What about him?" asked Swift.

"They couldn't get here in time to extract him, so we were called in to buy them some time," said Bob.

"They?" asked Swift.

"Look, I would love to tell you all about them, but seriously, I got to go," said Bob.

Bob grinned as he got up and started walking towards the black silent Huey that hovered inches off the ground.

"Swift, I'm really sorry this has to end this way because I really do admire you. But in fairness, I did offer you a way out with that MIG in Japan, but you refused my help and that's on you. I sure hope it was worth it," said Bob.

Just as Bob stepped onto the skid of the black Huey, Captain Swift called out the Man in Black once more.

"Hey! I have to know, who are you?" asked Swift.

Bob turned around and smiled before saying:

"I am you."

A faceless man in black jungle fatigues could be seen in the Huey ready to slide the door closed. Bob waved goodbye to Captain Swift as the faceless man started to close the side door when Captain Swift called him once more.

"Hey, Bob!"

"Yeah?"

Captain Swift looked Bob straight in the eye and fired his Colt.45 aimed for his abdomen. To his surprise, a small flash of light blunted the bullet downward into a spin unexpectedly piercing the top of Bob's leg sending blood splatter in all directions.

"Hey, you shot me!" cried Bob.

"It's nothing personal," said Swift.

Bob's seemingly jovial demeanor quickly went into distress as he quickly passed out from his wound. His faceless accomplices quickly pulled Bob in aboard the black chopper as it lifted out of hover mode and made an ascent up into the pre-dawn skies without making a sound.

"I bet he didn't see that coming," said Thunderfoot.

"No, he didn't," said Swift.

"Hey, look," pointed Langford.

To their surprise, the old man was still there smiling at them. Just then, a UH-1 Huey could be heard approaching, followed by the encroaching sounds of small arms fire. Billy Langford got up and reached into the spider hole to retrieve his M-16.

"That sounds close! I must have keyed twice before that guy knocked me out," said Langford.

Swift and Thunderfoot retrieved their weapons and quickly

chambered them. They instinctively took cover with Billy Langford as the gunfire got closer.

"We're too far from the extraction point," said Swift.

"How the hell are they going to know where to pick us up?" asked Langford.

"Him," pointed Thunderfoot.

He pointed to the old Vietnamese man who was surrounded by a bright blue light as his skin became translucent. It was then that the UH-1 Huey came into sight. They could see the incoming chopper had its side doors open and had two M-60 gunners began giving cover fire. Moments later, the helicopter came into land by the impact crater. Swift could see Crazy Eddy came in on a different helicopter than the one he flew them in. He could also see Colonel Wallace was seated in the Co-Pilot's seat. Swift instantly ran to him. Colonel Wallace opened the door and stepped out to talk to Swift as two US Army soldiers hopped out of the chopper and helped retrieve Captain Ky's body. They quickly wrapped him in a green poncho and loaded him onto the chopper.

"See, I told you I would come for you!" said Severson.

"Thanks, Eddy, I wasn't expecting you to," said Swift.

"Neither did the guy who sabotaged his chopper. I always have a backup plan for situations like these," said Col. Wallace.

"We lost Captain Ky," reported Swift.

"That's a shame. The South has lost a good man," lamented Col. Wallace.

"Yes, Sir, his wife just gave birth to a baby boy, too," replied

Swift.

"How sad, we'll make sure his family is notified. Did you by chance retrieve anything of value?" asked Col. Wallace.

"Negative, everything's too irradiated and too dangerous to move," replied Swift.

"Sorry to interrupt, but we got hostiles closing in quick," warned Severson.

"We also have a C-130 inbound that's going to drop a Daisy Cutter right on top of this position!" said Swift.

"Well then, we had better get the hell out of here!" replied Col. Wallace.

"Right, you take care of these two, they're good men," said Swift.

"You're not coming with us?" asked Col. Wallace.

"Negative, I have to complete my mission!"

Swift looked to the old Vietnamese man who extended his glowing hand towards him.

"What?" asked Col. Wallace.

"No time to explain, you'll just have to trust me," assured Swift.

"As far as I am concerned, Operation Pleiades is over!" said Col. Wallace.

"On the contrary, this is just the halftime show," said Swift.

"You don't have to do this!" pleaded Col. Wallace.

"You know I do. Colonel, it's been an honor and a pleasure serving with you," said Swift.

"All right then, Jay. By chance you return, I'll keep Pulsar open for you. Good luck and God bless you!" said Col. Wallace.

With a deep sigh, Colonel Wallace gave a slight nod as the two men saluted each other for the last time. Captain Swift then reached into his black backpack and pulled out his small journal and handed it to Thunderfoot.

"You keep this. I think you'll know what to do with it," said Swift.

"Good luck, Captain," said Thunderfoot.

"You too, so long Wayne."

"Never say so long, say until we meet again," said Thunderfoot.

"You're right, you just never know!"

Captain Swift quickly shook Thunderfoot's hand and patted Billy's shoulder.

"Thank you, Sir. It's been an honor and a pleasure, Captain."

"Likewise, you take care, Billy," said Swift.

He then patted the side of the Huey for it to take off before making his way towards the old man and disappearing into the mysterious blue-white light that pierced through the jungle. With haste, Severson's Huey lifted off the ground, taking AK-47 fire as they lifted above the treetops. The two M-60 gunners returned fire while Colonel Wallace turned his head back to speak with Thunderfoot. It was then that they witnessed a bright blue-white light shoot straight up into the sky.

"Where the hell did they go?"

"On a journey," replied Thunderfoot.

At that moment, a bright white orange fireball exploded below obliterating the crash site and the adjacent tunnel complex. The Daisy Cutter released such energy; it sent up a small mushroom cloud into the morning skies.

"Whoa!" exclaimed Langford.

"A journey where?" asked Col. Wallace.

"A journey, unlike any other with a Caretaker who will show him the way," replied Thunderfoot.

"Do you think he will find what he's looking for?" asked Col. Wallace.

"I believe so, Sir!" replied Thunderfoot.

The tired sergeant sat back in his seat and closed his eyes as the UH-1 Huey made the turn towards An Khe and flew into the early morning sky. With one last backward glance, the man known as The Chief watched the last twinkle in the stars and smiled.

CHAPTER XII
THE PERFECT CIRCLE

The Four Corners region, Arizona, present day. For Wayne Thunderfoot, it had seemed like a lifetime ago that he had traversed this very same red clay earth trail with his grandfather. And much like his grandfather before him, he too wore his hair long with streaks of grey under cover of a black Stetson hat. He walked in his dusty brown leather cowboy boots, denim jeans, and jacket looking like the retired Navajo Nation Police Chief with his silver-tipped turquoise bolo tie. He was taking his twelve-year-old grandson Joseph Wayne Thunderfoot to see the ancient petroglyphs before continuing on their day-long trip to Sky Harbor Airport. There, they would greet Joseph's father, Lieutenant James Mintaka Thunderfoot of the U.S. Army's 10th Mountain Division. He is returning from his second deployment in the war in Afghanistan.

"Are we close yet, grandpa?" asked Joseph.

"More or less, you'll know when we pick up the tourist trail."

The two walked up the dirt path along a rock face, and Anasazi Kiva ruins among many that lined the canyon. Once they had reached the top, they could see a three-foot-high wooden post marking the tourist trail to the large petroglyphs up ahead.

"It looks like we beat the last tour group," observed Joseph.

"There's more where they came from. But since we're alone among the Ancient Ones, let me show these carvings," replied Thunderfoot.

Wayne Thunderfoot pointed to a series of petroglyphs depicting strange beings that emitted light, others without faces walking by ancient peoples who looked up to the ovals in the sky and the stars.

"That's some weird stuff," said Joseph.

"You have no idea," replied Thunderfoot.

"Are you sure these are not different tribes?" asked Joseph.

"Something like that."

"So tell me, what happened after you returned to base camp?" asked Joseph.

"I went straight back to see Madame Nhi in Sin City to retrieve Captain Shindo's journal, but the faceless Men in Black beat me to it. My Nisei friend based at Pleiku kept his original translation notes hidden, so I was able to reconstruct it."

"What ever happened to Billy Langford?" asked Joseph.

"They say he married a good Native American woman and went to work for the NSA in Iceland. The last I heard, he walked away from his post during a display of the auroras and was never seen again," said Thunderfoot.

"What about Captain Swift? Will he return with the Sky People?" asked Joseph.

"I would like to think so."

"Do you believe in they exist?" asked Joseph.

"My grandfather and his grandfather, Ten Bears, before him did."

"What about you?"

"The ancient peoples…"

Unexpectedly, Thunderfoot stopped himself in mid-sentence as his attention was drawn to a large white tourist bus that pulled up. A moment later, a small group of Japanese men in their late 50's wearing matching white tracksuits and hats disembarked. There, they were greeted by a female U.S. Forest Service Ranger who happily led the group up the tourist trail and to the petroglyphs. It was then that Wayne Thunderfoot noticed an old Vietnamese-looking man trailing behind them that resembled the translucent being he encountered at Dak To.

"What's wrong, Grandpa?" asked Joseph.

"Nothing," he replied.

"You look like you've seen a ghost," said Joseph.

"Come on, Little Joe, you know ghosts don't frighten me."

He noticed standing next to the familiar Vietnamese looking man, a familiar tall Caucasian man accompanying him wearing a brown leather flight jacket; military issue gold-framed Ray-Ban aviator glasses, and a black ball cap reading Vietnam Veteran above the three service ribbons from the Vietnam War.

Wayne Thunderfoot looked at the man intensely as he dipped his aviator glasses to make eye contact and smiled back at him.

"What does that circle mean over here?" asked Joseph.

"My grandfather called it the Perfect Circle," replied Thunderfoot.

"The Perfect Circle?"

"It is the completion of a long journey," replied Thunderfoot.

"Like my father coming home from deployment?"

"Something like that," replied Thunderfoot.

"Do you think you'll ever see Captain Swift again?"

Before Wayne Thunderfoot could answer his grandson, he took one last careful glance at the familiar Vietnam veteran who looked back at him. The man was joined by one of the Japanese men and the familiar old Vietnamese-looking man. The three men stood along the wooden fence to pose for a group photo taken by the U.S. Forest Service Ranger. The three familiar-looking men stared directly back at Thunderfoot and smiled, reassuring him of what he had suspected.

"Grandpa?"

"Oh yes, most definitely!"

THE END?

For more of Captain Shindo's story, please read our expanded story The Lost Sentai available on eBook and Paperback.

ABOUT THE AUTHOR

American Mishima is the work of author Louis Edward Rosas, the son of Mexican immigrants whose father, Luis Sr., served in the U.S. Army in the Central Highlands of Vietnam. Louis Rosas, in his youth, grew up on glamorized war films and military aviation in the sleepy seaside plains of Oxnard, California. It was there he watched waves of replica Japanese warplanes fly overhead as they filmed WWII dramas including *The Black Sheep Squadron* out of the nearby Oxnard Airport. Instilled with an early fascination of the Second World War during the Post Vietnam Era, it was his exposure to Akira Kurosawa's Samurai epic *Ran* (Toho, 1985) that ultimately changed his views on war while creating a lasting impression of Japanese culture and history. Further inspired by the works of famed Japanese author and playwright Yukio Mishima, Rosas would go on to become immersed in the study of Japanese language, history, and swordsmanship, which led him to the practice of Koyasan Shingon Buddhism and Shinto. Rosas has also trained in Shinkendo, the ideal practice of the Samurai Code of Bushido in the modern world under its founder in Little Tokyo, Los Angeles, which helped shape the creative force that is *American Mishima*.

www.ingramcontent.com/pod-product-compliance
Ingram Content Group UK Ltd.
Pitfield, Milton Keynes, MK11 3LW, UK
UKHW021335100825
7319UKWH00023B/599